MY ENEMY, MY BROTHER

MY ENEMY,
MY BROTHER

by James Forman

Meredith Press/New York

MY ENEMY,
MY BROTHER

PROLOGUE

HIS LONG COLD FINGERS CREPT INSIDE THE SHREDS OF HIS JACKET and pressed against the numb center of his body where hunger was and had been for as long as he could remember. He could go away now, anywhere, if he had the strength, yet he did not move. It was easier to rest there in the cold nullity of approaching death. At first he had not been able to imagine his own death, though he had seen it come often enough to others. He could even picture his own corpse, but he always looked at it through living eyes. In the early days of camp life, there had been for him a terrible joy in evading death for a few more hours, in surviving to see another dawn.

Then slowly a change had come. He had found himself no longer distracted by the groans of the sick and dying. He no longer noticed the dead. There were so many of them that emptiness had become for him a densely populated kingdom. New arrivals only made him more conscious of the absences dwelling beside him.

When a free human being died, he lost his life, but here, when a prisoner died, he lost only his pain. The thought had occurred to him suddenly one morning, and had set him on a road which all seemed to take when they had nowhere else to go. But still he could not die. His heart went on beating, beating. It was no easier to die than to live. He had become one of a bare handful—as miraculous as the human wreckage of a disaster far at sea, somehow surviving through an odyssey of endurance, riding out typhoons on broken life rafts, snatching at passing sea birds, licking occasional raindrops from their cupped hands.

Daniel Baratz was healthy, compared to the average survivor of a concentration camp. He was smaller than a boy of sixteen should be, and thin to the point of emaciation. His eyes were so sunken it was impossible to guess their color, and his black ragged cap of hair had been shaved with a razor. At last he was free to get up and leave. The gate through the barbed wire stood open. He tried to find the strength to crawl with a yellow patch of sun as it moved across the camp compound, but even crawling wearied him. He curled up against a barracks wall in the sun, trying to remember, through an indifferent haze, a warm happy parlor and a piano. They came and went, the laughing figures, the music; and the haze engulfed them again.

What had kept him alive? Dan could not believe in a guardian angel. What sort of an angel would save a mere handful and destroy all the rest? He heard the piano again, and he began to cry silently because he knew he was giving up the easy death to which he had been so long resigned, and was returning to life which had become all bitterness and pain.

Not far away, leaning peacefully against a wall, was an old man. Dan was keenly aware of him because he was his grandfather. They had learned a communication more primitive than speech, like ants talking with their antennae. Without the other, neither would have survived to hear the guns below the horizon. It was Jacob Baratz's profession, watchmaking, that had saved them. At the camp factory they had worked together on the triggering mechanisms for land mines. A few extra rations, immunity from the regular selections of the unfit had been their reward. It had seemed only a postponing of the inevitable, but now it was over. The old man flexed his once-limber hands in the sun. Were they still deft enough for watches? Dan knew his grandfather's thoughts without asking.

Dan had loved the old man before the war when he had a whole family to love. He might love him more now, if he had the strength for such strong emotions. Jacob's ugly face would have looked well staring down in stony meditation from the heights of some medieval cathedral, and it had sometimes frightened him as a child. Years and the war had brought a certain nobility, and the lines of almost comic ugliness had settled into lines of determined dignity. Dan felt sure his grandfather would never die.

There was the thunder again, thunder that brought liberation instead of rain. Those who knew said it was no longer bombs but artillery. Dan did not know and scarcely cared. For years there had been rumors of invasions from the west, of German panzers abandoned in Siberian snow drifts. He had long imagined the prongs of the Soviet pincers, reaching from the pale distances of the Russian steppes toward Poland and the German fatherland. The guns were louder now.

Then there was another sound. The scarecrows stirred along the wall. Some pressed against the once electrified wires which sang with death no more. There they hung waiting like so much blown newspaper, held erect only by the pressure of an east wind, the wind from Russia.

Some of the faces twisted around, showing wild, grotesque, yet strangely silent emotions. They reflected years of straining at burdens too heavy for enfeebled bodies, years of fear

3

and starvation. As the features of flesh diminished, the eyes somehow enlarged, so that suffering took on an aspect of enormous surprise. Suffering did not ennoble. Dan had learned that much from camp life, but it did impart a heedless courage and a cold hatred that grew with the months. With the first sound of the Russian guns these emotions had erupted, had sent the inmates streaming across the deadline toward the ugly towers from which flickered the last panicky bursts of machine-gun fire. Many prisoners had fallen in that final fight, but the guns had been thrown down along with the gunners. The few remaining German troops whose job was to demolish the camp and its inmates had been slaughtered.

Nearby lay the body of a guard, Corporal Bodlander, a nonentity in death as he had been in life. He lay there strangely enlarged, a great frosted snowman, though inside he was nothing now but broken crockery. As he lay groaning and dying, his uniform had been stripped from him, for as he himself had said, even in Bavaria it had been a three-coat winter. It had not been Corporal Bodlander they had wanted to kill, but the camp Commandant, Horst. In his SS uniform Colonel Horst looked resplendent, a sort of satanic Hamlet; Bodlander was at most a gravedigger. So often Dan had imagined Horst squashed flat. It had been a daily dream, a dream they all shared, the arms wide, fingers spread, legs writhing in a circle, but it had never come to pass. Commandant Horst had reached the safety of the last retreating truck. Bodlander had tried, but he was too fat and slow to run away. He had almost touched the tailgate as the driver shifted gears and then, as the gap widened, with the furious prisoners closing behind him, he had lain down slowly, settling to his knees, then putting his head down to the ground as though trying to burrow into it. There he had died, with the graceless resignation of the last dinosaur accepting extinction.

4

Dan remembered the living Bodlander without sentiment. He retained no more capacity for hate than he had for love. Bodlander had supervised Dan's barracks and the daily march to the factory compound. As guards went, he had been a good one, punishing rarely but promptly after the crime, in the way dogs are trained, dutifully writing home to his *Liebchen*, and setting out seed for the birds at Christmas.

Bodlander dead was simply more useful than Bodlander alive. He had worn sturdy German boots, too large for Dan's left foot, just right for his swollen and bandaged right one. The foot had very nearly been the end of him. As it turned out, the infection had saved him. No sensible prisoner ever voluntarily appeared at the hospital. There were rumors of fatal injections. There were patients who returned having left any gold-capped teeth behind. But the ones who returned were few. In the end Dan had been forced to go to a section ominously entitled "Receiving and Sorting." But in fact it had been a dreamworld of a cot to himself and a bowl of canned soup. The patients were watched over by a fat and glowing doctor with fierce bushy eyebrows, like misplaced moustaches. He had inflated his cheeks and addressed Dan in recognizable Polish. With strong bristly hands he had opened and sterilized the wound and bound it with gauze bandages. For a week or more Dan had remained at the hospital in a state of vague euphoria, though there was always the one, ultimate fear to haunt him. Selection. Death by gas. The orderly shower baths where the Nazis killed to the *pom-pom* of ceremonial music were no secret, and over and above the antiseptic hospital aroma was a permeating and constant smell, familiar only to those who have lived near burning ghats and concentration camps.

But there was no selection in those last weeks. The doctor had protected his patients. The gas chambers had been blown

5

up to destroy the evidence when the Russian guns had first been heard. There had been an evacuation of sorts—the inmates who could still march, and finally the hospital staff. Only the doctor had stayed, either out of courage or a sense of guilt. Of those few Nazis who had not fled, he alone remained alive and untouched, serving without sleep among the survivors.

Dan was unaware of the cheering at first. It was so like the wind. Then he heard it and knew and was stumbling toward the wire with the others. From between close-packed bodies he first saw the Russians. They were big men in heavy overcoats, their voices enormous and unintelligible, sounding in unison like the voice of Jehovah. The prisoners cheered, a thin dry cheer pumped up from weary lungs. The Russians, the liberators, were driving on to Berlin with their motto, "Two eyes for one eye." The prisoners, now free men, waved cadaverous hands and their cheers rose higher, like the calling of gulls in a gale.

CHAPTER 1

THE FRONT LINE PASSED. THE SOUNDS OF GUNS DIMINISHED AND vanished, and the small concentration camp near Zambrów was forgotten. It would become anonymous amid the great complex of camps like Auschwitz and Treblinka, where millions had died. At Zambrów there had been about five thousand prisoners, most skilled munitions workers. Of that number, over half had perished within the barbed wire. Most of the survivors had been evacuated into Greater Germany, never to return. Among the hundred or so who remained, some set out toward homes and families which almost surely no longer existed. The rest sat, slept, and devoured the all-too-meager rations which the Russian Red Cross was able to furnish, mostly K rations from the United States in waxed containers which Dan pried open with jagged fingernails. At first the concentrated foods made him sick, but they were strengthening. His grandfather said they were too weak to walk very far, so they remained where they were, watching the Russians with their pitchforks shoveling the dead into bullock carts and spreading lime. A sweet and terrible smell hung in the air. Then those inmates who were able to walk were given a package of food and told to seek their homes. They had to make way for German prisoners of war.

The German doctor, Wildebrand, who had never left the camp and who would remain now to minister to his own countrymen, examined Dan's feet before the boy's departure. The left one was fine, the right still somewhat swollen. Since the SS boots were far too large for the long trek ahead of them, the doctor stuffed the toes with gauze and some crumpled pages of *Mein Kampf.* "What a pleasure," he said. "What a splendid place for that book."

On an April morning, with the trees in early bud and a trace of melting frost on the roadway, Dan and Jacob trudged through the gray gates which still bore the wrought-iron legend, "Work Will Set You Free." A Russian guard acknowledged their passing, or perhaps only nodded in sleep. Dan was afraid of the expanse around him, the solitude. He matched his step to his grandfather's and walked very close to the old man, who looped his arm around Dan's shoulders. They both felt it, the terror of freedom.

The sun was high in the treetops when they first rested. It seemed a great and curious eye hanging there, and under its scrutiny Dan felt as white and vulnerable as something that had lived forever under a stone. Now the stone was gone.

Jacob broke open a small chocolate bar from the box of K rations and they shared it silently before they continued down the long road to Warsaw. Whether it was the chocolate diffusing inside him, the warming day, or the monotonous security of the pace, Dan's spirits began to rise. Old Jacob still had a gray and wintery look. He had aged enormously in the last few weeks. He leaned forward heavily as he walked, but his eyes, the same dark-brown color as the soil of Poland, remained cheerful and undefeated.

When he began whistling Chopin's "Grande Polonaise," Dan, who had not heard the tune since the late summer days of 1939, when Warsaw was under siege, kept up as best he could with the opening bars. Then it was folk tunes—Polish, Russian, songs from Eretz Yisrael. The whistling did not last long. Dan had begun to limp, and he was the first to give up. They stopped often now, and their rest periods grew longer. Evening was coming on, and with it the cold. Occasional farmhouses revealed themselves in the distance, but it was not country they knew. They were too jealous of their freedom and too suspicious to trust themselves to Polish hands even for the warmth of a night's lodging.

With the first gray dusk they stopped for shelter in a shallow cave formed by the upthrusting roots of a fallen tree. The wind by then had a knife's sharp edge. It tasted of snow. They lay deep down, arms wrapped around one another, as they had many times before while snow sifted through the warped slats of the camp barracks.

Half sleeping, yet wakeful from the cold, Dan relived the bitter march that had brought him and his grandfather to the concentration camp at Zambrów. It had been midwinter then and snowing, no feathery Passover snow but a driving blizzard from the north which seemed to foretell the mortality of the planet. Spring would never come again. Once more he saw the staggering figures and the German motorcycle patrol, their black helmets gleaming in the headlamps. He saw Commandant Horst, majestic as always in his black fur greatcoat, ageless, handsome, serene, and damned, driving them like a cattle herder driving stock. Yet Horst had gotten away. He remembered how the column fell slowly apart toward morning, with the older men drifting back through it, still being borne along by the young ones, but sinking all the time. If the fallen could not be kicked into animation, they were left where they lay and the snow covered them. Dan and Jacob

9

were still stumbling side by side when the snow had stopped toward morning. Dan had moved with the jerky rhythm of an animated corpse, but from his pain he knew he was not dead. It was only when his feet passed into dullness that he became really afraid, and by then the eastern horizon was lit by a steely light.

They had survived the snow march. Many had not. . . .

But Dan's feet were failing him now, and each day the distance they covered toward Warsaw was less. The weather improved, and so did their accommodations at night—an overturned and partially burned German truck, an abandoned barn. There were Russians on the roads who, except for an occasional gift of food, ignored them, and there were people like themselves, wandering, following rumors of food and families. Many of them were bound for Warsaw.

When Dan had first asked his grandfather why they were going to Warsaw and not to the village where Jacob had a home and shop, the old man answered evasively. He said he wanted to see the loathsome city once more and then be able to leave and forget it forever. Dan could not believe this explanation, and eventually, in the privacy of the road, he received another one. During the last days of the fight for the Warsaw ghetto, Jacob and Dan's father had hidden a small box of family jewelry and other valuables in the basement of the house in which they lived. If it was still there and could be found, it would open the only path to food and clothing presently available in Poland, the black market. This came out in a dead and even tone. Dan answered and questioned in the same way. Their voices formed a monotonous strophe and antistrophe in a realm without real color or dimension. They were entering the outskirts of the city.

Warsaw was flattened: a city without buildings, without

10

pigeons, trees, gardens, without even the rustle of leaves. It might have been the face of the moon, with ragged specters poking through the craters, stooping to pick things up. A few streets had been cleared and an occasional sign tacked up. They began asking for Mila Street and by noon found their way to the ruined rail terminus at Umschlag Platz. From there trains had left for Treblinka. The remains of the ghetto were nearby. By afternoon Dan and his grandfather reached the old Jewish cemetery, where the ghetto inmates had planted a few vegetables between the headstones. That had been before the outbreak of typhus and the opening of mass graves, when corpses lay naked in the streets waiting with stony patience for the tumbrels to pick them up. It was not that the bereaved had become callous, but funerals were costly, and clothes could be worn by others or sold.

They did not locate Mila Street that day, but spent the night in some ruins where opposing walls had met in skeletal collapse, forming a tent. The morning sun found them once again exploring. With advice from an ancient janitor who seemed determined to supervise a block of buildings long ago demolished, they located their objective. Mila Street was deserted, razed. From the fire-blackened stump of a tree under the shade of which he had once sat, Jacob paced off a certain number of steps. "Here, right here we will dig." Dan had watched, feeling numb. Surely it was all unreal. But they began to turn over the debris and within half an hour uncovered evidence that even Dan could not deny; flame-browned ivory piano keys. His father's piano. He held them in his hands, trying to bring them back to life by imagining what they meant.

Jacob began digging in earnest. They were to watch for any evidence of a basement floor, for a box, and for the bored-

11

out leg of a chair into which jewels had been poured. "Keep digging, boy. Over this way." His grandfather's words came from a great distance and from a world in which he had momentarily lost interest, for in his mind Dan was playing with what he most desired to rescue from the meaningless ruin of his childhood. Piano keys. As he found them, he laid them out side by side into a sort of keyboard. There was no music in them, and yet he could hear playing. His father was playing, improvising stormy passages when things had gone badly at the law courts, light airs when all had gone well. Music to suit the mood, he had called it. His father would give the keyboard a last punishing blow and sit with hands suspended in the air while Dan stamped his foot and fashioned an appropriate expression. Thus both would remain with heads thrown back staring at each other until the last vibration had ceased. Dan's mother frequently watched this game, her head a bit to the side, smiling slightly but never quite understanding. And when the last chord died, Dan would be grabbed by his father, strong hands under his arms. "Up, around, and down . . . then through the streets of Warsaw Town!" as Dan crawled pell-mell through his father's legs. "Please! For heaven's sake watch out for the lamps," his mother would plead, shaking her head and finally returning to the kitchen. The smells that emanated from the stove, rather than her admonitions, would bring them to heel.

Standing with a handful of piano keys like so many broken teeth, Dan remembered it all. That was the good time of not knowing, when he had been a little boy.

Then there were the days of his beginning to know. War caught the Baratz family almost unaware, as a storm fills up the sky without releasing its thunder. His father traveled occasionally on business. He enjoyed the French, he said, for their good food, and the English for their sense of humor. But he never went to Germany. If the shot fired by the battleship *Schleswig Holstein* at 4:45 A.M. on Friday, the first day of September, 1939, reverberated around the world, Dan didn't hear it. War began for him that afternoon, when his father played out the "Grande Polonaise" with no grand gesture at the end. Instead, his head settled silently into his hands. Dan stood there transfixed, and his mother had run to him. "It's all right, darling, it's all right. Your father's just tired." But somehow from that moment Dan had known that the life he was accustomed to was over and not likely to come again.

The first German planes swarming over the city, their black shadows scything the rooftops, were an anticlimax. He had seen his father cry.

In his memory it seemed like the same day, though it was actually a few weeks later, when the German army marched in, strutting stiffly behind their panzers. He had watched with his parents from a window. His father had said, "What has become of the old-fashioned German with his nightcap and tankard of beer?"

His father was in special danger, as were all professional men in Poland. He was a lawyer, one of the few Jews to graduate from the University of Warsaw in 1924. He had always cherished the law, he told Dan, because where law ended, tyranny began. Not that the German administration lacked laws, but for a Pole who was both an attorney and a Jew it meant going in at the front door as a pig and coming out the back as a sausage. At least that was how he explained it to Dan; so when his grandfather arrived, a refugee from the countryside, the boy was not surprised to see the law office changed into a watch repair shop. Both men had good hands, and life continued. There was always music in the evenings. "Light and shadow, light and shadow," old Jacob would say of the playing, whether it was Stravinsky or Chopin or Bach. Music, his father said, was a law unto itself, and he would play German music when he felt like it, the good old men of music, never Wagner.

How many centuries had passed since then? The sun was overhead when they rested from their digging and ate the last of their rations, saving only a few bites for later. From now on it was beg or starve or find the box, which Dan had no faith was there. Even if it was, what chance had they of finding it, with charred sticks instead of shovels? When they went to work again, Jacob kept talking, for morale perhaps, or perhaps because he was an old man remembering. Dan found the familiar voice comforting, but paid little attention to the words. When he became aware of a bit of broken glass, an antelope with its horns and legs missing, he slipped lightly once more into the current of his own memories, seeing behind his eyes.

Dan remembered his mother as beautiful—homely, comforting, familiar, yet somehow beautiful. A malicious friend had once compared her to Queen Victoria. It was true she was plump and rather dumpy, but her hair was gorgeous, and all her own; she wore none of the false hairpieces so many women wore. He remembered combing her hair, and the comb was a ship sailing on dark and peaceful seas. Her face, too, was lovely in repose, like the faces of Renaissance madonnas in his father's book called *World Masterpieces*. Her tastes were simpler than her husband's, and Dan remembered his father chiding her as a "thing" person. She did have a passion for small bright objects—for buying, arranging, polishing them or just holding them in her hands. The

14

living room was full of their glitter, which set off the great dark piano, sitting in the center of the small room like a trapped mastodon.

It was she who had started Dan on collecting glass animals. "See how the light goes through them. How lovely!" When Dan asked for a live pet, she had said, "Glass animals are nicer. They get on together. No quarreling, no mess." Then his father had come home with a puppy. There had been a thunderous quarrel, much banging of the piano and doors, but the puppy had stayed. In the end it was his mother's bed on which it slept, a real concession on the part of a woman who became upset by shoes on the carpet and fingerprints on her good china. She wore rubber gloves to search the little dog for fleas, and when he died of overeating she wept all night. From then on, Dan contented himself with glass animals.

His father had no such taste for the tangible but dreamed of a distant paradise beyond the waves, of Palestine, the country of oranges, prophets, freedom, and sunshine. To all this Dan listened with eager eyes, but his mother had said only that she did not think women kept very well in the desert.

"What is it about women?" his father would wonder. "Always wanting to be in the same place they were yesterday."

"Well, it is nice here. It's small, but it's warm and we're together. Oh, hear that wind howling outside!"

She was definitely a homebody, with the rooftop horizon of Warsaw all she cared to see or know. Hotels and trains, ships on stormy seas: God forbid! They were not for her. And so, while other Jews were leaving Poland, she refused to go, reigning serenely over her possessions, unaware of dangers outside.

She would change her mind, eventually, but by then it would be far too late.

At first, living under the Nazis was endurable. There were insults and arrests. Houses were occasionally entered forcibly for no good reason, and valuables were taken. It was at this time that the jewelry went into the table leg, which was sealed and reset. But life went on, with Dan and his family feeling somehow safer in sharing the fate of thousands. Then one day his mother returned from shopping empty-handed. She would not look at him, and when she did turn around he saw a white face and hands clutched at her waist to keep them from trembling. That night they went out as a family into the pale-red light of sunset to examine the piles of bricks, the pyramids of sand, and barrels of water at the end of their street. Jews were at work there, building something which gradually took shape, growing, closing off the outer world. It was a wall.

That night, in their growing confinement, his father played only German compositions. He played them defiantly, for German music had been forbidden to Jews.

At first the wall brought with it an odd comfort, providing protection from German indignities. Life in the ghetto went on, differing little from normal life. Only the normal pressures were magnified. There seemed to be an intensification of human emotions: hate, love, greed, generosity. Food diminished, and typhus showed itself with the summer, but other normal things continued. A fine symphony orchestra gave weekly concerts. The streets were full of crowds, trundling carts loaded with onions and turnips and herring that Dan could smell a block away. There even developed ghetto fashions. Wooden-soled shoes became normal, jackets became colorless, and furs disappeared to the Russian front. Unhappily for Dan, school, which had been forbidden by the Germans, sprang up again in attics and cellars.

Dan found bizarre things to laugh at, like the wig factory

16

that flourished next door. As a result of typhus, women were losing their hair, and at the same time the more orthodox men, to avoid insults and street beatings at Nazi hands, were shaving their beards. So what could be more economical than a combined barbershop and wig factory? Everything was upside down. Janitors, who before the war said "sir," were now the men of power. Housing was short, but never as short as food. A black market burgeoned, and Dan at first wondered whether his mother would not rather starve than sell her things. All the troubles of that year showed in her face. The living room became bare. The piano stood alone, along with Dan's collection of glass animals which she insisted must never be touched.

The Baratz family had grown accustomed to ghetto life when, in the summer of 1942, another change came. "Resettlement in the east," it was called. Some thought it really meant resettlement; deportation to keep them from the danger of the front lines, farm work to feed Greater Germany. Bread and marmalade were offered as bribes to those who volunteered to board the trains, and in the beginning many accepted.

Resettlement took place during daylight hours. When volunteers no longer materialized, houses were entered. *"Alle Juden, raus! Raus! Hinunter, alle Juden hinunter!"* All Jews out, downstairs! Sometimes the search parties were near enough for Dan to hear the barking shouts and see the residents assembling in the streets. Those with valid papers formed on the right, the rest turned left and were marched eventually to the loading platform of the Danzig Station siding, where boxcars were waiting. Mila Street was threatened with evacuation, but a ransom collected by the residents forestalled it.

The summer wore on, and with it the growing acceptance

17

of a truth too ghastly to believe. There was no resettlement for those who were deported. There was only death. By the autumn of 1942, almost half a million Jews had vanished from the shrinking ghetto. One choice remained for the survivors, and Dan's father announced it to his family in a gentle voice, incompatible with his stark words. They could die like sheep in a concentration camp or die fighting in the streets of Warsaw.

Dan had prickled all over with fear and excitement. He was too young to believe in death. His mother had put her hand to her side and had leaned, whimpering, against the piano. "I'm too old, I'm too old." She had cried all that night, and in the morning Dan had helped her to dress. His father and grandfather were already at work in the basement digging out a bunker. That afternoon they bumped the piano down all the way at the cost of its legs. Its lid would form a kind of secret trap door.

Resistance began quietly all over the ghetto.

The Baratz bunker was connected with many others by passages cut from cellar to cellar and through sewers. Across the street was the Zuckerman bunker. In their own subterranean fortress, Dan's father was in charge. With Germans closing in street by street, the place quickly filled to capacity, then became overcrowded and congested. Its cavernlike walls were stalactited with the dangling necessities of life and the implements of self-defense. Food was scarcer than ever. The usual diet was broth tinctured with lamb and a slice of bread from a neighboring bakery which had gone underground. The baker had promised only the best for his fighting friends, but this meant a good share of sawdust nonetheless.

In the half-light of a few guttering candles, Dan and his grandfather made fire bombs. All that was required was a
18

gasoline-filled bottle, below the neck of which they fastened two little capsules, one of potassium chlorate, the other of sulfuric acid. From their bunker the supply went out through the subterranean byways of the ghetto.

At times Dan's mother helped them. She was dressed in an old fur coat, long hidden from the Nazis. It looked like the fur of a molting dog, but she wore it proudly, carrying the memory of her beauty with dignity. Her dark eyes reflected a spirit which seemed to have experienced deepest sorrow and mounted above fear into some higher realm.

Dan's father never changed. For him the world had turned dark and deadly, but it was the same world. His wife had awakened into a nightmare where none of the old values applied. She could study the manuals of survival and killing as she might once have perused a flower-seed catalog, and calmly pass the information on to Dan. With a wild windmill sweep and a crashing to the ground, she demonstrated how to hurl a grenade and then how to take cover before the air was full of steel splinters.

The Germans were never referred to by name; only as "they," absolute evil. While the beehive of activity went on below the streets of the ghetto, "they" prepared their final solution. It came to Mila Street in formation, SS troops marching abreast, doing the goose step in perfect unison. The Jews watched them over the sights of their guns and then opened fire.

Dan was too young to fight, but he saw his mother, who had always seemed to him so weak and feminine, aiming and firing. The first fight was won in a fog of smoke and the stench of burning flesh.

The Germans did not return the following day. Their dead lay in the street, changing slowly from white to yellow to a kind of coal-tar black, while the Jews below filled bottles with gasoline and asked God for a miracle.

During this time Dan acted as a courier between bunkers. Other strong points had fared less well. Some had been obliterated. Dan returned with news of Nazi preparations. An army was being massed: against the few hundred freedom fighters—the third battalion of the SS Grenadiers, two battalions from the 22nd regiment of SS police, the Polish police, and a Warsaw regiment.

The last fight began with an artillery barrage. Poles in their Sunday best stood smiling and nodding, watching the German gunners at work like children watching fireworks, while deep below ground Dan Baratz felt the first dull bumps of explosions like something going off between his teeth.

The following morning the infantry came on, cautiously this time, running from door to door, probing their way with flame throwers. Abruptly and unexpectedly during a lull in the fighting a voice called from the street in Yiddish, "All fighting is over. Come up and discuss peace terms." The news was pleasant to believe in the crowded, smoke-filled bunker. "It is all over. You will be sent to a factory near Krakow," came the voice again, measured and seductive.

"Fighters, stand with me," Dan's father had ordered, but a few went up. There was a brief silence, and then firing in the street. It was a trap. Those who remained below survived there one more night because darkness arrived and the enemy withdrew until daylight.

During that night, after an assessment of their dwindling arsenal had been made, the one-time lawyer, now leader of an isolated and last-ditch fight in the jumbled ruins of the Warsaw ghetto, spoke to his son. He began with a question.

20

"What do you intend to do tomorrow?" he asked.

"I will fight with you, Father, if you'll give me a gun."

"And you will kill many Germans."

"A great many, I hope," said the boy.

"In the end they will kill you. They will kill all of us."

"Then we'll be together."

"I see."

"Is that all?"

"Wait a minute. I want to tell you something, but my head is muddled. Let me think."

"It doesn't matter, Father," Dan said.

"Sit down, Danny, and try to listen. The day you were born I said to myself, 'Here's one for freedom. Here's the one they won't touch.' Will you understand if I ask you not to fight tomorrow?"

"I want to fight," Dan replied stoutly.

"I know, but I'm going to ask you not to. Not just for me and your mother, but for everyone here. Someone who has seen all this must come through, some young person who will be able to describe it so that it will never happen again."

"And what will become of the rest of you?" Dan asked, only to postpone a promise which was harder to face than the prospect of fighting in the morning.

"We shall win." His father smiled wryly. He could say nothing but the truth. "Whatever happens to your mother or to me is only an episode. What our enemies are trying to kill is immortal—out of their reach. I want you to go and hide in the forest with the partisans. It's all arranged. Will you do that?" Dan lowered his face, unable to speak. "Good. We must hurry." Dan felt the dry touch of his father's lips on his forehead. "I must get your mother."

She took his wrists tightly in her small dry hands. For a

long moment she stared at him as if to fix an image within her brain. He could scarcely look at her, for the candle threw upward elongations into the wasted fissures of her throat, turned her tearful smile into a gargoyle's grimace, accented the white in her hair so that she looked like an ancient and tormented version of herself.

Without warning, the dawn attack commenced with a great dragon's tongue of fire curling down from the cellar escape route. A machine gun began chattering like a battery of typewriters and Dan felt himself torn away from his mother into a nearby sewer channel. His grandfather was dragging him along, urging him to hurry as though he understood what was going on, but Dan could only think of his mother. Surely she was coming. Wrenching free, he started back along the passage, only to be blinded by an incandescent flash of light, then knocked flat by the concussion. Over him rolled the deafening report of the explosion, then blackness.

When Dan recovered, they were far along the interlinking maze of sewers. His grandfather was holding him in his arms. "Danny," he was saying, "you've got to help yourself from here on." Below them flowed the main sewer stream toward the Vistula River. For a time the Germans had flooded the whole system of sewers, but the resistance had managed to open a reserve valve which kept the drains free for those who knew them well. "Breathe, boy, breathe deep, then keep your nostrils closed," his grandfather ordered. Then they plunged in, hand in hand.

They moved forward slowly, stooping in the slimy dark with the water and filth up to Dan's chest. Once his foot slipped, and he fell face foremost into the awful brew. His grandfather fell, too, and a bitter curse rolled and reverberated down the distant tubes.

As the sewer widened toward the river and was entered by

22

subsidiary tunnels, the level of filth subsided, became ankle deep and sluggish. At last, Dan was able to ask what had happened back there. Why hadn't his mother come? "She never intended to leave your father," the old man told him. "She could never do that."

"Do you think they are dead now?" During the last few days he had become used to people dying.

"I think so."

"Were they frightened, Grandfather?"

"No. They knew what to expect. They're at peace. They were brave people, your father and mother. Never forget them."

He accepted this without further question. His home and family were gone, the ghetto, his entire remembered world. Everything should stop, but it did not. Life went on.

Presently he felt the cold air from the Vistula inside his clothing, and finally in the distance he saw murky light.

With darkness they emerged onto the bank of the river. Like two weary and dirty owls, they stood staring mindlessly into the dazzle of a rising moon.

His grandfather's sudden activity brought Dan back to the present. He was rooting around with the excitement of an old dog discovering a long-lost bone.

"Danny! It's the box! The table leg, too."

Both were rotted from exposure and seepage, and he broke them open easily to reveal a hoard of jewelry and bright gold coins. Dan felt an odd mixture of joy and sorrow. His parents' possessions meant food, now, and yet somehow it seemed unjust that things should have survived while his parents had vanished without a trace.

Jacob was counting the gold coins; a hundred or more, all told. One could imagine a Nazi's joy upon finding them, but

Dan wondered what a German official would do with the engraved and gold-inlaid fourteenth-century circumcision knife. "Danny, here's your father's watch!" The old man held it to his ear, his face wreathed in expectant smiles. "It runs, boy. Listen, hear her ticking?" The gold case was old. The works he had made himself. Whatever sentiments stirred within them at the discovery, the fact remained that they were suddenly rich, rich beyond the starving dreams of thousands of derelicts like themselves picking through the debris of Warsaw. The old man stood up, his knee joints creaking. He put his finger to his lips. If they were not careful, they would wake up the next morning with their throats cut.

With something to hide, they became distrustful, as though the glint of gold could be seen through their clothes. "Never turn your back on a Pole," Jacob said. Were they not all Poles, insofar as it meant being homeless, dirty, and in beggar's rags? An idle glance became a stare of burning suspicion. No recognition whatever seemed subtle deceit. They would have left Warsaw that very day, but it was growing late, and both were weary and hungry to the point of collapse. So they finished the last crumbs of the rations from the camp and tried to sleep back to back in a bomb crater where no one could take them by surprise.

In the morning they visited the black market. To display a gold piece was dangerous, but they were hungry. Dan hid one of the smallest coins in his pocket while his grandfather lurked at a distance, concealing their horde. Dan's contact in the black market was a freak among scarecrows, clad in a heavy wool sweater, gray breeches, and sturdy farmer's boots. He was a great roast of a man, all solid meat and sturdy fat, with massive, black-haired arms. He wanted to know where Dan came by such a coin. Red with laughter and full of good nature, he tested it with teeth that had never been seen by a dentist. "Robbed your mother's purse, son? We can do business. Tell me true, now, are there more?" Dan was evasive. "I can make you fat, son." Dan denied having any more funds, and they did business of a sort. The gold piece went for a mixed bag of moldy field rations which in normal times a good housewife would have thrown out for fear of poisoning.

Dan walked quickly away with the feeling that calculating eyes were upon him.

"Were you followed?" his grandfather demanded.

"I'm not sure. I don't think so."

So they left Warsaw without delay and with many backward glances. They were tired and hungry, but the presence of other nondescript figures on the road was sufficient to propel them along until dusk. At last, taking advantage of a moment when no one else was in sight, they plunged into the forest that encroached upon a road. There the tree trunks stood close together and twilight had almost passed. Dead trunks were strewn on the ground and covered with decaying leaves. Their feet sank silently into the soft carpet with every step and mud oozed up around them.

They went on until darkness stopped them. "Here, this will do," Jacob said. In the thick gloom of the ancient trees Dan looked down at a rotten log which would serve as a windbreak. It was scored and gutted with claw marks and in the earth beside it were the prints of enormous feet. There were still bears in the forests of Poland.

Silently they ate what they could of the black-market rations. Some were moldy, some hardened with age beyond the capacity of a human jaw. One day when they could manage a fire, they would make soup. Nothing could be wasted.

Jacob was the first to say good-night. "I'll wake you in the morning."

"You're my alarm clock."

"Age is an alarm clock. I wonder why old men wake so early. Perhaps an hour is more important when there's little time left. But boys should sleep late and hard."

Dan was preparing to do just that when the old man added, negating all he had just said, "Sleep with one eye open, Danny. You can never trust a Pole."

No, as long as he lived, Dan would never trust a Pole. He had once; they both had, as they struggled along the Vistula in darkness, with the burning ghetto of Warsaw behind them. All that had kept them going was the thought of a house in a forest, where a lifelong friend of Jacob's had promised to shelter any member of the Baratz family against the terrors of the Nazi night. The last miles had led through a marshland. Muddy to their knees and filth-encrusted, they had arrived at the forest toward dusk. Fanned by a wind from the plain, the pine forest with its millions of needles had shimmered.

Jacob, half carrying Dan, had pounded on the front door. A man had appeared, a small sad man with matted hair and tin cuff links, who seemed anxious to please. His eyes watered easily. So did his nose, the one feature of his entire face tending toward dignity due to its enormous nostrils. He had shown them into a small well-polished room heavy with hangings and a stale human odor, a room where people lived too comfortably without sufficient fresh air. He was a widower, he informed them, and delighted to have company, only they must be careful. Terribly careful.

That night Dan had eaten mutton broth with bread swimming in it. He was forced to eat it slowly because it was so hot. He would often remember that bowl of soup in moments of hunger, seeing again the globules of fat that re-

26

flected the lamplight like countless tiny suns. The soup had been pure joy until, thinking of his parents who would never taste food again, he began to cry.

Their relief was not to last. Within a few days there were hints that quickly matured into demands. How did Jacob intend to recompense his host for the expense and risk of harboring them? Only the promise in writing of the deed to Jacob's house and shop seemed for a time to satisfy him. It was highway robbery. Jacob said so, but they had no alternative.

In the following weeks a tedious routine developed. The days were not so bad with their host away. There were books and playing cards and housework to be done. But at night, when supper was over, it soon became plain they were to listen while their host expressed himself in a curious declaratory tone, in which almost every sentence was prefaced with a soft, sibilant s-s-s-s. He enjoyed describing some acquaintance encountered during the day, devouring him from head to toe, perhaps twice over, chewing up every succulent detail. If well attended with demure nods and comments from his captive audience, he usually proceeded to speak of his own goodwill, his love for Jacob and Dan in particular, and for Jews in general. If, however, he was ignored, his manner changed alarmingly. He might spit on the floor straight and hard as a peashooter, and in the light his eyes would seem to swim with venom. Something dark and irrepressible would force its way into the jolly stories, a note of foreboding with frequent mention of informers and of the Gestapo. He would tap his head and wink for emphasis. Once he had their fearful attention, his stories would contain tragedy, arrests, deportations.

More worrisome still were the words overheard when he spoke to his dog. Whether they were meant for their ears was hard to say. Certainly his monologues with mention of kosher slaughter and Gestapo mouse hunts were not fraught with tender regard for the people he professed to love.

Between themselves, Jacob and Dan talked of flight. Where? There was nowhere to go, and so they remained until that night when they were aroused by the beam of an electric torch thrust into their faces. *"Raus, Juden, raus!"*

Gestapo! Their host stood by ringing his hands and pleading. "I'm sorry . . . I am truly sorry." His sibilant s-s-s-s was more pronounced than ever. His face had gone all blotchy and red. He smoothed the air between himself and the now-manacled captives. "Please believe me. I couldn't help it."

That might have been the end of the affair for him had he not tried to retrieve a silver watch that had found its way into the pocket of one of the SS guards. There and then he was accused of harboring enemies of Greater Germany. He denied it piteously. "Keep the watch," he told the guard, "here." He offered the SS everything he could lay his hands on, then the deed to his house, to Jacob's house, if they would only take their prisoners and go. It was too late. The muzzle of a Mauser rifle was thrust into the fat of his belly and the trigger pulled. Oddly, it made little noise, only a kind of *purrp,* as if the cartridge had become jammed in the barrel. With eyes wide and wondering, their Polish host fell dead, and Dan and Jacob were hustled out to a waiting truck.

For three days Dan and his grandfather were kept in a sealed and crowded synagogue near Warsaw. There were no toilets and no running water. On the fourth day they were loaded into cattle cars on a siding and told that if any attempted to escape, all who remained would be shot. Then the car was sealed. The journey took two more days, though most of the time was spent on sidings. The prisoners took

28

turns sitting down because of the limited space. At Krakow the car was opened and all watches and jewelry collected. Krakow was the last stop before Auschwitz, and a woman went mad during the last short leg of the journey. She shouted about seeing a consuming fire. The men in the car beat her until she was silent.

At Auschwitz the boxcars were unloaded. The crowd stood in the full heat of midsummer, a frozen death on all their faces. Men and women were separated. Dan held his grandfather's hand. Perhaps it was the odd smoky sweet smell in the air which revived the madwoman, who began to shout about flames and damnation. Dan was glad when they were marched away.

"Don't leave me if you can help it," his grandfather said, and when no guard was near, "Tell them you are fifteen. Stick to it—fifteen years old." As Dan already knew, children were summarily executed at Auschwitz. Then they were marched to an anonymous room with brain-colored walls, like a transient cell in a monastery. There was only an SS doctor present, an expressionless man with the vapid eyes of a corpse. After a few questions he made a designation, left or right. Those who went left were useless: too young, too burned out. There was nothing on the other side of that door but death. "Left. Left. Right. Hurry up. Left." As the sentences fell, some tried to argue, many cried. There were no secrets about Auschwitz by this time.

Jacob was a strong old man. He had rested well and eaten better than most in recent weeks. He passed automatically to the right. With Dan it was otherwise. The doctor scarcely looked up. "To the left," he said with all the indifference of a postal clerk allocating mail. Dan stood dumbfounded, able finally to speak through the reflexes his grandfather had drilled into him. He was fifteen, and strong. No reaction other than impatience: an envelope without an address. Then Dan said he was a watchmaker, that he had made bombs in the ghetto. For a long instant the doctor stared at him and through him. Then he nodded him to the right.

From the preliminary selection they were marched double time to a barracks. Some said it was a converted horse stable. There they were stripped of everything but their belts and shoes. A barber with a straight razor and a rough and unsteady hand came next; then immersion in a barrel of gasoline for delousing was followed by a naked run through a shower and on to a commissary, where black-and-white-striped pajamas were handed out. A bowl of thick soup was next, then an orientation lecture on the value of hard work. As a last measure, lest they now regard themselves as free employees, they were tattooed with a number.

Of Auschwitz one thing could be said: It was clean and efficient. There were neatly spaced concrete barracks, gardens, and a daily routine that began early with ersatz coffee and a march to work by music. For Dan and his grandfather, work meant sorting out electrical fittings. There was thin soup at noon. Roll call came at six at night, then bread and water. At 9 P.M. they were bedded down. Nothing really was to be feared but the slow decay of the body and the spirit, a natural obsolescence which the German authorities planned and supervised by periodic selections. To fail during a selection meant to be handed a bar of stone soap and sent to a mass shower from which there was no returning. One could not avoid a selection; one could only do one's best to look strong and calm. "Run, to get a little color into your bodies," the veterans advised, and so they would hop up and down. Dan could still remember his grandfather's skinny old legs pumping away like the needles of a sewing machine. Time after time they came through while others did not. Then they would promise to say the Kaddish for the departed in three days' time, but more often than not they forgot.

Without the other, neither would have survived in Auschwitz. Dan had to teach his grandfather how to keep in step on the morning march to work. Otherwise he would have been beaten. Without his grandfather's prodding, Dan would have given up eating. "Anyone who becomes an enemy of food here will die," the old man told him. To survive meant to conserve one's energies from day to day. It was as simple as that. Together they survived three months of Auschwitz and then were marched to another, smaller camp. This time they were housed in tents. It was a privileged camp, designed for the employment of skilled workers: electricians, locksmiths, watchmakers. If they cooperated, they could expect fair treatment, the camp commandant told them. He was a small man, rising on the toes of his black boots, snapping a little leather crop against them for emphasis. "Human suffering," he explained to them, "ceases to pay dividends after a point. If you are worth your keep, that limit will never be exceeded here." In short, they had value as slaves. Infringements, however, were dealt with promptly.

When a boy, surely years younger than Dan, took advantage of an air-raid alert to steal food from the camp kitchen, he was promptly hanged before the assembled camp. "Bare your heads," came the command. Five thousand caps were lifted. "Cover your heads." It was supposed to be over then and the prisoners marched by in review, but the body that dangled there was so light the neck had not broken. It took the boy half an hour to strangle.

On the same day the camp inmates celebrated Rosh

Hashanah. "Blessed be the name of the Eternal." Dan could wish no one a happy New Year, nor could he fast at Yom Kippur. He could not worry about God, who had obviously turned His back long ago.

The sun was already high when Jacob awakened his grandson.

"You shouldn't have let me sleep so late," Dan insisted.

"You slept too hard for an old man to waken. Look, we have a fire."

Jacob had made a pot from a petrol can, had found a stream in the forest, and was boiling what remained of their rations.

"We should be home before nightfall," Jacob said as they regained the road. *Home*. To Dan the word was one long ago torn from the dictionary.

All day they traveled through a gently rolling countryside of abandoned fields and small stands of pine and birch. Here and there the land was scored by signs of battle, but the fighting men were gone and in their stead were wanderers with small carts or simply burdens on their backs.

"Do you know," Dan said, "I've only come this way in winter. With Father and Mother. It was lovely then, with the snow."

"It's lovely in spring, too." His grandfather's voice was confident.

But Dan could remember his grandfather's town and the trip there only in winter, all bundled up in the little car between his parents, their breath making smoke in the air. During the winter holidays he would watch impatiently for the first snow. Suddenly it was there, not flung from the sky but grown mysteriously in the dark like moss on the rooftops of Warsaw. His mother would be dusting herself with a huge swansdown powder puff so that her face wore a mask of pale-mauve pollen. She said that to be ugly was death, and she must try to be beautiful. His father would swirl his way into a black fur coat and don an elegant fur-trimmed hat. His mother's hat was fierce with feathers. It made her feel secure, she said. His own was leather, like an old-fashioned aviator's.

Best of all was riding close together in the small automobile over the ice-slicked roads, his father taking the curves just a little too fast. Each time his wife would admonish him, and when that failed, she would inhale sharply as though she had run a thorn under her finger. Then his father would wink. He was an expert winker, and could close either eye without the slightest change of expression on the other side of his face. When the driving game had lost its savor, he would tell tales of his tragic childhood, how his father had sung to him in his cradle, "This is not the little girl of my dreams. . . ," and how his prize rocking horse had broken its leg and Dan's grandfather had to shoot it.

Dan's father was always the butt of his own intricately embellished tales. His mother, missing the point, would reassure him. "Oh, that's all right, dear. You musn't mind it now."

He told of how he had once shoveled snow from his father's walk, hoping for a coin for his efforts. His father had looked out and said in a gruff voice, "Who did this! Who has stolen all my snow?" looking up and down the street for the thief.

This brought a confession from Dan. He was sometimes afraid of Grandfather Jacob. "He has such a great voice. And he's so ugly!"

"You talk as though he's some sort of gargoyle who'll turn you into stone," his mother said. "Your grandfather's a lovely man."

Actually, he's a sort of rawboned Gepetto," his father added. "You'll get to like him this time. All those clocks . . . I suppose that makes me Pinocchio."

"Dear, you have the nose for it."

"They say a long nose is a sign of virtue. With a nose like mine, virtue is inevitable. What do you say, Danny?"

Those were the good times, and he had surrendered the days too willingly. To him now they seemed one long day, when his childhood had passed without his even noticing.

By late afternoon they reached Jacob's home town, Góra, a place modestly famous for its medieval cobblestoned lanes and its church spire. Jacob's house was on the far side, on a street of whitewashed houses behind which fields stretched away to the forest's edge. Until this time Jacob had been optimistic, an old horse stable bound. Now gaping windows and heaps of rubble left him crushed. "Was there a battle here? My God!" Of course all Poland had been a battle-ground, and what high explosives and flames had not scarred, looting and neglect had. The years had changed Góra into a foreign place full of people Jacob did not know.

CHAPTER 2

Jacob's house was standing. They could see that from a distance. There was even glass in the windows. Dan remembered that the rooms had been warm and comfortable, the old battered furniture loaded with cushions. The big stone fireplace and the shelves of books had given off an aura of winter coziness. But now, as they drew closer, they saw a strange name on the door and a strange face appeared at the front window.

Their knock was answered by an extraordinarily tall man with a hostile smile. "Yes, please?" he asked. More remarkable than his height was a curvature of the spine that was oddly symmetrical with a generous and low-slung abdomen which he bore in a complacent manner as if it contained securities and gems. "What may I do for you, please?" He spoke so humbly, so politely, he might have been trying to sell them something. But it soon appeared that he owned the house under the local Russian authority. He was sorry, of course. The tragedies of war. Would it not be better if they considered moving to Palestine? So many Jews were doing so.

Surely it was the wisest course.

Jacob became angry. It was his house and he would clear it of strangers. The new occupant indicated that violence

35

would simply bring the Russians. What about the shed, then? Jacob was pleading now.

"You mean in the back? It's rather dilapidated."

"May we stay there?" It had been his watch repair shop before the war.

Now their host had an opportunity to display extreme generosity. His hands were together, his head nodding. "For the time being, of course. Until you make your plans."

So the old shed was theirs. The lock had long ago been forced, and the window smashed, but it had a roof. A worktable and some tools remained. Jacob sat down heavily. "Damned hooligans," he muttered. He looked defeated. The crease between his eyebrows was deeper than ever, and the edges of his mouth were turned down. With the delicate tracery of veins in his cheeks, he looked more than ever a weary old monkey.

For a long time he sat there with his head in his hands, silent with the patient suffering the concentration camps had taught him. Then he stood up and began to move about the small cobwebby shop, touching each object, each bit of rusty machinery. "It's all here," he said. Then he stood in the center of the floor and looked about, nodding. "All here." It was almost a miracle.

It was dark now. Dan lit an end of candle and they made a fire of small scraps in an oil drum. The old man continued to brighten. They had some money, they had a shop. All would be well. He was not finished yet. His body showed none of these symptoms of an organism breaking down: no shortness of breath, erratic pulse, bad stomach. His body had been kept young by unremitting work.

"Yes, you and I, Danny. We'll manage. Glory be to God. We'll get along here together."

36

They slept that night on loose straw, as they had often slept in the concentration camps, and Dan dreamed of winter visits before the war. Jacob and his father were hitching horses to a sled. Then they were off through the snow, his father laughing and snapping a whip, his grandfather's beard streaming back like a meteor.

On their last visit, early in 1939, they had been talking of Germany, of how the Nazis believed in a god, not of justice, not even of victory, but a pagan god of the hunt in full cry.

Then his mother had said, "Hush. That's nothing that concerns us now. Look, Danny, how the sun sparkles on the snow. Like diamonds." He remembered her expression in his dream. She was beaming, and yet he did not know whether it meant happiness or tears.

When they were ready to leave, his grandfather had asked, "Will you stay here with me, Danny? On some summer holiday, just the two of us? Will you?"

Dan had answered "Yes," because his grandfather was no longer as frightening as he had been.

"We'll do it soon, then. Maybe this summer."

But summer had never really come and he had not seen Góra again until now, when everything had changed. The dream was a happy one until it seemed in his sleep that gas was being pumped into the room. He was choking while everyone else was laughing and he could not make them hear. Then he awoke with his fists clenched, coughing because the fire in the oil drum was filling the shed with smoke.

In the weeks that followed they cleaned the shed and caulked the roof. Dan found the local black market and they were able to eat, not well, but as well as any. The new owner of Jacob's house visited them now and then. Sympathetic as

37

usual, he even brought blankets, urging them as he did so to go to Palestine.

By early summer Jacob had found a few customers. Some were old residents with whom he could pass the time, some were new, speaking Russian and communicating with him by sign language. As Jacob said, if nothing else, there was plenty that needed fixing in Poland. Dan worked at times under his grandfather's supervision, but there was little enough business for a master watchmaker, let alone for an apprentice.

So, once the shed was sound, Dan turned to gardening. The ground behind the shed was rough and unproductive, and the season was late. Schools were not open that summer nor would they foreseeably be open in the autumn or winter. Dan passed most of his time idly and without much purpose or prospect. When winter came, he made trips to the nearby farms, where food was occasionally available at a price. Thus the better part of a year rolled by, good only because the ones before had been so much worse.

In the early spring of 1946, he found himself lingering more and more often along the roadway to watch a growing community of vagrants who were building a shantytown in a deserted field not far from Góra. Just to watch them did him good; they were so much worse off than he. On one such occasion he was approached by a small figure whose costume appeared to be made of machine waste. At first he thought it was a child or a dwarf. Only as it drew closer did he realize it was a boy of his own age, wild and wiry.

"You!" said the boy. "You're not one of us. Go away!"

"Go away? I was just watching."

"Now! Go away!"

"A person can watch."

The face that confronted Dan was a pale, set mask; the

eyes, staring intently into his own, were harried and desperate. The lashes were very long and oddly feminine.

"Good-bye," said the boy with cold articulation.

"Hold on, now. This is a public road."

"I said good-bye. You see, I'm polite. I have said a pleasant good-bye."

Dan hesitated. He had been told what to do for no reason long enough. But the pleasure of watching these refugees at work was hardly worth a fight. Though the stranger reached only to his nose, he did not regard him as small. He seemed larger still when he dug into a pocket and came up with a knife which he flashed in Dan's face. Somehow it came as no surprise. It went with that fierce, handsome smiling face, and it was a challenge. Anything might have happened had not a third party arrived, angular, long of limb, his red wrists jutting out of frayed sleeves. He wore spectacles thick as magnifying glasses and heavy Russian boots with the laces untied. In any other place he would have looked a clown. The newcomer calmly stepped between the two.

"Slow down, Gideon," he said, placing his palm lightly against the knife. To Dan he added, "Gideon won't do you any harm until he knows you better. My name's Sholem." He put out his hand and Dan's jerked out to meet it. There was an immediate liking between these two.

"Is it a secret, what you're doing here?" Dan asked.

Sholem asked, "Are you a Jew?"

"He looks Aryan to me," interjected Gideon.

"How we fall into using these Nazi phrases," replied Sholem. "Anyway, I trust you, Dan."

"I've lost the knack of trust," offered Gideon. His voice held a quality of indictment.

"Do you remember hearing about Hachsharah? I mean

before the war," said Sholem. When Dan nodded, he went on. "Well, we're like that. Helping emigrants to Palestine, except that we're in a hurry. So we're building a way station for emigrants with funds from Youth Aliyah. We can use all the help we can get, if you're interested."

"We're all right as we are," Gideon protested.

With this mixed encouragement Dan visited the emigrant camp only occasionally. He did not really believe in running away, but their brave efforts appealed to him. Without tools, or materials, or enough funds, a town of sorts was arising through sheer sweat. Despite his size, Gideon worked for two. Sholem worked just as recklessly until his cough got the best of him.

"How long have you had that?" Dan asked him one day.

"My cough? It's the first thing I remember. I was born with it." He leaned forward, touching his chest and smiling gently. "I know what I have."

"Once you get to the Mediterranean, you'll be fine."

"I just want to see it," Sholem said.

Then Gideon, the realist, interrupted. "He always says he was born with it. It was the Germans gave it to him."

"You were in a camp, too?" Dan asked. Nothing had been said until now of those unmentionable days.

"Well, yes, in a way. An experimental camp."

"He means Sachsenhausen," interrupted Gideon. "Where they took a keen scientific interest in the inner workings of the Jewish body."

Then it all came out. Sachsenhausen was a camp where experiments were conducted. Pain was necessarily involved for the subject, and normally death. Only in the latter eventuality was Sholem an exception. Perhaps it was his resistance to physical pain that had saved him. In any case, he had been protected by one of the doctors there at the time when exper-

40

imentation was usually replaced by extermination. The experiments had a seemingly pointless pattern. Questions were asked and then a pain stimulus administered; more irrelevant questions and more pain in a sequence of ten repetitions. The injuries were then inspected and recorded in a medical record book and the process repeated. At first the pain was so enormous that it could not be subdivided. Sholem would open his eyes to find the pain, but a red film was between him and the world. Then he would scream. Eventually the screams would give way to rhythmical groaning, and as the days passed he tried to form each groan into a short prayer. It had to be a prayer, never a curse, because Sholem, as he himself readily admitted, lacked the quality of hatred. He failed to understand Hitler or the Nazis, but he could not hate them. After a while he did not think of them at all. He no longer groaned or prayed, but simply closed his eyes when the experiments began and thought of Palestine. He would live through this and he would go there. Israel filled his life, and as long as he could concentrate he remained safe, hidden in a secret place inside himself where no pain or terror could enter.

Dan was speechless with horror. "I would want to go back and kill them," was Gideon's reaction.

He touched a finger to his head. "He's a queer one, Dan." And it was true in a way. As Dan became better acquainted with Sholem, he realized that the boy's essential life went on within a strange silent shell from which he peered through eyes that were calm and appallingly dark behind their thick lenses. Dan could not see to their ghost-ridden depths, but he felt that Sholem was a stranger to all the world. Yet he was not unfriendly. In his face Dan found great kindness and dignity.

Gideon, it turned out, had never been in a concentration

camp. He came from a local farm, long since burned down. His father had raised potatoes in the very field where they now worked. When a German dispatch rider was ambushed by partisans on the Góra road, hostages were taken, among them children. Gideon's parents hid their boy away in a forest cave stocked with eiderdowns and potatoes. It had been a particularly cold and snowy winter, with the forest full of hungry croaking ravens. The ravens had stood hunched over in the cold like so many tiny rabbis. Many of them had died around Gideon's cave when the men with tommy guns arrived. These were the "green ones," the men in fur caps and sheepskins who were feared by Poles and Germans alike. They took Gideon's blankets and food. As an afterthought, because he had fought back harder than they expected, they took Gideon as well.

Among the partisans he had learned to eat strange food: bear and rabbit and venison. Often it was eaten raw after forcing out the blood between two wooden paddles. At first Gideon had carried dynamite sticks and other explosives for the partisans. He had felt proud when the wild, cutthroat men stubbed out their cigarettes whenever he approached. They'd even let him join them on a raid near Góra when a German supply truck had been destroyed. The following day he had returned to his parents' farm to reassure them, arriving in time to see them placed against a hay rack. They were shot down without pomp and buried on the spot without circumstance. A second volley had been directed at him as he ran shouting from cover.

"Were you hit?" Dan asked.

"Just a memento," Gideon replied. "In the forest one dies of serious wounds." He was rather proud of a scar on the left side of his throat.

42

"Gideon's a fighter," said Sholem. "He's killed Germans."

"They killed my family, so I killed them." Gideon described the first time. He had seen a German soldier and a girl picking flowers in an empty field. It couldn't have been better. He held his shot, he said, deliberately. He held it for the better part of a minute for the pleasure of saying to himself, "That's a dead German." Then the soldier had raised a field flower to his nose. How sentimentally Teutonic! The explosion of that shot in the stillness had been stunning, delightful. His eyes as he talked of it were hard and eager. He looked to Dan like some cruel immortal finding his spiritual feast in the agonies of a dying race. After all, it had simply been a matter of business, killing without mercy, with utter contempt.

Unlike Sholem, who had never known hatred, Gideon had passed beyond it into a mood approaching cold professionalism. The veterinarian did not hate the mad dog but he destroyed it. The executioner had no feeling for the condemned but he did his job. In such a way Gideon described his attitude toward the Germans.

"I don't think I could kill anyone," Dan said.

"I know I couldn't," said Sholem.

"You don't know. You haven't tried." Then Gideon described one of those mornings when an ambush was planned. His body had seemed to be weightless. He had felt immortal when he loaded his gun. "I don't know. Somehow on those mornings I'd see the world clearer. I'd pick a flower for my buttonhole. I'd try not to step on an ant in my path. I developed a certain respect for life, a fondness for everything, even the Nazis."

"Then a Nazi comes along, unsuspecting," interjected Sholem.

43

"Yes, and you feel a divine love for him. That's really it. When you take aim at an enemy and fire, you feel like a god."

"But if you were a god," said Sholem, "you could give him back his life."

"You know our friend here's a pacifist," said Gideon. "He expects Palestine will be a land of milk and honey, just as it says in the blessed Book." Well, Gideon didn't share this expectation. If it were true, he wouldn't get along there, not on some desert farm with nothing to do but plant and hoe and water.

"That's the way it should be." There was in Sholem's voice the first note of fierceness Dan had heard. Palestine was the secret dream of Sholem's life. "I'm sure I'll find my father there," he said.

"Your father?" exclaimed Dan. "I thought your parents were dead."

"I'm certain my father's there. He left on a ship when the war was just beginning."

Gideon said nothing, but the lines in his face as he listened to this exchange showed his perpetual outrage at life. Later he remarked in private to Dan, "That's what I mean about Sholem. You know, he's a good person, but sick."

"You mean his cough?"

"No. Up here." Gideon touched his forehead again. "You know the way he trusts everybody, even after all he's been through. The way he trusted you for no reason at first. It's the things they did to him there." Dan must have looked unconvinced, for Gideon added, "Well, you can see it in his eyes. Take what he said about his father being in Palestine. His father's dead. He was one of those people who went down with the *Struma* off Istanbul. Sholem's seen the list, but he

44

just can't face the idea that his parents abandoned him."

"You can't blame him for that."

"I'm not talking about blame. Wait until you know him better. You'll see what I mean."

During the following days Dan got to know them both better; their pasts, their hoped-for futures, the wounds they bore. Their wounds, like his own, were beyond surgery. Both his new companions were unreachable in different ways, and he felt for them differently. Sholem had no secrets, and yet he lived apart, behind a sheet of glass, untouchable. Even so, Dan had grown to love him.

Gideon, on the other hand, was deeply immersed in the world at hand. His barbaric face with its savage eyes and thin predatory nose was a forbidding mask. He was the sort of boy Dan would have ordinarily disliked and feared at school. Tough, cynical, a winner at games, Gideon knew his bagels. He was absolutely fearless, and he had an immunity to pain which was due, he explained, to a series of mastoid infections. "When you have an earache that lasts for the first four years of your life," he said, "nothing hurts after that." His parents were dead; the fate of the rest of his family he recounted with evident relish as he flipped through a tattered photo album. "That's Aunt Esther. She died at Dachau. And that funny little guy, that's Uncle Simon. I've never actually heard what became of him. Not worth saving anyway. And little Abraham, poor stupid brat. He was gassed at Treblinka along with his parents. See them? Right there. Abraham's sitting on old Granny's lap. Some storm troopers shot her." And so it went. Well, Gideon would get even. He had already taken some measure of revenge on the Germans. In future he meant to be a fighter pilot. He was built for it, light-boned and muscular. Often as he and Dan worked side by side, he pictured himself sliding silently through the sky, getting the sun behind him, then slashing down. "You'd feel like a god, doing that," he said.

Gideon pictured himself so frequently in the role of righteous executioner that Dan was heartily sick of it. Now as they faced one another over a two-handed saw, he was concluding dourly that his new acquaintance was not only a criminal type, but by no means a great thinker. Just then a third character entered their group with startling suddenness. She came with a flash of red hair in sunlight. Dan took a sharp breath. His mother's hair had been that shade once, natural at first, then dyed. It had become gray overnight when dye ran out in Warsaw.

The girl wore a beret, a man's heavy coat, and brown woolen stockings that drooped over her shoes. She walked quickly toward them, the great-coat flapping around her ankles. She had the gait of one used to walking a great deal.

Her face was pale and slightly freckled, with smoky-brown circles under friendly eyes. The otherwise sullen set of her cheeks was suddenly contradicted by the authority of her smile.

"Gideon," she called, thrusting up her right arm in what resembled a Hitler salute. His arm went up in greeting. On coming together they embraced, old friends, it seemed, though Gideon had never mentioned her. Then she turned to Dan.

"My name's Hanna," she said.

Dan was embarrassed by the unusual experience of meeting a girl. "May you call me Dan?" She should have laughed at this, but she didn't.

"She's a bit scrawny and funny-looking," said Gideon, "but aren't we all? She was a green one like me, a partisan. You'll get to like our Hanna."

46

Dan liked her already. She was snub-nosed and not really pretty, but the sum of her face seemed more than the total of its parts. Her smile was direct and spontaneous, and her eyes, lacking any childlike quality, were full of life and enthusiasm. Then there was the red hair.

"You think I'm funny-looking, too," she said to Dan, who was staring. It was half question, half declaration.

"No, I was just looking at your hair."

"The nuns cut it," she told him. "For lice, you know. They didn't do a very good job."

"No, I mean I like it."

"I don't," she replied. "Red hair is angry-looking."

"It reminds me of someone."

"A girl?"

"Well, yes, I suppose," he said.

There was a touch of ginger in Hanna's hair, which his mother's had not had. In a certain light she didn't seem to have any eyelashes.

Hanna behaved with people as though she had known them all her life. She was an explosive, merry talker, with laughter like dynamite that had been bottled up inside. Dan, despite himself, could not hear that laugh without wishing to laugh himself. Very quickly the human barrier he felt with most people dissolved, and he found he could talk freely with her. Unlike most of the others, she had no reticence about describing her experiences during the war. Her mother had gone to America to prepare the way for the rest of them. But her father, brother, and herself had been caught by the Germans at the home of a Polish fisherman near Ustka. He had agreed to sail them to Sweden that night. The fisherman and her father had been shot as they tried to bar the door. Her brother had been cut down in flight by an ax. She herself had hidden in a cellar. The house had been burned down over her head. She would have died there had not some nuns found her and taken her to a convent, where she had stayed until joining the partisans near the end of the war.

"You must want to go to America," Dan said.

"Why?"

"Well, your mother's there."

"She's a deserter. I try not to remember her or use her name." Hanna had hurt eyes but no tears. It seemed to Dan an affliction of the times, a necessity against dehydration.

"And what about you, Dan?"

"Me?" He talked about his grandfather, Treblinka, the other camps.

"I mean before that, in Warsaw."

Though they were constantly in his thoughts, he had never volunteered to talk about those days. "It's easier to get over if you talk about it," she urged. He wasn't sure it was something he wanted to get over, but he began to tell her, from the earliest times, when he was still young enough to sit on his father's knee. He used to curl up there with his eyes closed, pretending to sketch his father's face with his fingers, touching eyes and cheeks and nose. "It was just a game. We had all sorts of foolish games." He told her about his father's piano, and how his parents had quarreled solely for the pleasure of reconciliation. While it lasted, it had all been very good.

As he talked, Hanna had focused so intently upon him that her eyes, opening, closing, appearing to change size and shape, seemed to give back silent agreement to all that had been said. And it surprised him when she commented, "How lucky you are."

He gave her a questioning smile. "To have lost all that?"

"No, to have such wonderful times to remember. What a featherbed that must be to fall back on."

48

As he thought about it, he concluded perhaps she was right. In moments of particular misery, his thoughts always returned to the security and warmth of that small apartment with its good rich bakery smells. His childhood had become fossilized inside him, a treasure that was inexhaustible. No matter what came along in the future, he would have that to steady him.

"Then your parents died there, in Warsaw?" she asked.

He had not wanted to end the story.

"Yes, in a bunker."

"I wish I'd been there with a grenade." She had strong wrists and square fingers to hurl such a weapon.

"Then you'd be dead now," he said. "You don't wish that."

Here Gideon intervened. "You don't know old Hanna here. Skinny, like I said, but cheeky. She's killed herself a soldier."

"Shut up, Gideon." Her anger was sudden and genuine.

"Without help. I'm telling you, Dan, she's a fighter."

"That's enough, Gideon," she told him. It was enough for Dan to see that resolute mouth and fighting chin to know she was a match for any boy of her own age.

The early summer days passed into July. More and more of Dan's time was spent with his new friends. He saw very little of his grandfather, who now had enough work to support them without putting a drain on their hoarded reserve. The refugee camp as originally planned was finished. Dan and the others went on to enlarge it, for the flow of refugees never stopped. Like so much dry foliage left over from winter, they blew always toward the south.

It was not the work that drew him nor the talk of Zionism, nor was it Sholem or Gideon, whom he now regarded as his

49

best friends. It was Hanna. He was fond of her for many reasons. She reminded him constantly of his mother, not so much by her appearance as by the comfort he felt in her presence. She was not beautiful, not even pretty, but she had a trim boyish figure and a graceful way of walking. Her elbows stuck out sharp as knives, and so did her shoulder blades, but there was fine downy hair at the nape of her neck, where the fragile knobs of her spine seemed to end, that Dan wanted badly to touch. Then, too, he liked her confident manner, her way of doing things without waiting for other people to do them. It wasn't pushiness, for there was a certain magic in whatever she did. Her every action was so direct, gay, and complete that there was nothing to do but accept it.

Often they talked of Palestine. Hanna loved the history of the old days, of Saul and David and Solomon, the brief years when Israel was more than a dream. While they worked, or during the respites when they sat and ate, they would speak as if they were already there. She wanted to take care of farm animals, or perhaps grow things.

"I'll be a shepherd," Dan said once, as though committed already to another person's dream.

If Israel was for all of them an ideal, Sholem was their high priest, the keeper of the flame. His thick glasses were so powerful they seemed to suck Dan's eyes from their sockets when he tried them on, but Sholem had a special vision of Israel behind his eyes. There in a realm of incense and flowers he imagined Israel as a marriage contract between God and all Jews. To live elsewhere voluntarily was a kind of adultery.

Sholem had postcards of Israel. He often caressed them with the supple fingers which were the only thing about him truly beautiful. These were the cards a cousin had sent years before from Israel, cards that had drawn his parents there. And though the images were faint and fading, Sholem saw in

50

the deserts dancing air, palm trees, fertile fields. There were pictures of a kibbutz called "Promise of the Future." As a youth his cousin had farmed it, building up the rock walls with his bare hands, carrying baskets of earth on his back, planting vine twigs and lemon trees and fighting off Bedouins with an old pin-firing rifle when the need arose.

"Promise of the Future!" They all talked of it. Their talk disturbed Dan, for it sounded as though they meant to go there soon. He did not want to lose Hanna, though she was Gideon's girl, he supposed. He did not want to lose any of them.

There was more than one way of getting to Palestine, it seemed. If one had money, there was no problem obtaining travel permits, tickets, whatever one wanted. Very few had money. Most had to rely upon the Mosad Aliyah Bet, the international organization for illegal immigration. Some European countries, particularly Italy and France, cooperated with this Jewish agency. Others, supporting England's desire to preserve a friendly and peaceful Arab world, did not. For those who were too poor to cut corners and too impatient to wait for help, there was a last recourse—to become an infiltree, a person without passport or documents who depended solely upon his own wits and body to make the journey to Palestine.

"You wouldn't simply start out on foot," Dan protested.

"If I could only move one inch toward Israel in the next year, I would start," Sholem replied. Gideon and Hanna agreed. The Jews were a tide that had to flow. No one could stop them. And when one thought about it, the hazards were not so great. Once over the Czech border, they would not have to fear the Polish government. Once into Italy, they would be free of the English.

They all, in different ways, urged Dan to join them.

51

Sholem did not persuade directly; he simply lived and breathed Israel. For him, the old admonition, "If I forget thee, O Jerusalem, let my right hand forget her cunning," was a way of life. Gideon urged him directly. "Come on, Dan. We can use you, if you're not a coward." When Dan responded with a lifting of the shoulders, Gideon would become sarcastic. "I suppose you think we Jews haven't an enemy in Poland. Only our friends hate us." And he told the story of the pious cat, Poland, and the frightened canaries, the Jews. The pious cat had eaten the first bird because the bird, being kept behind bars, was obviously a criminal. Punished for this good deed, the cat had decided he had been mistreated for making a mess of feathers and blood. So he swallowed the second canary neatly and whole. Once again punished, the cat had reasoned out the commandment, "Thou shalt not kill." So he approached the third bird speaking softly and reassuringly, but the canary, unable to bear the strong feline atmosphere, dropped dead of suffocation.

Hanna's arguments were harder to resist.

"We'll all be happy there. We'll live the way you used to as a child."

"It's just running away," he told her.

"No, it's searching out. We'd be building something. People should live in their own country. There's something odd about people who don't, as if their clothes don't quite fit."

"This is our country, though."

"You're afraid to go. Is that it?" she asked.

"It's my grandfather," Dan replied. "He'd never go."

"But there's no better place for old people."

"Jacob's all right. He's a strong old man."

"I mean later."

"That's why I have to stay. Can't you see?"

"You'll have to decide soon, Dan."

"Yes, I know." Lord knows, he had thought about it, turning things this way and that in his head like an hourglass sifting always the same sand. Now time was running out. It was still summer, but the woods had already been touched with a tawny brush. There was no chilly premonition in the air, but the insect chorus was louder at night and the darkness came earlier each evening. If they were to succeed on their own, it had to be before the hard cold. Gideon had already begun collecting things: some rubber ponchos, winter-white German surplus, two Russian knapsacks lacking carrying straps, a bayonet, a Czech belt ax, one sewing kit, a few candle ends, and other miscellany which Dan thought looked rusty, worn out, or useless. They were obviously going.

"And soon," Hanna told him in a coaxing voice. It was hard to resist. Her hair had grown out during the summer and enfolded her head like a reddish acorn cap. In damp weather it was so curly that it looked like bunches of grapes.

"I wish I knew how it will turn out for you," she said.

"I'll speak to my grandfather tonight," he promised. "I'll talk him into coming."

Jacob was working in the late August sun, hoping to soak the arthritis out of his joints. "There's no curing old age," he said to Dan. "May it never happen to you." His weathered face in the exploring red rays was as homely as a plowed field. It seemed to Dan to have closed up a good deal. It was bigger than ever in the nose, smaller in the chin.

Dan felt he couldn't leave the old man, even though things were going well for him in Góra. His tools were bright and

53

he did not lack for jobs. The shed, poor home that it was, was his as long as he paid a nominal rent to the new owner, who no longer spoke of eviction. But they were all that was left of a family, and it seemed to Dan they should stick together.

He could not face the issue directly, but he casually mentioned Sholem's kibbutz, "Promise of the Future." There must have been something suggestive in his tone, for old Jacob raised his eyes with the polite attention of a gentleman whom nothing can surprise. While Dan described it as a place for old as well as young, Jacob again began to work on the mechanism of an antique clock, as though everything had been said already and what remained was only the acting out of a ritual.

"So many are going . . . some by train."

"Like so many long-nosed lemmings," commented Jacob wryly. "Sometimes I think they're right, and then I wonder if they aren't off to destroy themselves and finish what Hitler only started."

This was a setback, but at least Jacob had stopped working. He was a good listener, and he heard Dan out with evident interest, seeming to concur with everything he said.

"Danny, you can't know how much you sound like your father. I remember once. . . . You recall how he used to keep that telescope on the roof and watch the stars? We were up there one night and he talked about following a dream. He said God didn't give the Jews anything but dreams, and children to make the dreams come true. I think you must have just been born. I advised him not to do anything rash, to think of his new responsibilities. Now I wonder sometimes if what I said then kept him from going. Well, I talk too much, that's a Baratz failing. And it's your turn, now. You want to go to Jerusalem."

"Only if you do."

"I wonder what sort of clocks they have there. Sundials? Hourglasses? Electric clocks?"

"All sorts."

"I doubt old ones."

"Old ones, too. All out of order," Dan insisted.

"Danny, I'm just a small-town tinkerer."

"You're a great watchmaker."

Jacob stared at Dan as though hunting down any hint of mockery or patronage. "If you want to go with your friends, it's best. A bird must fly even if the sky is full of hawks. I envy you, with all your discoveries ahead of you."

"I won't go without you."

"All my life I wanted to go on a trip. Never did. You know, Dan, I've never left Poland, and now . . ."

"Now's the time, Grandfather."

"No, I think I'm too old. I've been in this soil too long to put down new roots. I want to die under my own roof. Not that I'm in a hurry. There isn't much use being dead. But you, Danny . . . I won't let you stay. I don't think your generation has a chance here."

"Will you come later, then? When I've found a place for us?"

"Me? In Palestine? I'd be like last year's brown leaf still clinging to the branch with new buds all around." Against this half-amused opposition Dan pleaded, nearly in tears, until his grandfather finally said, "Don't worry. I have money. I'll be there in the fullness of time."

The old man would make no further concessions and Dan had to accept this partial solution.

"I'm not sure age is well qualified as an instructor. Maybe a man profits less from the passage of time than he loses. But

I suspect I won't have many more chances to lecture to you, Danny, so indulge an old man for a few minutes." Dan sat with his head bowed, trying to make sense of the words. In the camps he had learned not to cry, but he felt the wells behind his eyes filling. "Now I know you have a friend with a lot of spiritual ideas about Palestine; it's the land of milk and honey, all that. And I say, splendid. Without such ideas how could we Jews have kept a thread of hope? But those ideas are dangerous, too. Remember, there hasn't been a Jewish nation in Palestine for over two thousand years. Long generations, in which the history of Palestine has been written in hysterics. I'm not worried now about the English or the Arabs. I'm worried about you. To the Jews, Hitler was a prophet. He kept all his promises and perhaps he taught us a new idolatry; nationalism. I should hate after surviving here to go to Palestine and fall into the hands of Jewish Nazis. When you get there, Danny, be a Jew and be proud of it. Your ancestors have paid a price for the privilege. But we mustn't become closed off again in a spiritual ghetto. We must interchange with the world. We must give and take, but never beg. We must be ourselves, not imitating those who persecuted us, not playing the persecuted man who's owed a living. For many people, Jewishness has come to mean matzo balls and herring. It ought to mean dignity and charity and humor, and, most important, what we've seldom been granted: tolerance. No more eye for an eye, tooth for a tooth. Leave the old Bible ways behind. Well, I don't know if that makes any sense, but it's probably the last speech I'll ever make. You know it's getting cold out here. We should get the fire going."

Though impressed by the intensity of the old man's speech, Dan was too caught up in his own emotions to make sense of what was said.

56

Outside, the dusk thickened into night, as their small fire took over from the daylight. They ate together in silence. Then Jacob said, "There's a girl going with you. Hanna, isn't it? Has she a last name?"

"I've never heard it," Dan admitted.

"But you like her. Is she pretty?"

"She's skinny, with a lot of freckles."

"Homely, then?"

"Oh, no. I wouldn't say homely."

The old man looked at him, smiling. "The best philosophers are beardless boys. I wish I were a boy again." And somehow in the firelight he did not look old. At least there was nothing ruined in his face, nothing broken in those steady eyes.

As the September days passed, they waited with dwindling hope for the refugee agency to find them places on a train south. Then one day it was decided, not in words so much as glances. They could wait no longer.

At dawn they would set out. Dan spent a last sleepless night beside his grandfather and arose in the dark. He did not waken the old man, since he would have to pass the house again on the way out of town. The refugee camp was dark and still under a star-stabbed sky when he arrived. A light showed from one canvas tent, and he entered. Several young people were crowded together, all exceedingly tense and self-possessed.

Sholem, a black prayer shawl thrown over his head, was bowing toward the promised land and leading them in those beautiful rhythmic Hebrew prayers to which he had dedicated his life. "Hear, O Israel, the Lord our God is one God, and thou shalt bind these words for a sign upon thine hand . . . ." Dan glanced around to locate his friends. He recognized

57

the Szoszke twins, their pinched little faces white as cold cream. So they had decided to go. He felt sure they would never make it. Zeev and Pola Kilman were there, too. Dan hardly knew them. He smiled when he saw Hanna in the shadows. Her lips were moving. Gideon was beside her, his mouth set. "May the will come from thee, Adonai, my God," prayed Sholem, "that thou walk me in peace, and march me in peace, and support me in peace." The world's oldest prayers were a thin cry which seemed to rise like smoke above fear and darkness.

No one moved when Sholem had finished. Silence drained around them as they sat, reluctant to make the first move to go. They were all afraid, now that the time had come. Through the tent flap Dan could see the sheds and the tops of trees taking shape against the growing light. He saw the candle pale until it no longer cast a circle of yellow light. One by one the stars vanished in the west.

Sholem stood up. "Follow me," he said, his voice no more than a breathless wisp of sound. Like gypsies they gathered their belongings into bundles. First Sholem left the tent, then Gideon with Hanna beside him, her coat whipping out like a flag in the north wind. Dan followed, the others close behind him.

Full daylight brought the small procession back to Góra, where Jacob met them on the road. He had parting gifts for Dan: a tight roll of American dollars tied up in a dirty sock for disguise, and a gold pocket watch. "This was mine and then your father's," Jacob told him. They embraced. As Dan pulled away, he tried to smile, but his face trembled and his eyes clouded over.

"You've promised to follow me," was all Dan could manage.

58

"Write. Tell me about it. And Dan . . . Dan, be a good Jew. Never a Nazi, Dan." The old man's lips continued to move as though by themselves. He was crying. It surprised Dan, and then he realized how natural it was. Never before had it occurred to him in so many words that his grandfather loved him. He turned away with difficulty as he felt the magnetic pull of the others, of the road to Palestine.

It was a long way no matter by what means one traveled. As he waved to his grandfather, he sensed in his heart it would be a long time before they would see one another and be part of the same world again. Perhaps it would be never. On the first rise of the dusty road Dan paused and, shading his eyes, looked back. There was Jacob, still standing in the road. Dan waved one last time, but the old man was feeling for something in his jacket pocket and did not notice. "I'm doing the right thing," Dan reassured himself. The hoot of a distant train made him shiver, and he trotted after the others.

CHAPTER 3

THE ROUTE THEY PLANNED TO TAKE LED GENERALLY SOUTH TO Krakow, then west of the white Carpathians. They could cross Czechoslovakia in a week, with luck, and Austria in another. Once into Italy, they would be relatively safe, and the Alpine path would all be downhill to Trieste on the Yugoslavian border. From there they would find a ship to Palestine.

It looked simple on the map, eight hundred kilometers, more or less. Dan could cover it all with his hand. The first sunny days were easy ones for the eight who had chosen to go. They began each morning's march with a song led by Hanna in a small tuneless voice. Four of the group were almost unknown to Dan. The Kilmans, Zeev and Pola, had been among the partisans toward the end of the war. Zeev carried a "comet," a quart can full of hot coals which was a stove in daily use, a weapon if attacked. His sister Pola was fat, suspiciously so for anyone who had lived on a partisan diet. At the end of each day's hike, these two lagged well behind the others. Then there were the Szoszke twins. As twins, they had been particularly suitable for Nazi experimentations, and had known Sholem at Sachsenhausen. They were almost as devoted to him as they were to one another. When one had

60

been deafened during the experiments, the other had driven a pencil into his own ear drum. His hands had been manacled before he could do more damage. Dan found it difficult to communicate with them. One was completely deaf, the other half so, and they spoke to each other with hand signals. The partially deaf one would speak only to Sholem; when Dan approached them, their sad grave mouths became set in an expression imploring no further penetration. So he left them alone, though he felt pity for them. Only love of Sholem had brought them out on the road, and Dan did not think their devotion would prove strong enough to carry them all the way. The hard core of the group was of course Sholem, Gideon, and Hanna. These three had the same high and sacred aim: never to stop, never to turn back until Palestine was reached. They were always in the lead, and as Dan watched them he felt confident they would not fail. Hanna marched like a drill sergeant, as though there were a procession behind her. Her face shone with a passionate happiness. She was subject to no one, and freedom was s clean garment she would not soil. Gideon walked with a curious sliding motion, as if he did not wish to leave footprints behind him. His hands were usually out from his sides as if expecting opposition. Dan presumed these were mannerisms he had learned as a partisan. Sholem was the obvious leader of the small tribe, though he looked fragile and coughed a great deal. He constantly encouraged the others, particularly the twins; yet his innermost self remained sealed away in impenetrable privacy. He walked with the aid of a staff, his long legs opening and closing with angular regularity.

Dan never doubted his friends, only himself. The realization that he might never see his grandfather again continued to haunt him. He felt uprooted, scarcely able to believe he was actually on the road to Palestine. As irresponsibly as a cricket, he had leaped off into the unknown because of someone else's impossible dream. Or was it because he fancied another fellow's girl? It was easier not to ponder the reason, just to set one foot ahead of the other, each step a confirmation of his foolishness.

At first they followed the Vistula south, then west and south along the banks of the Pilica through rolling forests of pine and birch. They forced themselves to tramp swiftly and steadily, until marching took on a repetitious pace, one day duplicating another from dawn to dusk. Usually they sang in the early morning, but by noon silence reigned except for the shuffle of feet. Toward sunset, talk would break out again.

More and more, the forest country gave way to fields of barley and wheat and tobacco, much of it neglected and all of it leopard-spotted by autumn.

Mid-October brought the first heavy rain. Chilled and blinded, they sought shelter in the midst of a pathless waste. They finally came across the remains of a flattened cottage, a roofless hen coop, a meager pile of clumsily cut firewood, and a cave which turned out to be an abandoned coal-mining shaft.

They were all exhausted and for the moment disillusioned. When Sholem suggested a prayer of thanks for the shelter, Gideon commented bitterly, "Oh, it's snug and cozy, all right. I feel like a corpse in a coffin." For the first time they did not pray. It was no loss to Dan. He was too hungry, cold, and footsore to care. He drew off his broken shoes and examined his toes. They were cracked, and the color of dried clay.

The following morning they pulled themselves together slowly and glumly, more dispirited than when they had arrived. They had a hard time rousing Sholem at all. He wasn't asleep, just withdrawn, and Dan had the odd feeling that he didn't really exist. He questioned him anxiously, "Are you all right?"

"Yes, wonderful, thanks," came Sholem's reply. In his face was the usual sweetness, though the flesh was more tightly drawn over the bones.

At least the sky had cleared when they set out. The air was sharp with a young friendly cold that made them feel its teeth without biting.

This was coal country north of Krakow. That morning they saw the first gray trace of the Carpathian foothills. Here, too, were industrial plants, some destroyed or abandoned, and the scarred sites of battles. Very often the river bridges had been blown up. "At least we won't have to burn them behind us," thought Dan.

On the road they met occasional displaced wanderers, discouraged in their search for relatives or for a home. Many had given up and were on their way back to some camp for the winter. Infiltrees without passports were being seized, they heard, particularly in large cities or near borders. The necessity of giving Krakow a wide berth added another day's hard walking.

They were racing against winter, and a day lost was not regained. Sholem insisted on taking the Sabbath as a day of rest. They all needed it, but Gideon raised a protest: They simply did not have time for religious amenities. He was overruled, and they went on the next day, refreshed. Here the hamlets, interspersed with woods, were protected by loosely engirdling hills. From the top of one such hill they first glimpsed the mountains, a gleam of sunlight on snow.

"I don't know what it is about mountains," Hanna said. "They're never as high as I expect them to be."

"You wait," Dan told her.

"They'll slow us up," said Gideon. For him the mountains were an annoying obstacle. "And winter's due early this year." They had already seen wild geese flying south.

Two more days took them to the Carpathian foothills, a land of tall black pines and shacks, their steep slate roofs polished by rain. The valleys grew deeper and the rivers rushed down them with the wild laughter of a gang of children. Here the shepherds carried old-fashioned crooks and were as unfriendly as gnomes. Overhead loomed the snowy mountains that meant the border of Czechoslovakia.

Leaving Poland was their first real hazard, for if they were intercepted by a border patrol they were certain to be interned. Even minor roads seemed dangerous, so they took to the woods; towering black pine closely planted, and leaf-bearing trees which seemed so completely and suddenly shed of their foliage they might have been inadvertently planted upside down.

All was silence save for their own voices and the occasional outpouring of mountain streams. There was no end to the forest. With dusk, bare roots seemed to grab at their ankles.

"It's like something out of a fairy story," Dan said.

"We'll be lucky if all we run into are witches," said Gideon.

Something twittered through the gray sky like a flung black glove.

"What kind of bird is that?" asked Dan, whose imagination was getting the best of him.

"Who cares?" replied Gideon. "You can't catch it, and if you did, it wouldn't be worth eating."

The pine trees seemed to suck up light so that it was black where they walked long before the sky above was dark. In that early night, the bats were skittering on leathery wings.

Up ahead Sholem was pointing his stick. Hanna shouted

back at them through cupped hands. There must be something to see, but Dan was too tired to run. He made out a vast black shadow frowning through the lesser blackness of the pines. It was a castle, ancient, stony, and crumbling, but still massive. Emerging from the forest onto what had been a road, he saw the sign. "Drachenberg." Dragon Hill, Gideon translated. It must have belonged to a Prussian family, to judge by the name.

"Someone's been here recently," said Hanna. "You can see tire marks."

Whatever its history, Drachenberg was a refuge. None of the weary travelers hesitated to enter the black doorway, though it seemed to squint malevolently at the intruders as if it had murders to hide.

Inside, it smelled of bats, and was cold as an ice plant.

Gideon lit a candle stub. The ceilings were high and arched, the walls battered and pocked by bullets. The floors were littered with bottles, books, and what seemed to be shreds of bandages.

Studying one of the bottle labels, Sholem said, "This is Russian. The Russians must have used this place as a hospital." That accounted for the damage.

A search for food was organized. While Hanna and Sholem started a fire of bandages and broken furniture in one of the many vast fireplaces, the others went off in three directions. Dan led the way down a narrow flight of circular stone stairs. Behind him were Zeev and Pola, complaining all the way. They were hungry. They were tired. This was all a waste of time. "You mean going to Palestine?" Dan asked them. No, they hadn't meant that, but as long as he had brought it up, yes, it was more than a waste of time. It was hell. Too much of him agreed with them for Dan to make any rebuttal.

From the mossy stone walls oozed bright drops of water.

Underfoot were feathers from burst pillows and glass from cracked mirrors. Eventually they came to a bare circular room from which several low passages led in various directions. Zeev and Pola sat down on the stone floor. Their stubborn refusal to search farther only increased Dan's determination to examine every nook and cranny—for what, he didn't really know. He explored one corridor after another, his feet crunching on broken glass. By the time he had reached the third one, only the Kilman's rebellion kept him going. Halfway down it, he poked his head into a side door and suddenly he began to laugh out loud. Pola and Zeev came on the run, and holding the candle high, he laughed at them, too. Staring through the candle smoke, their eyes were as round as if they had glimpsed a treasure trove of jewels.

It was a larder. Broken into, to be true, looted and rat-gnawed; but there were dried meats hanging from the ceiling, long thin dried sausages, round cheese, and bright cans of undisclosed contents, even racked and moldy bottles of wine.

The result was a feast, very nearly a bacchanalia.

They all gathered around the fireplace, feeding the flames with old books which had been gnawed by rats.

"Do we have to use books?" Dan objected.

"They're all written in German," said Gideon.

"And slow burning," added Hanna, as she tossed another to the flames.

None of them were accustomed to drinking wine, and the meat turned out to be smoked ham. With the expression of a polite child at a party who declines too quickly a second slice of cake, Sholem refused to eat swine.

"Meat is meat," said Hanna. She spoke for the rest of them.

Sholem ate only cheese.

Dan devoured great slices and hunks of the smooth brown flesh. He drank the wine, which must have been very old and seemed to have lost most of its color. For a time he saw nothing, heard nothing, was aware of nothing except the good taste in his mouth and the warmth going down and spreading through his body.

When his senses cleared enough to notice his surroundings, Dan saw a brand-new rosy world full of fine people. Even the Kilmans looked so happy it was a plasure to watch them. He felt a rush of joy at seeing so many smiling faces.

Gideon leaned toward him. "Did you know Hanna is really a little white rabbit?" he asked. "Yes, she is. Have you ever listen to her talk? 'Bibble-bibble-bibble.' That's the way she talks. Like a rabbit. 'Bibble-bibble-bibble.' "

"Bibble-bibble-bibble," echoed Dan.

Gideon doubled over, nearly joining his nose to his knees, wheezing with soundless laughter. Even Sholem laughed out loud until his merriment deteriorated into a deep cough which he controlled by rocking back and forth.

Hanna looked at Dan with a desperate smile, the corners of her mouth shut down tight over a huge mouthful of food. She swallowed and her eyes widened with the effort. Gasping, she laughed right in his face, laughter that was as natural and necessary as breathing.

He laughed in reply, self-consciously.

"Don't you know how to laugh?" she demanded.

"My mother used to scold me for laughing too much."

"So that's what stopped you?"

"Bibble-bibble-bibble. Listen to the white rabbits," interjected Gideon. He waved a bottle in their faces, and once more laughter spread from one to another. Hanna's whole face laughed, her eyes narrowing into slits, and Dan became involved in her mirth until he choked and squirmed with laughter. He was being tickled inside. Oh, Lord. His eyes filled with tears and the whole world seemed lit by starlight. He could hardly breathe for laughing and he rolled on his side in real pain. Gradually the spasms subsided and he lay back laughing in bursts, rubbing his left fist backward and forward into his eye.

Aware that the others were looking at him, Dan rolled over onto his stomach. For the first time in memory there was more food than he could eat. For a time he ate sparingly, simply for taste. Hanna was beside him, staring into the fire. In action she was boyish and athletic; now in repose she seemed the most feminine girl he had ever met. With a boldness he did not often feel, Dan told her, "You're awfully pretty, you know."

"I am?" He had meant it, and he had also hoped to embarrass her, but Hanna simply widened her smile and stared back at him. It was Dan who finally looked away toward the fire.

With the feast in shambles before them, Sholem rose to pray. Counting on his fingers, Dan realized it was the Sabbath eve. Dan was ready to hear him out, but the twins stood up and began to dance around their angular hero; then the Kilmans, dancing clumsily like trained bears; next Hanna and Gideon, and finally Dan, who did not want to be the only nonperformer. So Sholem stood helplessly in the midst of the turning circle, grinning foolishly, the firelight splashing from his thick spectacles. Finally the Kilmans collapsed to huddle by the fire, and one by one the others followed them until only Sholem remained standing.

Faintly Dan heard the damp books hiss in the flames. He

was warm and full. When Sholem turned his back and walked into the shadows, Dan watched him dimly as though from a dream.

That night Dan dreamed he saw Sholem walking in a pine forest. When a wolf emerged from between the trees, Dan tried to warn his friend, but he had no tongue. The wolf and the boy walked slowly toward one another, and as they stood face to face, the wolf about to spring, Sholem put out his hand. The wolf licked his fingers. Together they walked off and were lost in the trees.

Dan woke early with a cramp in his shoulder. It was damp and the fire was low. He built it up again, counting the sleeping crowd in its light. Only Sholem was missing. Most of them were awake, stretching, hungry again by the time Sholem returned.

"Where were you?" Dan asked him.

"Walking. It's misty outside."

No more was said about it.

During that day they rested and ate, putting aside the food which would keep best on their journey. There was little laughter that day.

"Why are we all so sad, I wonder?" Dan asked Hanna.

"Because it's been so fine here, and it can't last."

Next morning Dan awoke shaking with cold. He didn't touch the fire, knowing that he would shiver himself warm once they were walking. There was a heavy fog when they left which began clearing away about the time they stumbled upon a narrow-gauge railroad line. The rails were rusty and it seemed safe to walk beside them.

"Look, animal tracks, and footprints," Gideon said.

The tracks looked big enough to belong to a wolf, and they

were fresh. Taking no chances, they walked at the base of the embankment where they could gain the woods in a hurry. Without expecting it, without the joy or anxiety of anticipation, they came upon a stone marker. There were no guards, no border gate, no barbed wire, yet the stone told them they were leaving Poland.

Gideon took one step beyond, then turned back and spat. "If I didn't hate Poland for any other reason, I'd hate it because it's damp and cold," he said.

Czechoslovakia was just as damp and cold.

When the railway curved north, they left it, plunging now into the flank of the wilderness, the big woods, bigger and older than recorded memory, upon which man's puny gnawings left scarcely a trace. Here there was no horizon. Dawn came early and remained dawn until the sun was directly overhead. Then the tall dark trees strained the weak sunlight so that they seemed to walk in suboceanic depths. After the sun passed through the zenith, dusk came early and lasted as long as the dawn.

"Can you believe it?" said Zeev. "I used to think there was nothing like picnicking in the woods. Better cold bread and beans than hot roast at home."

This was the third night since Dragon Hill, and supplies were running low.

"Did you ever have Chinese food?" asked Dan.

"Chinese food? Just give me some gefilte fish."

"Well, I like Chinese food," said Dan stubbornly. He remembered one meal of it in Warsaw before the war. It lacked all disgusting proofs of mutilated animals; everything was minced and blended with the vegetables. "No ghosts to haunt you, no skeletons, my father used to say." Zeev pointed out that this could just as easily be said of gefilte fish.

They talked about food that night until Gideon lashed out

70

at them. He was unable to stand such gastronomic visions on an almost empty stomach.

Next morning the voluminous and sinister silence to which they had grown accustomed was broken by the startling yelp of a farm dog in the distance. Echoing among the great tree trunks, it sounded like a pack of hounds in full cry, but it was good news. They had come to the end of the forest.

Progress was quicker in the farm country. The government policy in Czechoslovakia did not hinder emigrants moving south, but the peasants were aloof. It had not been long since the German soldiers had left with a promise to return, and they were hostile to any strangers. All that could be learned from them with sign language and a few common words was that they were poor and had no food to spare. If any help was to be had, it lay to the west in the American displaced-persons camps.

There, behind barbed wire, they would find food in abundance, after a dusting with DDT. All pledged to avoid such a fate to their last breath, but sometime during the night the Kilmans vanished.

"And good riddance," was Gideon's reaction. Dan was inclined to agree with him, but Sholem was desolate. Any defection on the part of others he took as his own backsliding. How had he failed them? He wanted to set out in immediate pursuit. It took the combined efforts of Dan and Gideon to keep the group on its way south.

Another Sabbath arrived. It was November. Thin clouds overhead resembled puffs of frosty breath, and snow was in the air. For shelter they found a shepherd's abandoned lean-to, part stone and part timber. It was well located on a hillside with a clear view in all directions.

Sholem and Hanna gathered twigs for a fire. The others

climbed halfway down the hill to an orchard where a few small misshapen apples had been overlooked by the pickers.

"Lord, this tastes good. I'd forgotten about apples," said Dan.

"They're sweet enough," replied Gideon, "but you've got to look out for worms."

Meanwhile, Sholem had found some bacon in a dark corner of the hut. It was slippery and green on the surface, but they cut it into soapy lumps and managed to roast it over a small fire. Again Sholem refused to eat pork, though he clearly needed nourishment more than the others. The only food that seemed to keep him going was spiritual. It refreshed them all to hear him talk of Palestine. His words had a biblical flavor. His voice came from deep recesses within him, and he seemed to see it all before his eyes. "Every tree, every blade of grass, has its spot on earth from which it draws its strength," he would begin. "Men have those roots as well." To him, Palestine was a pastoral paradise where they would live at peace with the birds and the little beasts of the desert, far from the barbarous cities and the conflicts of mankind.

The twins gave him their enraptured attention, seeming to hear with their eyes. Dan also hung on Sholem's words, though it was the only time he ever thought of the future. It was hard enough to survive the present, day by day.

Only Gideon ever registered disapproval. He would watch and listen with his head on one side like a gundog, waiting. "Castles in the air," he might say. "Somebody's got to put foundations under them."

On this particular occasion, fatigue and hunger must have prompted him to take his dissent a step further, for he said, "Do you want to know what I honestly think about all this talk? Do you?"

"You're bound to tell us anyway," replied Hanna.

Sholem leaned forward with eager anticipation.

"I think this world is just one big free-for-all, and the winner will be the guy who gets up first while all the others are still flat on their backs. And all of God's good guys—the martyrs, the rabbis, the Sholems—are just going to lie there with their jaws broken. The one bastard we ought to have learned something from is Hitler. We don't need bees and flowers. We need blood and iron."

"That's not Hitler. That's Bismarck," Hanna corrected him.

"Bismarck, then. You know what I'm talking about," Gideon said. "I'll never forget the way you stalked that German on skis and took your time and killed him." Hanna's face began to lose color. "And you were proud of it then, Hanna. You weren't worried about whether he had kiddies at home." Gideon obviously enjoyed telling her story, but the blood had vanished entirely from Hanna's face. Without fighting back, she turned and slipped out into the darkness.

"You see?" Gideon shouted. "You see what this flower talk has done to her? A year ago, six months ago, she wouldn't have done that. She'd have told you the story herself. We can't become soft. You know what it means to die like a Jew? It's like saying 'to die like a dog.' Well, if we're not going to become extinct, we must give it a different meaning."

He looked from one face to another, but none seemed ready to help him or come to his support.

"Damn fools," he said, and, turning, followed Hanna into the dark.

"Poor Gideon," Sholem said. "He's tired and hungry. We all are. I don't blame him for losing faith. But we'll bring him around. My voices . . ."

"Do you hear voices?" Dan asked suspiciously.

"Yes, I hear yours."

"I mean when you're alone."

"Sometimes; inside me. It's like a voice telling me what to do."

"In your imagination?" Dan asked hopefully.

"Of course," replied Sholem, smiling. "How else would one hear voices?" He had done a great deal of thinking at Sachsenhausen, he said. About God first of all, and then about Palestine. God was an enormous thought, big enough to shut out pain and fear. It didn't matter what one called Him, Jehovah or Allah, or even, like the Germans, Gott. He was one God and He belonged to all the world. But the world was in darkness and did not understand this. It was up to Israel, which had waited so long for something to live for, to be the bridge between the darkness and the light.

Now a new age was dawning, a time to abandon the barbed wire and surrender one's arms. It would be an age of greatness, a new renaissance. People had said so before, but Sholem had no doubts. This time the world would not forget. Soon would come the day when the young herdsman and his flock would walk side by side with the wolf.

As Dan listened, he thought he heard in Sholem's voice the genuine intonations of prophecy. Just then, Gideon returned with Hanna, and began to apologize.

"Sometimes I just lose my temper."

"You need sleep," Dan told him. "If I slept as little as you . . ."

"Shut up," said Gideon.

Sholem unquestionably remained their spiritual leader. He kept them toiling toward Austria through cold days and colder nights. Up to this point it had been the twins who had held them back each day, but clearly now Sholem's chest was

74

giving out. He still denied it, and insisted, "We must all stand on our own feet," when Hanna would offer him a helping hand.

Dan had liked Hanna from the start, but he respected her now. There was something uncanny about the way she kept clean on this march, as though grime did not exist for her. Never once had he heard her complain of hunger or exhaustion. Never had he noticed her lose her temper, and it was with this steady good nature that she finally persuaded Sholem to take her arm. He had allowed no one to touch him until now.

More and more he leaned on Hanna, and as his strength diminished, his companions worried. Both Dan and Hanna revered him as they would a holy man.

"You know what he told me today?" Hanna said. "He told me we ought to go ahead and leave him to come alone more slowly. I almost cried."

"He'd go to hell instead of heaven just because the poor souls there needed help."

"And we'd follow him all the way."

"I know. What can we do? He's sick. You only have to touch his hands to know how really bad he is."

There were herb remedies. Some people said that being buried up to the neck in the soil could draw a fever.

"It would only kill him faster," Hanna protested.

"Of course," Dan agreed. "There's nothing to do but get on with it and hope we reach a warm climate. Unless we give up." But Sholem less than any of them was ready to surrender.

So Hanna rallied her faith. "He'll make it on willpower alone, if need be."

"But he can't work miracles," Dan cautioned. "Listen to the way he coughs."

"I think sometimes he is a bit of a miracle."

"Our Moses? I hope so," said Dan. But he had his moments of doubt, when he thought of Sholem as a misguided Pied Piper leading them into oblivion.

The following day they stumbled along under a dull yellow sky. Rain showers fell intermittently. Dan assumed they were lost. Even Gideon could make only a pretense of locating them on a map, which made the sudden appearance of a great mist-shrouded river all the more a shock.

They stood on its steep bank, dumbfounded, until Dan said, disbelieving, "Could it possibly be the Danube?"

"The Danube!" Gideon searched his map. It could only be the Danube, the Gypsies' dustless road that led to the sea. They had passed into Austria without even knowing it, and were much farther along than any had dared to hope. Under the dull autumn rain they enjoyed their discovery, the small houses along the bank, a castle on a rocky bluff downstream. There were no boats in sight and no bridges, and the joy of discovery gradually gave way to the problem of crossing.

Sholem began to cough. He had learned by now to camouflage it by continually clearing his throat. The others understood his device and tried to ignore him.

"Well, we can't stand here dripping," Hanna said.

They took shelter as best they could in a grove of evergreens by the bank. The branches were dense, but the rain still filtered through and settled on their clothes in tiny pearl-like globules. Better than nothing, it was no real refuge. Rather than setting out in one direction or another at the rate imposed upon them by Sholem and the twins, Dan and Gideon would quickly explore east and west along the bank.

Dan plodded east through a thin gray drizzle. The houses he approached were locked or abandoned. The only boats

76

had their bottoms broken. At one point he heard through the mist the haunting conspiratorial voice of river traffic. Somewhere out there a barge full of Rumanian Jews had been marooned in 1940 while the Nazis hounded them. Well, he would settle for less than a barge, but modesty was unavailing. He found nothing of interest except a signpost that indicated it was fifteen kilometers to Vienna. This small ray of hope he took back with him through a mist that had grown so thick he heard a cough before he knew he had reached his comrades. Then he saw Sholem standing like a big water bird, hunched against winter weather. Hanna had tried to get him to relax, but he had refused as long as Dan and Gideon were out searching.

Gideon had already returned with only a hard loaf of bread to show for his efforts. He announced truculently that they couldn't stay here living on prayers. When Dan mentioned the sign, Hanna snatched at this hope. They must go to Vienna and get a doctor. Sholem instantly opposed this, and Gideon backed him up.

"Sholem, you need a doctor," she urged for the first time openly; adding, "So do the twins. You only have to look at them."

"We can't afford it," Gideon replied.

Dan revealed his American money.

"Fine," said Gideon. "With that we'll be taken into custody for sure."

The old Hapsburg city, which none of them had ever seen, was a powerful magnet. Hanna spoke wistfully of its Baroque palaces and fountains and the famous Opera. "Just what we need," sneered Gideon. "Maybe we can see a performance of *The Gypsy Baron*." There was some talk of Austrian food, of dumplings and strudel.

"And barbed wire," Gideon reminded them.

"Possibly Zionists," Dan said for counterweight.

What decided them was the river. In Vienna at least there would be bridges. "We'll go then, and cross tonight," Sholem told them, finishing the argument. As if to prove they need have no concern for his health, he set out ahead with a stiff jerky pace that made him look like a clumsy puppet.

Throughout the wet afternoon they walked steadily down the widening valley of the Danube, past hay-stacked meadows, castles, small towns with needle-pointed churches, and factories moth-eaten by war.

They would have reached Vienna by late afternoon had not one of the twins begun to lag, and then, with a cry, not from his lips but from his brother's, fallen face down. It was simply a matter of fatigue and hunger. Dan helped him to sit against a tree. Sholem produced a small lump of chocolate, and the boy, looking like a wide-eyed famished squirrel, took the gift in both hands and devoured it. Finally, with Dan giving him a supporting arm, they moved on again. It was a cold, foggy evening when they arrived in Vienna. Few people were abroad, and the streetlights were gay and warm through the mist. The gray outlines of buildings did not show the destruction of war.

Dan had feared that the bridges might be patrolled, but the first one they found was unguarded, and they crossed over. At the far end Sholem announced a decision. For the sake of their health, the twins must stay behind. While one, his face as hollow and sickly as an El Greco child's, translated in hand signals to the other, Sholem openly wept. These were the earliest, the most fragile, of his disciples, and he loved them.

"I wonder," he said to Dan. "It's a great deal to ask, but if you could let them have just a small loan . . . I'll pay it back, naturally." Reluctantly Dan surrendered a ten-dollar bill, part of his small hoard of that green and universal currency his grandfather had obtained on the black market. Sholem seemed overjoyed in passing the money along. At least it would get them a meal and a doctor; in the end undoubtedly the money would lead them to a displaced persons' camp, which was, though no one mentioned it, about their only hope of ever reaching Palestine alive.

Clearly the twins were desolate, but they had never questioned Sholem's decisions. They did not now. The fog soon engulfed them as the others went their way with heavy hearts. They were now reduced to half their original number, and Dan felt those four that remained were somehow invincible. If one faltered, the others would hold him up; if one failed, all must surely fail.

They agreed it was safer not to be seen in Vienna during the day. They found no shelter, so they tramped through the fog all night. By morning it had vanished, leaving a varnish of ice everywhere. They rested for a few hours in an abandoned shack, continuing that afternoon through uplands of spruce, pine, and copper beech. Toward evening it rained again, steadily, a cold steely rain that put the chill of the Ice Age into their bones. To make matters worse, the road had been washed out and they had to ford a stream full of floating ice. Their feet were numb and heavy. They all complained bitterly except Sholem, who for the first time leaned heavily on Dan's shoulder. Fortunately the area afforded numerous huts, used by shepherds only in the summertime. They came across one now, and were able to make a fire. By morning the rain had stopped, and they went on climbing. The wide pastures swept down from one rocky ledge to another like stairs. Through openings in the clouds they saw the variegated gleam of the mountain walls on either side, jagged peaks piling up against the sky. Beyond them lay the sea and the great unknown toward which they were moving.

"The sea" had become a magic word. It meant the warm plains of Italy, and help that was waiting there. *"Thalassa! Thalassa!"* They had adopted the catchword at first in good-natured imitation of Xenophon's staggering legions. Now it was an incessant thought that Dan could not put from his mind. At each turning of the road he longed for it. How much farther could they go? Yet each turning brought only more mountains, and God knows they were feeling it now. Even Hanna walked with a weary roll, and Sholem's cheeks burned with a telltale flush. At night his cough kept them from sleeping; a hesitant, restrained cough, but regular as a dripping tap. "My God," and again, "My God," Gideon kept muttering, not to Sholem as much as to the cough. Dan kept silent, but he shared the longing of the others to press a pillow down over Sholem's mouth and hold it there. He felt guilty for it.

"You're half dead and don't know it," Gideon told Sholem the next morning. Sholem smiled at him without resentment. It would have been infuriating were it not such a part of his nature. "Maybe I'm beginning to find out," he whispered.

Only Gideon never appeared to tire. All day and at all hours of the night he had a dependable flow of energy. Nor did he seem to mind the cold. "It's the truth. My temperature's always been a couple of degrees above normal, like a dog's." In one way only was he fallible, and that was in map reading. Two days out of Vienna they found themselves following a road that no longer tallied with the chart. To make matters worse, Sholem required more help than Hanna was able to give. He appeared to have shrunk and grown much older. In spite of protest, Dan drew his arm across his shoulder. With the added burden, Dan's legs became so tired and his muscles no longer had any feeling. His feet continued to move sluggishly, with no sensation of touching the ground.

"It can't get any worse than this," Hanna said.

Then it began to snow.

Both Dan and Hanna agreed they would have to stop for a few days. Gideon, who now led the way, objected. "It may seem bad, but if you want to know my own humble opinion, it can get a lot worse. What we need is warm weather."

"But look at him over there. Just look at Sholem."

The boy huddled beside the road, eyes open but scarcely seeming to see.

"Well, what?" Gideon demanded.

"Can't you see it written on his face?"

"What? What the hell are you talking about?"

"He's sick."

"Hell, I know that."

"I think he has influenza. He may be dying, Gideon."

Gideon placed his hand against Sholem's forehead, and a change came over his face. From that moment they searched for shelter and for help, but it was night before they finally found a house. The door was locked. They knocked gently at first so as not to prejudice the inhabitants, then louder. Gideon was about to smash through a window when a light appeared under the door, and presently, with much rattling of keys, a crack. Into the opening the jaundiced face of an old woman was inserted, all sharp nose and flabby gourdlike cheeks. It reminded Dan of the hard breastbone of a chicken. They tried to communicate, first in Yiddish, then louder in snatches of whatever other languages they knew, at last wildly with hand signals. To no avail: The door slammed in their faces, only to open again fully as Gideon was about to test it with his shoulder.

An old man with rivery white hair stood there, his expression one of concentrated austerity. He did not want them to come in. A large knife in his left hand was proof of that. But he was willing to talk, or as it turned out, experiment with a variety of animal sounds and gestures. They tried everything: gobbling sounds for hunger, hands folded beside heads for sleep, groans for exhaustion, coughs for illness, to all of which he listened patiently, smiling slightly, the knife still aimed.

Then Dan tried the word "Italia," simply for directions. The man fixed on it, repeated it with amusement, and finally wrote out on a piece of paper, "Yugoslavia." Then he pointed at the floor, all around. There was no doubt where they were. Italy was not far, but as the travelers well knew, the Yugoslavian border was swarming with British patrols and sprinkled with detention camps full of luckless Jews.

Their reluctant host finally indicated a small whitewashed chapel where they might rest. Here Dan, within whom hunger crawled like a long-legged centipede, took the initiative. Recklessly he displayed an American bill, and this more quickly than anything else brought results: bread, cheese, some dried meat. Finally they asked for medicine. "Medicina," tried Gideon, because they had had luck with Italia. The old man shrugged, smiled, and they got the impression that given time and some more money, he might find a doctor. Dan handed him another bill.

The chapel stood neglected and isolated in a gap in the woods, at a dead end. Its roof was sagging. Inside, it was bare and depressing as a sealed tomb.

"I feel like a butterfly in a killing box," said Dan. "I don't like it."

82

"I don't like any of this," said Gideon. "Satan must have had a good deed in mind, so he put hell on earth and called it Yugoslavia."

"It's too cold for that," said Hanna. "Give me hell any time, just for the warmth."

"Why stay here, then?" said Gideon. "Are we waiting for the next Ice Age? It's on its way tonight. By morning we'll be frozen solid. No more problems."

"You know we have no choice," said Dan.

"What I like least of all are those people. That man and the way he smiled. I don't trust him. Maybe I should use this pitchfork." He indicated an old farmer's fork leaning against the wall.

"And what, Gideon?" Hanna demanded.

"Kill him. *Kaput.*"

She flinched at the German word.

"They're all right, Gideon. We're none of us saints."

"There are saints." Hanna reached for the fork and Gideon let her have it. There was loose straw on the floor and he began kicking it together.

"I don't trust these people," he said, simply to end the conversation. For a time they were quiet, collecting the straw. Outside a melancholy wind hummed through the trees.

The one reason they might have to stay for several days had not been mentioned. It was, of course, Sholem. He sprawled loosely in the corner as if he were about to fall apart. His skin was pale. His shoulder gleamed whitely through his rags.

He had to be forced to eat, so Dan, though saliva rose sudden and sharp around his tongue, suspended his own appetite and held food to his friend's lips. Sholem turned his head away, but when he was made to understand that the

83

others would not touch food until he had eaten, he opened his mouth and tried to chew. His wasted throat moved with difficulty, but food went down.

They had all finished eating and were arranging a blanket of straw over Sholem when Gideon stiffened into an attitude of acute awareness. His cheeks sucked in nervously, his eyes widened. He had the stance of a deer that smells hunters upwind. Shaking his head in evident disgust, sufficient to baffle the others, he stalked out into the night.

"What's that all about?" asked Dan.

"Did you hear anything?" Hanna asked back.

Dan listened at the boarded windows. At first there was complete silence, then a faint scurrying. Rats or field mice? He opened the door a crack. The cold wind made him gasp. Sharp stars pierced through the blackness, unromantic as pointed daggers.

In one corner of the chapel drooped a great dead Christ, with a neat hole in his side, a fallen head, and a crown of thorns painted on his wooden hair. He was shrouded by a gauze of spiderwebs in which hung moths like so many bits of rigid satin cloth. Beneath the cross lay Sholem, mercifully asleep. Dan and Hanna heaped the rest of the straw over him.

"What are you listening for?" Dan demanded. Hanna had turned a disturbed and unseeing face toward him, as absent and preoccupied as a mask of Siva. "What is it?" The impatience in his voice cut the fine thread of her concentration.

"I wish Gideon would come back."

"No, really, what is it?" There was more to it than that, he felt sure.

"I don't know. It's just a feeling, a premonition." She dismissed it with an embarrassed laugh, but Dan was serious.

84

"My mother had premonitions," he said. "They always made me nervous." He was edgy now, not because of what Hanna had said or because of Gideon. The memory of the time he and his grandfather had been taken had returned to his thoughts. "Maybe it's the cold that makes us edgy."

"Or maybe it's being so near to where we want to go. Just a day or so, and all downhill into Italy. And we're sitting here. It's tempting fate. I wish Gideon would come back. He didn't take that pitchfork, did he?" She put her finger between her lips.

"I never knew you were a nail biter. And don't worry about the pitchfork. It's right here under the straw."

"You're a good person, Dan. I mean, you're . . . well, humane."

If she hadn't seemed so serious, he would have laughed. "Not particularly," he said.

"Really, I have a feeling you'd never let me down."

Again he denied this, but her words came as a command he would have to obey.

"Don't underrate yourself." Her smile was so straightforward, so dazzling, he had to look away to hide his pleasure. Yet every word she said was a shackle of confidence, binding him.

"I mean it," she said. "I do. You don't have to look away, Dan. You're so conscientious, sometimes you make me feel a rotten sort." He could only shake his head. "Do you know I was sort of afraid of you at first? You looked so forbidding. But you've a very aristocratic nose and nice eyes." She put her hand gently on the back of his neck. No one had touched him in quite that way since his mother had done so years before.

"I wish you'd known my family," he said.

"Funny, I was just wondering what you were like as a little boy."

"Anonymous, I think. Anonymous and forgettable."

"My father used to say I was hell on wheels," she said, yawning.

"Hell on wheels? What does that mean?"

She yawned again. "I guess I was, anyway. Where's that Gideon?" She didn't sound very interested anymore.

Presently her eyes closed. He realized she had fallen asleep almost as she was talking because her breath became a purr. Not a snore, but a kitten's purr.

Dan tried to sleep. It was late and he was exhausted, yet his legs would not obey him. They kept trying to run of their own volition, like a dreaming dog's. He envied the girl the effortless progress of her sleep. With pale lashes resting like crescent moons upon her cheeks, she looked pretty. She was smiling in her sleep. Dan had always avoided touching people, but now he placed his hand over hers. The knuckles lay under his palm like the ridges of a small backbone. The touch of the incredibly living flesh informed him instantly and in a completely unfamiliar manner that there was life and hope. He felt a wave of fondness so uncommon that he became giddy.

"Hanna," he whispered, too softly for her to hear. "Hanna." With the word on his lips and the thought that life was good and the future a thing to savor, he finally fell asleep.

After what seemed a matter of seconds, he woke with a jolt as though the earth had gone over a bump. Gideon was back, but there was something wrong with him. Across his face in the early dawn light passed shock, astonishment, outrage, then downright fear. He screamed something at them. Hanna was groping awake. In confusion, Dan struggled to his feet.

The old farmer stood there, grinning like a jack-o'-lantern. Beside him were several soldiers, heavily armed. Then another man appeared, a small bag in his hand.

Gideon slashed past them. He had nothing but his life to lose. He broke through one of the boarded windows as the stranger with the bag shouted something in English.

Hanna put her hands to her throat as though shielding nakedness. She glanced once at Dan, then sprang for the window. Dan followed her through. Ahead were dark pine woods. Gideon had already plunged into them when a whip seemed to crack through Dan's mind. Sholem!

For all his madness, Dan loved him. Perhaps he loved him more because of it, for his madness was more beautiful than the good sense of others. So he turned back, through the window. Sholem sat in the heaps of straw like an owl scared blind by converging flashlight beams. Scooping the pitchfork out of the straw, Dan advanced toward the group of strangers.

"Don't be daft, boy," said the English doctor. He had the round good-natured face of a young Friar Tuck. "Put that thing down."

Dan felt a great weariness settling upon him. "Yes. Yes. All right," he managed in English, letting the pitchfork fall. Under him the ground seemed to slide.

"You're a long way from home, lad." He heard the English voice fading as he fell.

Dan was only dimly aware of being carried out. He felt the touch of snow on his face. He saw the faded parsnip face of the old woman from the night before. She looked at him closely and spat. From her chin a few hairy roots seemed to spring. One of the soldiers rebuked her and pushed her away.

From the forest Dan could hear the deep baying of dogs.

CHAPTER 4

THE BRITISH DETENTION CAMP OCCUPIED A BARE HILLSIDE two miles from the Italian border. Twenty army barracks were laid out in two neat rows. Each was fitted with a stove and iron cots, and all were surrounded by a high barbed-wire fence. The only camp building outside the compound was the hospital. Behind it were the pine forests.

The inmates were Jewish infiltrees caught on their way to Palestine. Most were young, and all were uncooperative. They would do nothing to enhance their surroundings, for to do so would be to admit defeat and lend an air of permanence to their imprisonment. It was all the guards could do to get them to march around the grounds twice a day.

At first Dan would not even eat. He felt possessed by a consuming lethargy, without hope, disillusioned and doomed. He communicated with no one, but wrapped himself in his own dark and spiraling thoughts. It was only a day's walk down to the soft vine-covered Italian foothills, another to the sea. From the hospital he could see the water flashing in good weather, and he felt a fierce longing for freedom, the most ordinary, physical freedom. With sensuous clarity, he imagined himself taking that walk. Then he would look at the barbed wire, at the guards, and life would become a cheat and a disappointment, a mere passage from one unreality to another. Even Kaph-hakal, that hellish torment in which a sinner is tossed from one end of the world to another, would be better. At least in passing he might see Palestine, he might see Hanna and Gideon safely on their way.

"Eat up, lad. No good starving," an English soldier encouraged him. "Your mate's coming round. He'd be dead without sulfa. Both of you lads are lucky to be here."

Dan had heard it said once that the average Englishman had a smaller vocabulary than a Laplander. Of course he didn't know anything about Laplanders, but his own limited English was sufficient to cope with this soldier.

"And how long will we be here, then?" he asked.

"Ar, that's the burning question, ain't it?" The guard gave a half-boyish grin which suggested honesty. "If I were Attlee, I'd have us out of this bleeding cold place in no time."

"I suppose work will make us free?" said Dan.

"How's that, mate?" The soldier did not understand the joke. "I'd eat the flaming food if I were you."

Here, in comfort, Dan's boredom and hopelessness had somehow increased. Pain and hunger were no longer present to distract. The one good thing was Sholem's health, which drugs, rest, and regular food had improved. His spirits had never failed, and he tried to cheer Dan. "You can't simply sit there and rust," he would say. "Eat. Exercise, keep in good condition. We won't be here forever." He spoke constantly of Palestine, as though he were there. He described houses nestling among enormous green trees, geometric fields, flocks grazing in the meadows, shepherds piping tunes that were sweet and sad as those sung in the temple on the Day of Atonement. He yearned for natural happiness, to go to bed tired from honest work, sweat-drenched in summer, stiff with cold in winter.

89

Dan would listen absently, the mushrooms sprouting in his heart. He admired Sholem's faith, but could no longer share it. "Sometimes I feel shaken," Sholem confessed. "Then I shut my eyes and I'm all right again. Try it. Shut your eyes." With a shrug, Dan obeyed. "Tell me, what do you see?"

"Nothing."

Sholem was obviously disappointed. "The first thing I saw was God."

Dan's grandfather may have known the number of whiskers in Jehovah's beard. Dan didn't know what had happened yesterday, let alone what tomorrow might bring, and before his closed eyes was nothing but gray emptiness.

"Naturally," Sholem continued, "God appears in the shape one imagines Him. It's logical. Otherwise, one would see only emptiness. Do you know how He appeared to me first? It was after I'd been burned with microfilm, and He appeared as a cool drink of water."

Dan opened his eyes. "If I were to see anything, I'd want it to be an armored tank to get me out of this place."

"Stop worrying. You'll get out. I promise. Think how long we Jews have been on earth and survived. We're deathless, in a way. We'll get out, but we must keep up our strength. Every day you must be more ready." When the spark failed to catch, he tried another approach. "You want to see Hanna again, don't you?"

"Why? She ran off fast enough. Anyway, she's Gideon's girl."

"You should have heard her talk about you."

"Go to hell."

"I mean it. When she talked about Gideon, it was only to apologize for him. Dan, we only have a little hope and a little love. They're like seeds planted in all of us, and they have to be nourished."

90

Life was hard, but love seemed harder still. Dan had loved his family, and he had lost them. He had never really had Hanna to lose, and yet he did love her. He could tell her so when she wasn't there, but he couldn't understand why he felt as he did. She was not really good-looking. She had never shown him any special attention. Then why? Whatever arguments he presented to himself pro or con, he always arrived at the same conclusion. He loved her and felt sure he always would.

By the time he admitted this rather sheepishly, Sholem had won him back to hope. All that night they talked, comforting their hearts with the thought of friends and the Promise of the Future.

They talked until the sun rose, each adding his store of anecdotes. By breakfast call, Dan's attitude had completely changed. He ate with determination, though his bowl of gray and glutinous mush was an affront to his palate.

"What is this?" he asked in anguish.

"I don't know. I've never eaten it before," Sholem replied.

"It seems to me I've stepped in it once or twice." To get it down, Dan put on lots of catsup. "I feel as if I'm mixing cement." Still, it was nourishment.

After breakfast he went into training, beginning with a set of exercises: squatting, hands on hips, hands over head, legs apart, legs together. Before him was the window, beyond that the fence and the forest. He threw open the window and breathed deep of the snow-heavy air. With a little effort, he could imagine the soldier promenading there was not a guard, but a protector.

"Close that perishing window!" the guard shouted. Then, looking more affable, he strolled over. "There's no getting out of here, if that's what you're thinking. You'd have a rum go in this weather."

Dan would have shut the window, but the guard was feeling conversational. He'd just been detailed back from Palestine. He didn't think much of the Arabs. "The way Churchill said, you give them a job and they finish off the tools. Still, they're better than the Jews."

"Why?"

"Well, because we British like the underdogs, I suppose. Old Arab, he'll take a shot at you in the night, but he'll give you a pot of coffee when you come around investigating in the morning. Bloody Jew doesn't even offer you a cup of coffee when you've spent the night protecting him."

Dan slammed the window down hard, making a jagged crack in the glass.

That night from bruised gray skies rain began to fall on the sea and on the Italian coast. In the hills of Yugoslavia it fell as snow. Dan yearned to make a dash through it, under the wire and away. Without Sholem he would have a chance, but to leave Sholem would be like leaving part of himself. So he stayed and watched the mounting snow, an endless fall of flakes from a brimming sky, until the camp became a colony of white temples and the great weight of snow bowed down the forest trees. Outside, the marching boots of the sentry made no sound.

When Chanukah came, Sholem fabricated two yarmulkes. Dan would not wear his. Undaunted, Sholem begged a candle and broke it into eight stubs, for the eight days of pure oil. Dan sulked. If it were not for Sholem, he would already be in Palestine.

Lying in bed, he imagined himself there. When dreams took over, he became an autumn apple, the last one hanging on an autumn tree, wind-worn, falling, never landing, tumbling into deeper sleep and another dream of perfect happiness and freedom. In this dream he swam ashore from a boundless sea. He walked through wide cool meadows with sheep at his heels. There was no one else in this dream, only the silence, the sheep, and the birds passing by overhead. Then he sat down in the tall grass, and as he waited, the grass parted and Hanna appeared. She touched his hand with remote, cool fingers. They embraced, never saying a word, while the sheep ranged politely about them. Then, as he was about to kiss her lips, she began to cough, a convulsion of coughing followed by an eruption of blood that brought him wide awake, gasping with horror.

Sholem was coughing in the night. When Dan lit a lamp, he saw that his shoulders were thrashing like the wings of a crippled bird. His face had a pewter sheen.

"Are you all right? Do you need the doctor?" Dan asked him.

"It's nothing. Go back to sleep," Sholem assured him.

In the next few days, all the gains that Sholem had made disappeared. It seemed to Dan the flesh visibly fell from his bones, like wax melting in the heat of some inward fire.

"Have you been hemorrhaging?" Dan asked him one night.

Sholem denied it, unconvincingly. He refused to be touched, but one night when he lay helpless in sleep, Dan felt his forehead.

"You've got to go to the hospital," Dan told him in the morning.

Pride glowed in Sholem's dull eyes for a moment. "No. If they put me there, I won't come out again." As if this were a dangerous admission, he added, "The warmth of Palestine is the only thing I need. Tell me how it is there, Dan. Tell me how it is." So Dan talked about the palms and the desert, and the Promise of the Future basking under the sun.

"Tell how we'll go together."

And Dan described a night in spring when they would break away and take a ship to Palestine. Finally, Sholem slept. Dan could hear his lungs bubbling every time he breathed. He could stand it no longer, and called for a hospital orderly. One look at Sholem was enough.

"How did this go unreported?" the orderly demanded. He wrote out a hospital pass. "We'll have him picked up in the morning."

Dan was left alone with his friend and his thoughts. He didn't think he could stand it alone without Sholem. On the first dark night he would rush the wire. He was rested and well fed. There was a new solidity to his body. With a little luck, he could make it.

He sat through the night beside Sholem, who wakened occasionally and worried because Dan was not asleep. "I'll get sleep enough later on," Dan said, and added falsely, "We'll have you well in no time."

Sholem had enough courage to look into his own dark. "I don't want to die," he said. "I mean to put up a fight. But if I lose, I want to do it well."

"Don't talk like that, Sholem. I hate it. Go to sleep."

For a while Sholem was back in Sachsenhausen under torture. His body groaned and cried out while his withdrawn self watched idly. He was breathing hard and deep. "Do you know how to see God?" he said. "Close your eyes. To hear Him, you must stop up your ears." From Sachsenhausen his thoughts moved on their inevitable course to Palestine. Dan came to realize that no matter what, Sholem would never be less than Sholem. Even now his face remained alight with the most perfect hope. There was a day coming, he told Dan, when men wouldn't belong to different tribes or religions or clubs. Then there wouldn't be any wars because there would be no cause. But until the last man was included, there would be no real human society.

"Sleep, Sholem. Sleep now."

The sick boy nodded to himself, as if with each nod he drove his point home a little deeper. Dan tried to get his glasses away so that he would not roll on them in sleep, but Sholem clung to them, muttering, "No, I can't see. Everything's so far away." His breathing came irregularly, with terrible effort.

"God," Dan prayed, as he had not done within memory, "make him well or give him peace." He heard a rasping distant voice repeat, "God." Sholem did not speak after that, but seemed to drift away. Dan put his glasses on the table between their beds.

Toward morning Dan nodded and fell asleep. When he woke, it was very cold. He could see his breath in the air. Outside it was still snowing.

Sholem's covers had fallen off and his body emerged from them, pitiful and appalling, as from a winding sheet. "That's no way to sleep," Dan said, taking hold of one hand that trailed to the floor. It was heavy and cold. With sudden terror he saw that Sholem was regarding him from behind a narrow slit of open lids, his eyes the color of weak milk.

"Wake up, Sholem. Sholem! Oh, God, no! No! You died without letting me know!" He felt betrayed.

Dan sat beside his friend, his hands gripping together until the knuckles were white. "My fault," he repeated with miserable insistence. "My fault. I should have stayed awake." But he knew it was no one's fault. Sholem had known he was doomed from the start, and his death had been as civilized and lonely as his life.

Dan could not cry. He did not know how to behave with

95

the dead. Their enormous deafness and rigidity demanded privacy. This was no longer his friend. He felt himself in the presence of some wise old prophet upon whose face resided a terrible marble repose.

He went to the window and eased it open. The sharp air made him gasp. There were no guards in sight. If a dash to the wire offered little hope, at least it represented involvement. A backward glance stopped him. Sholem's glasses. They should be on his face. Returning to render this last rite, Dan noticed the hospital tag wired to the foot of Sholem's cot. Even in death Sholem seemed to help him, and placing a kiss on the high pale forehead, he left him to the English who would parcel him up for a foreign grave.

A guard stood, shifting from one foot to the other, at the main gate. Dan showed him the hospital pass. He offered to remove his boots and display his feet, hoping the scars would pass a hasty inspection. But the guard waved him on, saying, "Straight to the hospital, mind. I'll have my eye on you."

Remembering to limp, he made slow going on the drifted road. A half-buried truck winked its headlamps at him as though in real distress. A gust of snow blotted out everything, and he was tempted to run for the woods. It passed quickly, and the guard was still watching as he entered the hospital door. An orderly showed him into a waiting room. Two doctors were there examining a dark X ray that might have been a cyclonic storm in the Baltic Sea. They ignored Dan, and finally left the room together.

Dan stole to the window. No bars, no wire beyond. In a moment he was through and clumsily running. Behind him came a muffled exclamation and a shout. Then he was staggering through close-grown pine trees in a shower of snow, rolling and tumbling. The wind played tricks. He seemed to hear shouts of pursuit coming from every side, the howling of dogs on a scent. So he stood for a moment breathing hard, alien and lost in the white and soaring gloom. Then he ran again, always downhill toward the warmth of the Italian plain.

Often he had to stop, for his old boots were in shreds as hard and stiff as wood. They hurt at every step. How long he floundered through the pines was impossible to say. There was no sun in this stormy world, and the faint light never varied. It must have been well toward evening when he came upon what seemed to be a road. There was no trace of vehicles, but it was recognizable as an empty white slash through the trees. There Dan should have made better time, but exhaustion was catching up with him. He felt oddly taller, and his feet were a great way off. He could feel the impact of the road under them, but very little seemed to exist in between. "I can't get tired," he thought fretfully. "I must not get tired or sleepy." He began to repeat this aloud in time to his feet.

He could scarcely think rationally anymore. His head seemed full of snow, and he pondered how it got there. He was no longer capable of surprise. His brain felt about to freeze solid. Only his teeth had renewed life. Moved by some reflex, they continued an annoying chatter. It never once occurred to him to turn back.

Darkness was coming now, swiftly. He could scarcely distinguish the road. "Hurry! Hurry!" he urged himself on to Palestine. Sholem urged him on. He could see his friend's eyes, his smile. "But it's so cold, Sholem." The deadly chill seemed to coil around his heart. At first he did not realize he was down, crouching on all fours, because he could no longer feel his own body. It seemed indistinguishable from the snow. He was turning into a snowman! Someone would give him a carrot for a nose, two lumps of coal for eyes. This made him laugh. Surely there had to be some corner where he could curl up and get warm. Again Sholem urged him on. Or was it his grandfather tapping him on the shoulder? "You must stay awake, Danny. The Nazis will shoot anyone who can't keep up. Get up, Danny, get up!" Squinting, he saw motorcycles passing, the slogging backs of prisoners. The endless procession swept past him on the wind. His grandfather and Sholem were pulling him. He stood up, bobbing like a cork through water. "Hell is white," Sholem whispered, and then it was not white anymore but rich green, the vineyards of Italy, the sea. "Look, Sholem. Can you see it?" Dan smiled at his friend. The hot Mediterranean sun beat on his back and on the top of his head. Then something roared and flamed inside him. The world turned black and an immense silence seemed to press him into oblivion. Stars, sun, bright grains of snow, spun round into darkness. Dan huddled at the core, forgotten, lost, infinitesimal.

He lay face down in the snow. A thick white powder formed swiftly on his back.

CHAPTER 5

DAN AWOKE TO BLINDING LIGHT. HEAVEN, OR THE FIRES OF Hell? Through half-closed eyes he saw Jesus Christ walking toward him over water. The faded picture hovered like ecto-plasm on the wall beyond his feet. Dan was in a wobbly brass bed under much-mended and rather damp sheets. The room was small and shabby. Besides the bed, it contained only one chair. Unupholstered and hung together with wire thongs, it reminded him unpleasantly of an electric chair. Like music, there drifted on the air the sound and scent of frying oil. At a more subtle level he was aware of unwashed clothes and de-fective plumbing.

Dan tried to sit up. His head spun, and he clung to the mattress. At that moment a face looked in at the window, so briefly it was no more than a shadow passing before the sun. Presently voices rose in exclamation.

Footsteps approached, and a man entered. Shaped like a soda-water bottle, the man had a dark brilliantined love curl on his forehead and a brilliantined moustache like two tiny rolls of barbed wire. Incongruously, his eyebrows were heavy, Cagliostrian, his eyes protruding and expectant.

Dan lay back, too weak to fight, expecting the worst. The man leaned over him, the great eyes boring, his bulk exuding a wave of garlic and rancid oil.

The man babbled at him in a strange tongue. Dan whispered back in another. The man tried French. Finally, hesitantly, Dan responded in English. The man stood back, grinning.

"Whatta you say? Eh!"

Dominic Barbasso was delighted. They both spoke American. He had spent some years in the States: Newark, the Bronx; he named the great cities where he had lived. "You feel better? I please to hear. I like find out from you . . ." Dan hid nothing, and in return he was informed that this was Muggia, a small Italian fishing town not far from Trieste. The people here were poor, very poor. They understood the plight of a poor Jew seeking a homeland. Perhaps they could help one another. With this, Dominic tugged at a watch chain hanging across his globular vest and pulled out an old watch. He winked at Dan. "The watch for expenses, eh? Whatta you say?"

At first Dan was confused, until he recognized his father's watch. Then he was furious. The little tin-pot Mussolini! He tried to seize the watch, but he wasn't strong enough. Dominic pushed him back onto the bed. "Danny, resta you'self." He tried once more to grab for the watch and failed. "You waita one minute." The explanation was simple. He and his wife were poor. Perhaps there would be a reward for runaway Jews. On the other hand, there was a boat leaving for Palestine before the week was out. "You agree? For the expense?" A poor out-of-work Italian in Muggia had to eat. "What you say, Danny?"

Defeated and suspicious, Dan asked what sort of boat it would be. Dominic gave a great sigh like a burst inner tube. "A Greek boat, a caïque. I no fool with you. I like to help, my boy. I lika for you to get good impression. You hungry? I bet you hungry boy."

A large bowl of spaghetti was produced, and a plate encrusted with grease and tomato sauce. This Dominic dusted with a rag. He breathed on it, then polished it again as though to give a high luster. He handed the still filthy dish to Dan along with a sticky fork and spoon. He asked forgiveness. There was no grated cheese but he endeavored to make up for this with a heaping mound of spaghetti topped with ornamental worm of tomato paste and a dousing of rancid olive oil.

Over this repast Dominic said a prayer softly, intimately, finally cupping his hands over his breast as though to imprison the blessings which flowed from the words. "Now eat. Good food. We take good care of you. You get your money's worth out of old Barbasso."

This was the first mention of money, and with it came Dan's realization that his pockets were empty. He was penniless. Still, the food was welcome, and Dan ate until he could hold no more.

His host ate from the bowl, then sat back in the wooden chair mining his teeth with a metal toothpick. The process elicited loud appreciative sucking noises.

"Good?"

Dan nodded.

"You betcha is good. Now sleep, rest." He patted Dan on the head. "You trust Barbasso."

For three days Dan lived on pasta and tomato sauce. Because of it or in spite of it, he felt stronger every day. He got to know his host, and to enjoy his mannerisms: his clumsy air of a trained seal grappling with human emotions, his tittering helpless laughter when amused, the little cough which was his invariable comment on the best of his phrases. Barbasso had been a fisherman and a pastry salesman. In the First World War he had been wounded at Caporetto. Proudly he

101

displayed an old belly wound which was located near the center of his torso and looked like a second navel. He grumbled about the government, which had no appreciation of its heroes. His stomach was still a discomfort to him, his liver was worse, his constitution in ruins. How much of all this was fact or fancy Dan could not say, but to Dan he was as good as his word.

On the third evening Dominic led him outside. He showed him the horse and wagon which he'd been driving downhill through the snow when he'd found Dan ten miles from town, showed him now the way to the sea. It led down narrow streets of houses roofed with orange tile. Behind them in the distance rose the bleak hills of Yugoslavia. From them the shadows advanced as the earth rolled on its axis into darkness. Barbasso led him by a stone fountain, by artisan shops, loading platforms and warehouses on the waterfront, by fishing boats pulled up on the beach. The snow here was thin and melting into muddy shapes. They passed the customs house unchallenged, and there on the sand Dominic said good-bye.

They parted as friends. Dan was to walk until he saw a small fire by the water's edge. "And take care, Danny. The English, they always looka for trouble."

There was no sound except the waves lapping the sand in flurried gasps. Corks lay bobbing in a thick yellow scum. Overhead the stars came out, sparkling like chips of ice. In the sea, Dan could just distinguish the black silhouettes of ships that Allied bombs had wrecked.

He walked so far that he began to suspect a trick. Maybe Dominic had simply gotten rid of him. Then he saw in the distance a flame, motionless in its contained lipidity. It burned close to the shore, laying an oily orange stain on the water. There were indistinct figures, some walking, some

102

standing by the fire. So this was to be his last night in Europe. Ahead lay the sea, and Palestine.

Dan gave an involuntary grunt as something round and hard was thrust into his back. Turning, hands above his head, he faced the muzzle of a carbine, and behind it a British uniform. He was subjected to an intensive scrutiny. Then the gun was lowered and the soldier addressed him in Yiddish. He was from the Jewish Brigade. There was a Star of David patch on his shoulder, if Dan cared to look, and they were both where they were supposed to be, waiting for a caïque.

The slow moments gathered themselves until midnight had passed. The emigrants stood in little groups with an air of hushed and reverent expectancy. Their rags fluttered in the wind. Many were barefoot; others had wrapped their feet in rags. Most of them were thinner than Dan. Their cheeks were hollow; their bones stuck out. Toward morning a few lay down on the sand. There was weeping and prayer. At last a silent ghost of a boat appeared. It was low in the water. Its smokestack looked like a coal-black candle and was almost as tall as its two masts.

The caïque ground onto the sand and the refugees crowded around it, knee-deep in the icy water. Sailors began to pull them in over the sides. There was no time for Dan to meditate on the fact that he was leaving Europe forever. He scrambled aboard and helped an old woman to follow. Presently the sailors put their shoulders to the boat, the engine stirred. For a moment the caïque stuck and then it pulled away. Soldiers on the shore gave a muted cheer.

Some of the Jews prayed aloud in a babble of tongues. Others wept. Great tears ran down their cheeks, forming a moonlight sheen on careworn faces. They were slaves at the moment the collar is struck off. Some were too frightened to

103

pray. The boat was loaded to the gunwales. They might drown and never see Palestine. They might be eaten by fish and cast up on the sand to be picked at by unclean birds.

Silently they passed beyond the sea mole. A dog barked at them, a sea bird swept overhead. The water was calm beneath the stationary stars.

The morning was misty. It was warmer on the Adriatic. The sun's rays drew up little spirals of mist, like rings from a giant's pipe. They floated lazily above the ship. Far away Dan could see the mountains of Yugoslavia, where clouds were building up over the peaks. Below, the sea looked dull and brown.

It would take a week or more to reach Palestine, they were told. Those who grumbled were reminded of the *Knesset Yisrael*, which had been nearly a month at sea, with water and food being rationed, before Palestine was sighted. They should welcome the time to relax and plan for the future.

Dan felt mixed emotions on first seeing his fellow passengers in the light of day. He felt pity, then anger, that they should be so mean. They reminded him painfully of human inequalities and the depths to which Jews could be driven. There were Russian Jews in battered black hats and long gabardine coats; Hassidim with flowing earlocks; survivors from camps with scalps still showing the effects of the razor, their flesh pale as scoured pumice stone. Then, as he looked longer, he began to see a worn beauty in their faces, as if, like the earth, they had taken part in all the catastrophies of nature. The record of their race was etched there. The gray flesh was a parchment recording the painful march of civilization, wars, migrations, persecutions. The harsh history of Europe had left its mark, but they had survived, and even the

104

ugly ones wore their ugliness proudly, as if it were a kind of beauty.

If the passengers were a mixed lot, the crew was more so. The majority were Greek, and they spoke not with their mouths alone, but with their faces, eyes, hands; their arms flailing the air in emphasis, modifying each gem of wisdom as it spun from the speaker's lips. There were a few Spaniards, exiled Loyalists from an almost forgotten war. The helmsman, Ah Feng, was a little Chinese man with a face like a wrinkled yellow apple. The Greek captain called himself Odysseus, and was drunk more often than not. His spray-splashed oilskins made him look phosphorescent.

On the third day out they were passing south of Corfu. That morning an old man had announced to Dan that there was a storm about. He could feel it in his bad shoulder. By afternoon Dan had only to look at the sky, which had turned the color of dirty steel. Shreds of tarnished clouds veiled an angry sun. The sea had grown dark. It was licked and stroked by foam from the rolling crests.

To add to the general distress came another alarm. A ship was sighted. Long, gray, indistinct, it vanished as quickly as it had been seen. Perhaps it was only vapor exhaled by the sea, but the rumor persisted that it was a British destroyer.

That night Dan tried to sleep on his improvised berth, a hard, narrow shelf against the caïque's outer hull. He could hear the waves sloshing and gurgling along the outer planking. He had managed only a few moments of shallow unconsciousness when he felt something cold crawling on his neck. He sat up and brushed off a cockroach. Then he noticed a file of bugs crawling down the wall, over the hand of his sleeping neighbor and up inside his sleeve. Dan leaned over and nudged him, pointing to the roaches. The other made a grimace, brushed them off, and with a shrug fell back to sleep. But Dan was fully aroused. A cockroach stood looking at him thoughtfully from the headboard, waving its mandibles as though gesticulating in nervous conversation. At that moment a wave hit the ship and the cockroach fell.

The storm was picking up. By morning several passengers were seasick. A woman had gone into labor. There was still speculation about the British destroyer. Was it a destroyer, and had it seen them? Had it a right to stop them? Legally, perhaps, a few argued, but in fact no power on earth could stop them. The British must realize that even if they stopped this little ship, others would set out.

Dan did not join the argument, but he was sure of one thing. He was never going back. He would drown first.

By afternoon this had become a very real possibility. Low clouds writhed overhead like coils of a brown snake. The floundering caïque buried her bow in the smother, then struggled upward like a rocking horse, waves creaming over the wheelhouse.

The caïque had a draft of only four feet, and when the big waves began lifting her propellers out of the water, the engine was shut down to spare the bearings. Only two small storm sails propelled them along, and each icy wave struck with a shock that was felt from stem to stern.

Dan lay down and tried to stay flat. He wedged himself against the wall, but even the floor flung him away. He was reminded horribly of a carnival fun house he had visited when he was a child. The other passengers were strewn about in no better shape, clinging to piles of disorderly baggage.

Assorted tongues and dialects voiced their anxieties. The British destroyer had been seen again. It had struck a mine and sunk off Albania. The captain was drunker than ever.

The helmsman had been seen praying to a heathen idol. They were sinking. Those who were able turned to their Pentateuchs. Next to Dan, a Talmudic scholar with black caftan and side curls bent so low over his Torah that his beard rested on the page. He read aloud in awe and fear and humility, "Save us, O God, for the waters are come in even unto the soul." His hands shook as he turned the pages and he mumbled of angels turning the unworthy away from Jerusalem.

Dan could hardly hear him above the roar of the sea, but what he heard made him afraid. He was secretly relieved when the prayers ended in seasickness and the rabbi lay down, mute and unsavory, among the other sufferers.

Throughout a terrifying night the storm held them at its mercy. But through the mixed blessings of prayer, a ship sturdier than she appeared, and a tenacious crew, they did not sink. By morning the sunlight flamed through shattered clouds. Little by little the clouds shredded away and the gale became manageable. The wind of freedom seemed to swell the caïque's sails.

"We make fly." A black deckhand from Guiana grinned through pearly teeth.

And they did fly south into the Mediterranean, toward the green continent of dark-skinned tribes and wild beasts. Water sloshed about in the forecastle, was atomized and blew away as mist from the rails, made glittering glassy fans of spray on the deck. The pump manned by Jewish volunteers stuck, choked, and pinched the hands that plied it, but they were alive and on their way. Behind them Europe sank forever into the wine-dark seas of Greece.

The sea remained rough, with waves that broke and swallowed their own foam. Dan could see far below the surface.

107

Now and then a rain squall would dash across the surface, driving passengers to cover. By the second day the storm had passed entirely, though the sea remained heavy, each wave a watery slab in which the ship buried herself, trembling. By evening a golden finger issued through the thinning clouds, a portentous sight that led to jokes about God. In the morning the skies had cleared entirely; the waves were tiger-striped and lion-maned, and it was good to be alive. The only sad note was that the woman who had given birth during the storm had died. With the Greek flag lowered, she was put over the side, a stranger in life and in death. Though an orphan born in a storm, her baby did not die. They called him Israel. Many parents, having lost their own babies, vied so passionately for the child that the captain had to decide the issue by a drawing of straws.

Dan lay back with his head on a coil of rope. He looked like an underfed Byzantine saint with a large halo. The sun felt good and he was almost asleep when a child said to him in Yiddish, "I had three throw-ups yesterday. Two through the mouth and one through the nose."

"Well, you're a lucky one," Dan told him.

"I am. I'm going to Palestine."

The rabbi joined them. "It's a good thing to see a man sitting silent and not sinning," he said. "That is particularly true when he is sitting on a ship that is going to Israel." This sounded like Scripture, and Dan nodded and smiled and hoped the rabbi would leave. Yet it was true. He wished that Sholem could have been there to feel the spring morning and see the sky which fell away to heaven like an endless blue tunnel full of puff-ball clouds. "Sholem." He whispered the name. It sounded heartbreakingly forlorn. He had been Sholem's protector, and he had failed to save him. Now he

108

could only hope to carry forward his ideals insofar as he understood them.

By the next morning the waters had turned as brown and oily as the Nile Delta. In the distance was Sinai, the cloudy coastline of a dream come true. But the passengers were given no time for dreaming. Instead they were organized on the stern deck, where a Haganah veteran addressed them. They listened with reverence; this was Israel speaking. With luck they would go ashore at Caesarea before the following morning, they were told. There Herod had built a city in honor of his Lord. There, too, twenty thousand Hebrews and their sage, Rabbi Akiba, met martyrdom. The Crocodile River still flowed to the sea where Akiba was skinned alive. Unless they listened carefully, disaster would strike at them. They risked detention pens at Haifa or endless confinement behind barbed wire on Cyprus. Fifty thousand Jews were on Cyprus already.

As soon as the boat reached shallow water, they must go over the side, destroying their papers as they went. Haganah would have people waiting on the shore to meet and hide them from the British. The British must not be underestimated. They had a real stake in the future of Palestine. Their empire depended on Arab oil and Arab friendship, a harmony which the unchecked arrival of immigrant Jews could only disrupt. And if the British were thorough in ferreting out illegal Jews on land, they were more deadly at sea. Some immigrant ships were protected by iron plating and steam hoses. Their caïque was small, too low in the water. They must rely on stealth alone. Silence would be their most powerful ally once night had fallen.

For the rest of that long day, the passengers were warm and friendly, bound together by a thousand invisible threads.

109

Each of these people had a hard protective shell which had been a means of survival. Now they were one, inside a single shell. They began to sing in impromptu choruses, not in a brave attempt to hide past grief, but in the joy of comradeship.

Dan felt himself bursting with a million barrel-organ tunes. He began to whistle. It was not really happiness, but rather an overmastering relief of mind. He had arrived. For the first time he was quite sure. He had arrived, and his chest was too small for his heart.

An Asian wind, a wind that had filled sails and piled up waves and shattered on templed coasts, a ceaseless warm wind, drove them along toward the cloud banks of Palestine. Water creamed around the bow. The sea was blue and full of light. It was Noah's flood that still covered the world. With the first red tinge of evening, flying fish flung themselves onto the deck, as though deliberately offering their flesh to the hungry fugitives. Dolphins danced in the glassy water. Their backs were olive brown, their bellies pale and shimmering. Their pointed snouts split the water as they danced in pairs, swimming from side to side, crossing and recrossing, twisting on their backs as they leaped before the bow.

Evening lent a dreamlike quality to the air. A shower of golden dust poured from the sun, which rode on the horizon for a moment, then settled, dipping itself into the sea. To-morrow was the Sabbath.

No longer did the caïque parallel the distant coast. They were heading toward shore through phosphorescent water. The wind had died. They moved under slow power so quietly that the ship seemed suspended above the earth, with stars above and below. Barely visible, a seagull floated on motionless wings, its cry weird and restless. Smoke streamed from the caïque's black stack like an unfurling tattered flag.

110

Dan felt freedom like pure oxygen about him. It eddied in the air from the approaching land. It filled his lungs so that he wanted to shout despite all warnings. They were leaving the night behind. It had been long and full of nightmares. Many had been lost in it, but he had survived. With the dawn would come the first day of his new life. He felt vigorous and strong, ready for the happiness ahead. Promise of the Future. He would live well there, as Sholem would have lived, in joy and humanity. He would be granted a ripe old age as nature's reward for grasping her secrets of survival. Oh, to be happy was a fine thing. To understand the reason for one's happiness was bliss.

"Listen! Isn't that the surf breaking?"

The words were whispered about. They could all hear the waves breaking on Palestinian shores. The rabbi pulled out a little bagful of Palestinian soil and emptied it into the sea. Others toasted one another in whispers, "To life!"

Then someone cursed out loud. The crew began shouting, and at almost the same instant searchlights blazed in the night. Destroyers! British destroyers! They must have been waiting with their engines cut, for there had been no warning sound above the voice of the breaking surf.

In the brilliant light the refugees looked falsely happy. Their lips, drawn back in tension, resembled smiles. As the destroyers' engines throbbed to life and edged suddenly closer, someone ran out the Zionist flag, and the caïque, employing its hitherto silent auxiliary engine, made a ponderous dash for the shore. Green water foamed around her bow. Pressure mounted in the boilers until the engines visibly began to disintegrate. Speed quickly dropped and the destroyers, only momentarily caught short, swept around in graceful arcs. Marines crowded the decks, prepared to board with leather shields and lead-tipped clubs. A loudspeaker sounding from behind the galaxy of searchlights demanded immediate surrender. If they surrendered, the passengers would be escorted peaceably to Cyprus. Cyprus, where thousands languished in garish purple shorts and shirts made from the linings of their tents there. Never Cyprus!

The destroyers edged closer, looming enormous over the helpless caïque. As the waves from their propellers caught the little ship, the refugees panicked. Men looked for weapons and found none. Women clutched their despair between their hands like twisted handkerchiefs.

Then a woman threw herself over the side and vanished without a sound. Others plunged in, swimming toward the shore. By way of discouragement, the destroyers set off a string of depth charges, then closed in with lifeboats crowded with marines.

Dan knew only one thing. He was not going back, and he was not going to Cyprus. Slipping to the shadowed side of the caïque, he stared down an instant at the gurgling black tide below him. He had never been a good swimmer. "Daddy isn't going to hurt you. Daddy only wants you to see how nice the water feels." So long ago, and yet he remembered it still. He felt the same terror and revulsion he had then. Closing his eyes, he took a deep breath. "Sholem," he whispered, "I need your courage now." Then he leaped into icy water, cold as the death that faced him.

His shoes dragged him down, and he kicked them off with difficulty. Flashing lights blazed everywhere. There were shouts and the beating of oars as others were hauled into captivity. Dan struggled through the cold currents, moving like a muskrat, with only his eyes and nose above the surface.

He was using up his energy too fast, so he rolled over on

112

his back. In this position he knew how to float almost tirelessly. Slowly the tide carried him from the drama of searchlights and ships and broken hopes. Numbly he heard surf; or was it the ringing in his own ears? Coughing stinging saltwater out of his lungs, he began to thrash again, first with his right arm, then with his left, moving in circles until his body passed beyond the point of outrage.

He could swim no more. He barely managed to roll on his back again and float on the surface, where he counted the unsteady thuds of his heart and waited uncritically for the moment when he would sink. His body ebbed and flowed with the currents. It seemed to grow enormously, to contain within it a galaxy of stars. The waves pulled at him, tumbled him over, and the water entered his lungs.

CHAPTER 6

DAN LAY IN A WASTE OF BRACKISH WATER WHERE THE SEA HAD flung its harvest of weed and shells. It was daylight and the wind was still. Waves broke among the rocks and raced in toward shore. Sandpipers were printing the beach with their delicate graffiti.

Dan was only dimly aware of all this. It couldn't be the land of milk and honey. There was a smell of rot and decay in his nostrils. A few meters up the beach a sea turtle lay dead. A thin dog was feasting on its entrails, closely observed by a vulture. The vulture crooned and gurgled, ruffling its feathers with hungry annoyance. Occasionally, overcome by the dog's slobbering enjoyment, it tried to share in the feast, stabbing and yanking at the carcass with its fierce beak. At each approach the dog, shivering with fury and starvation, would assault the vulture, which flapped into the air with a thunder of wings.

Despairing of the turtle, the vulture approached Dan, its head tilted quizzically on its long neck. Dan watched it dully, felt the cool of its shadow, and defended himself only when its beak struck the back of his neck. Staggering to his feet, Dan threw fistfulls of sand and shells at the bird. "Damn you! Damn you!" He raged in vain at the terrible thing called life.

"I'm not dead," he screamed at it. "I'm alive." He was a cat

114

with nine lives. If not nine, certainly two—his own and Sholem's.

Weak and dizzy, he lay down again on a shining crescent of sand. He was alive, and he would stay alive. Once more Atropos had opened her shears and permitted his thread to spin. Surely there was a reason. The warming sun revived him. The cool air of morning filled his nostrils, and hunger rumbled inside him. There was no sign of the Haganah; scared off by the British, undoubtedly. No sign of British patrols, either, though they might appear at any moment.

He sat up, still dizzy. He ought to do something. He could try to hide, or go inland, or follow the beach one way or another. Then he saw an old man approaching. He paid no attention to Dan, but with evident remorse stooped to bury the great sea turtle in the sand. Perhaps it was because his hands and feet were gnarled and knotted like the turtle's that he felt pity for the creature; perhaps because he loved the sea and what came from it. He was a stocky man, barefooted and roasted by the sun. His long striped shirt had faded to the same milky blue as the morning sky.

He moved over to face Dan and nodded a greeting. He must be a fisherman, Dan thought. The man's dark and salt-swollen hands held a length of bleached rope. The man spoke in Arabic, and when Dan did not respond, he looped the line around the boy's waist and yanked Dan to his feet. The man set off determinedly, and Dan was obliged to follow on rubbery legs. They walked along the beach for some time, through huge blocks of masonry that had tumbled from the cliffs, by fishermen and their nets, by children who were guiding wood-chip sailboats in puddles left by the outgoing tide.

Ahead were some shacks made of driftwood and stone, and

115

the old fisherman led Dan toward one. Dan stumbled to his hands and knees, but his captor pulled him firmly and gently through the entrance. Dan's eyes were red with weariness, and he couldn't see where he was going. The man helped him to a bunk, where he toppled forward, his face and arms on the bed, his legs on the floor. His legs were carefully raised, his forehead touched by a horny hand. Then the fisherman departed. "He smells like Neptune," Dan thought. "There must be saltwater in his veins, not blood. Saltwater." Then he fell asleep.

Dan slept until the following noon. He awoke coughing, his throat and lungs still raw from the sea. The small room was lit by fluttering firelight, and smelled of fish, cardamon, and garlic. The old man was preparing a meal. He nodded as Dan sat up and indicated a place by the fire. Dan joined him, sitting cross-legged on the sandy floor. As he watched and waited, saliva collecting inside his mouth, his host took a small brass trident and stabbed it down into a wooden bucket full of saltwater. When he pulled it out, a squid writhed around the prongs like a nest of vipers. The old man leaned forward and calmly bit the sea creature on its neck. The writhing slowed, an inky liquid oozed out, and the squid gradually grew slack and still. Cut into ringlike sections, it joined a chowderish brew sitting on the coals.

Dan was too hungry for niceties. He ate what he was given, and the nourishment shot through him with the healing properties of plasma. The fisherman watched him eat with pleasure. Then he prepared a water pipe for himself. His brown face softened as a pale cloud streamed out beneath his tobacco-stained moustache. When he caught Dan's eyes, he smiled. Did he mean this was the good life? They could not communicate in words, but Dan returned the smile with real gratitude.

116

The following days were lazy, thoughtless ones for Dan. Whether he was a prisoner, a companion, or a prospective apprentice he did not know. For the moment, he did not care. The only clue was a framed photograph of a boy. It hung on the wall of the hut, partially obscuring an age-yellowed picture of an Arab woman. With the odd sensation of a second birth, Dan knew instantly that he and the boy who stared so enigmatically back at him looked like brothers.

His daylight hours were spent on the beach, sometimes learning to mend the nets, mostly lying in the sun or collecting sea shells. At dawn the sea was the color of opals and mist trailed across it like scarves over the bosom of a beautiful woman. Later it grew dark, almost indigo, running away from the land when the sun was high. It was the sun that purged him of his European poisons, the sea that washed him clean, so that he could almost say Sholem was right. Nothing mattered as long as the world was simple and good.

Daily, Arabs came and loaded their donkeys and camels with hampers of sand. They were building something, somewhere. The fishing boats came and went, regular as the dawn and the dusk. His old Arab fisherman sat on the sand every morning repairing the nets. As he worked, he sang in a gravelly voice, his lips pursed. His hands were blunt and ingrained with salt, the fingers fat as sausages and crisscrossed with the burns of fishing lines. Few of the scars were fresh. They seemed as old as dry riverbeds in the desert, but they did not prevent his hands from performing with dexterity the fisherman's arts. Spare sailmaker's needles and wax and the net itself were held between his toes which, like his fingers, were swollen by saltwater. Clearly he had never worn shoes.

Dan admired the old man, so like his grandfather and yet so different. Both were artisans in their own way. How many pleasant hours they had been given by the using of their hands. Dan lingered day after day, watching the sea and the sun and the quiet old Arab, tempted by the thought that here was a chance to live in peace. But it was too lovely, too clearly a siren's song. With a lifting of his spirits came restlessness. He must not forgot Sholem or the Promise of the Future. He felt sure that he would find Hanna and Gideon there.

In the end Dan was spared the pain of initiating a change. His idyll was abruptly concluded on a windy morning when the salt spray rose in clouds, dusting the shacks with white crystals. Seabirds, their cries shrill and whirring, rode against the blast.

The old fisherman was already on the beach with his nets and tackle. Dan was about to follow him when two figures barred the door.

Large and glowing with health, they looked somehow immortal, as though no seed of decay could flourish in such hard flesh. The taller of the two wore a bushy moustache and a smile. He stood alertly at the door, long sinewy hands at his sides. The other, clearly in charge, was stocky. This one made a quick search of the small room, pulling back bedclothes, opening drawers, prodding in corners with heavy hands.

Apparently satisfied, the shorter intruder ordered Dan outside in a voice that was harsh and slightly shrill. Dan complied; there was nothing else he could do. The three of them stood in the dazzling sunlight.

"We're following up a rumor," the stocky one addressed Dan in Yiddish. "It's gone around that this old man has been harboring a Jew. You are a Jew, I believe?"

"I don't know who you are."

"Haganah. You're from the Greek caïque, the one called *The Ark?*"

"I didn't know it had a name."

118

"And your name?"

"Daniel Baratz."

The taller man, who as yet had said nothing, fingered through a notebook, evidently found a relevant entry, and showed it to the other.

"I see you've had experience with explosives," said the leader.

Dan's astonishment at this information was matched only by his slow realization that his interrogator, though muscled like a wrestler, was a woman.

"Baratz, you're coming with us."

"Hold on, now."

"It's useless to argue, Baratz."

"I have a right to know where I'm being taken."

"Baratz, your rights begin and end with me," she told him. The only concession he managed to win was a moment to say good-bye to the Arab fisherman.

The old man seemed to know what was happening. He made no move to prevent it. What would have been the use? He simply spread his hands in the age-old gesture of the bazaar huckster, humble, humorous, and knowing.

Dan could only project his gratitude by an uncertain smile. "You've been like a father," he said in words he knew the other could not understand. "Stay well, old man. I won't forget you."

"Come on, Baratz. He can't understand you. We're in a hurry."

So he went.

They directed him to a waiting car, an ancient and decrepit Ford that should have been scrapped before the war. Somehow it ran with jolting determination along the coast road. As they progressed, Dan heard from his kidnappers

119

what they knew about the old Arab. For as long as anyone could remember, he had been a fisherman, born into a fisherman's clan. In his old age he had fished alone with his son, until they'd run into a floating mine. The mine could have been German, English, even Italian; who could say? The explosion had been heard up and down the coast. The boat of course sank. The son was never seen again, but miraculously the old man had dragged himself ashore. Now he spent his time on the beach, mending nets and wandering along the seaside.

Presently they entered a city. "Ascalon," was all the woman said. It had been the Ashkelon of the Philistines, later a Roman city where Herod was born and where Salome lived. In 1270 the Sultan Baybars had laid it to ruin. Now the streets were narrow and crowded. Dan saw veiled Arab women, Bedouins wrapped in black abas, British soldiers strolling as though off duty. That was all he glimpsed, for the woman abruptly shoved him down on the floor of the back seat and pulled a rug over his head. "Don't worry," she told him. "We have the right papers."

The car stopped suddenly and Dan was thrown against the seat. He struggled to rise, but he was held down by his captors and summarily blindfolded. "It's all right, don't worry. Simply a formality," he was told by the woman. He received a reassuring pat on the shoulder as if he were a large and emotional specimen of another species that needed pacifying.

Dan was guided in darkness around a corner, down some steps, through a door that slammed and echoed. The cloth was removed from his face and he saw a room full of desks and discolored cardboard files bulging like ill-made sandwiches. Indifferently shaved clerks were drinking glasses of tea. An overhead fan stirred the dust on the floor.

120

At a second door the woman knocked and said something in Hebrew. The door clicked open and Dan was pushed into a small room full of blinding light. It hurt his eyes. Before him was the silhouette of a desk, and behind it a heavy-shouldered bull-necked form that sat in the brilliance like a stone. From this presence exuded an aura of well-kept living leather.

Dan was forced into a chair and a voice floated from the glare like oil in water.

"Your name?" He gave it. "How do you spell that, please?" The questions covered everything: his life in Poland, the camps where he had been imprisoned, his journey to Italy, the caïque. "You say you swam ashore?" Dan nodded. "No one else managed to get ashore alive. Did you know that? A few bodies were washed up. The rest were taken to Cyprus. You are either very enterprising or very lucky."

At this point the questioning stopped. "Well, Daniel Baratz," the man said, "here is your first Hebrew word—*chavera*." Dan repeated it hesitantly. "That means 'comrade.' Perk up, Dan. You're permitted to smile here. Be of good cheer. You're among friends." Standing up, the man behind the desk touched a button and the spotlights flickered out, leaving only one unshaded bulb shining from the ceiling.

At last Dan got a good look at his interrogator. The man was large, but lithe. His face was the product of sun and wind, the features frozen except for one eye which was alive and darting as a hawk's. The other, Dan would learn later, was glass, and except for its stillness it would have been hard to tell which was false. Clearly this was a man of power who accomplished what he set his mind to, a man who was willing to pay the price for fulfilling his dreams.

Leaning forward across the desk, he offered Dan a hand in

121

greeting. "Just call me Chavera," he said. Smiling, he continued to stare at Dan with his one good eye. It was a trick he knew well, and his gaze never faltered. "What really interests me, Baratz, is you," he said. Since Dan did not know exactly what was implied, he kept quiet.

"We need you," the man continued.

"I don't understand. Need me for what?"

"We have a rule here," said Chavera. "An eye for an eye. When the British compel us to take measures, we cannot compromise. We take them. Many of your friends died at sea. Surely you want revenge."

"I had no friends on the caïque."

"Relatives, then. We are all blood relatives here, Baratz. Tell me. . . . You have made land mines. Wouldn't it give you satisfaction to see a mine fashioned by your own hands go off under a British truck?"

Dan hesitated. He was afraid of this man, who was clearly a despot; a not unkindly one, perhaps, but a ruthless man of iron will, a born leader feared by enemies and regarded with apprehension by friends.

"I don't want any more trouble," Dan offered.

"Life is trouble. Only death is not." There was a reckless set to Chavera's mouth, but his eyes seemed contemplative now. He was a man accustomed to loneliness and brutality. "Will you join us? Yes or no."

"Join who? I don't know who you are."

"Our organization. Just repeat after me: I, Daniel Baratz, do give my body, my soul, and my being without reservation or qualification—"

"They told me you were Haganah, but I don't—"

"Let us say we are affiliated with Haganah, when it serves our purposes."

122

"Then who are you?" Dan insisted stubbornly.

"Irgun." Now the man's voice was soft. "Have you heard of us?"

Dan had heard. He had seen their symbol, an arm holding a gun with the caption, "Only Thus!" Founded ten years before to combat the Arab radicals, the Irgun had since turned upon the British. Their members were men and boys; women, too, it seemed. They lived to fight and kill, not as soldiers fought, but as gladiators, with only two alternatives: their own death or their victim's.

Dan had not risen from the dead to seek death again. "I don't want to get involved," he said.

"Involved?"

"In killing."

"Everyone here is involved. Completely."

"I have plans. It's a matter of duty."

"Duty to whom?"

"My conscience," Dan said. He couldn't mention Sholem, who would only be a joke to these people.

Chavera pressed his hands on the desk and seemed to be comparing the length of his fingers. Then he stared at Dan. "I will tell you something about conscience," he said. "The Jewish conscience. We Jews have always been the world's cuspidor. We've become accustomed to push ourselves from place to place, saying 'please,' and 'dear sir.' No home of our own, not even a bed of our own. Now our Procrustean friends, the British, would like to fit us to their bed. We may lose our feet in the process, but what difference to a Jew who is accustomed to using only his knees? At last, Baratz, some of us have developed a conscience. We want to stand up and take our place in this world. But England has her hands on our shoulders, heavy hands, and the Arabs are egging her on.

123

'Cut off the Jews' feet,' is the chorus," He leaned farther forward, transfixing Dan with his brilliant eye. "Dan, there is going to be a war here. The world is a stage on which there is always room for one more war. Now the stage is empty. It is our turn. What do you say?"

Dan said nothing at first. If they knew how he really felt, they would despise him. But Hanna, if he ever found her, would understand.

"You don't have to give me your answer now. Think it over."

Think it over, Dan thought, grinning sourly: the condemned man pondering his sentence, the target contemplating the arrow on its way. Delay would not protect him. There's a kibbutz. I want to go there. It's called Promise of the Future!

"Right here!" Chavera's clenched fist struck the desk. "Right here. We're the promise of the future."

Dan was adamant. Chavera stared at him with cold, unbelieving anger, his face lacking all sympathy. Lighting a cigarette, he blew out a long wriggle of smoke like the ghost of an escaping snake. When it cleared, his expression was still fixed with a sort of thoughtfulness. Evidently he expected something more, but Dan was determined to say nothing.

"Very well," Chavera murmured. His capacity for molding others' lives into patterns of his own choosing had evidently failed with Dan. Rubbing his chin on his sleeve, he gave a last contemptuous smile. "Okay. If you don't want to help, to hell with you. Take him away."

His original captors, who had said nothing during the interrogation, seized Dan. In Chavera's presence they were puppets, but puppets forged of steel. Dan went unresisting through a side door and down a corridor, where he stood for a moment as a heavy door was unlocked. Then he was thrust unceremoniously inside. His head struck the back wall, and he settled to the floor in a sitting position. Before he could recover himself, the door was slammed and locked. The back of his head felt warm and sticky and began to ache.

Hours later, someone brought him stale bread and coffee. A bucket of water and a bar of soap were also provided.

"Is that all?" he asked.

"This is charity. You're paying nothing."

Again the door was slammed with no indication of how or when they would dispose of him. Days passed. He would die of the mold and the damp. Worse than that was the solitude. At least in the concentration camps he had not been alone. Dan had a sudden need for people around him.

When the door finally opened and he was beckoned outside, Dan was ready to swear to anything. What he saw caught him completely by surprise. A deeply tanned young man stood there in khaki pants and white shirt with a Star of David suspended from his neck by a thin chain. It was Gideon. With a growl of delight he bounded toward Dan. They embraced with a grotesque effusion their past relationship scarcely warranted.

The big woman stood at the exit. No one else was present, and Dan asked her uncertainly, "Am I to go now?" Only then did she look directly into Dan's face, with the vacant stare of a person torn out of profound meditation.

"Why are you still here?" she asked.

So they went together through the door into dazzling light. Dan had to shield his eyes. Gideon laughed at his gropings. "You'll get to like it," he said. Palestine obviously agreed with him. He was so tanned that the scar on his throat was almost invisible. In spite of the fact that his fingernails were chewed down to the quick, Dan sensed in his old companion a new repose.

"You know, Dan," he was saying, "you're a bit of a local hero."

"What for? For managing to get here alive?"

"You might say that."

"Sholem didn't make it. He didn't even make it to Italy."

"I know. Poor devil. He never had much chance."

"How's Hanna?"

"Fine. When they contacted us about you, she wanted to come here." Gideon showed Dan a small pickup truck. "Nice, isn't she? Our little armored car." It was the supply truck from the kibbutz. There were metal sheets affixed to both sides of the cab.

Gideon swung into the driver's seat. Dan climbed in beside him. The engine sputtered and gasped, then roared like an airplane. Gideon snapped the choke in and out savagely. Then they lunged into the street, very nearly running down an Arab woman in a blue dress. She screamed and fell backward against the curb.

"You know, she wears that color dress to fend off the evil eye," Gideon commented dryly.

The truck coughed and jerked past open shops and taverns where Arab men drank their endless cups of Turkish coffee and played at backgammon. Gideon wrestled with the truck as if it were a colt in need of breaking, and they bucked their way into a marketplace. Here were camels and donkeys, beggars and mystics. Everything was for sale: flounder, onions, cheese, peppers, halvah, spun sugar sticks, trays of belt buckles and rhinestones, charms, and false teeth.

"Hello! Baksheesh!" Excited children yelled in at the windows. They ran along holding the headlamps and the door handles; anything to touch a car.

126

Gideon leaned on the horn to no avail. Then, as the market crowd began to thin, he gunned the motor into first, then second gear, accelerating so quickly that the truck arrived screeching at each blind corner before there was any need of third or fourth.

Behind shaded walls rose slim minarets, tremulous and white in the heat. On every side were the pale-purple blossoms of anemone and the orange-red of crowfoot. They passed an ominous sign painted halfway across the road in red paint, "Blood will be spilt." At last they emerged into open countryside. The air smelled to Dan as though God had opened a vast greenhouse. Above his head heaven's blue was streaming.

"Wonderful country," Gideon said. "You'll love it."

The truck picked up speed until they screeched to a halt at a British road block. "Don't panic," Gideon muttered. "I've got papers. Just leave it to me." They had no trouble. Grinning triumphantly, Gideon gunned the truck forward. Driving like an animal miraculously trained to manipulate a mad machine, he propelled them over the coastal plain. The scrub desert, the cultivated fields, and the drying wadis came at them at an incredible speed, and Dan could do nothing but cling to his seat.

"I wouldn't mind seeing a bit of the countryside, Gideon," he offered nervously.

"Sorry, early curfew," was Gideon's reply.

Buses full of Arabs and Jews, donkey carts, women carrying home water pots set gracefully on their heads—all flew past them.

"Damn women," Gideon said. "Think they're the lords of the road."

By midafternoon they arrived at Ramleh, the city of Gath which David had captured from the Philistines. It was a quiet town now, of sun-dried mud brick and sleepy men. Dan saw fine fruit orchards which seemed to be tended entirely by women.

"They don't even have any toilets," Gideon informed him. "Do we?"

"Damned right. Water and electricity, too."

"I hope you have some shoes," said Dan, looking down at his feet, which had been bare since the night the caïque was attacked.

"We'll fix you up with everything you need."

A flock of sheep held them up on the far side of town. Gideon thumped on the horn and cursed loudly, plowing his way through. After this they had clear going for another fifteen kilometers, only to be caught behind a convoy of buses laboring up slopes and holding doggedly to the center of the road. No amount of hornblowing forced them to yield, and when they topped the rise, they accelerated and swept fiercely downhill, leaving a cloud of blinding dust behind them. For half an hour Gideon waged a ceaseless battle with the buses, managing to steer, change gears, brake, accelerate, and curse almost simultaneously while breathing in sand and diesel fumes. Finally in a suicidal burst of speed they passed and careened around a blind curve where they were slowed to a walking pace by a straggle of Bedouin camels. Hunched over the wheel, Gideon pressed through them, impervious to comments by camels and their drivers alike. One of the Bedouins threw a stone and missed.

Now there was clear road ahead, and Gideon pressed his foot to the floor. "It's good to be a fighter again," he commented.

"You seem to enjoy it," Dan replied, thinking they were talking about the drive. He was quickly disillusioned.

"Would you like to hear some bloody tales of the horrible fight for freedom in tormented Palestine?" Gideon asked.

"No, thanks. Not with that introduction."

"Have you ever heard about old Trumpeldor who went through the Turkish lines to fight at Gallipoli? Have you heard how he died later at the siege of Tel Hai? We're fighters here. All my life I've been like a bowstring drawn all the way back. After a while you just have to let go. One day, maybe soon, I'll die for this country. I just can't imagine myself being middle-aged. No second thoughts, no tears. I just feel it."

"I wouldn't mind killing or being killed if it solved anything, but it never does," said Dan.

"Here's a present. Me to you." Gideon was handing him something.

It was an old Webley revolver which he had pulled from the glove compartment.

Dan stared at it. That was no gift, but a threat. "No, thanks," he said.

Gideon looked at him, a look that was both amused and contemptuous. "I don't understand you, Dan. How could you turn down the Irgun? What an honor! To be invited to join by Chavera himself."

"That man would give an order to the devil who was shoveling him through the gate to hell," Dan said.

"He's a great hero."

"Don't you mean an exterminator?"

"Go to hell," Gideon said with passion.

"Thanks," Dan replied. "I hope that's the last of your moral advice."

"You'd better give a thought to what you're saying, Dan. I don't want to wound your sensitivities with the facts of life,

129

but if we aren't at war here now, we soon will be. Listen, I'm just as much of a pacifist as you are, only I know how to shoot. And you'll have to learn, my friend. David may have won a war with a sling, but we need machine guns and airplanes now." Gideon talked about Messerschmitts that were rumored on the way. He yearned for atomic bombs so that the land of Israel as he envisioned it could expand over Asia Minor.

Dan began to realize he was another wild dreamer, Sholem turned inside out. He wanted to believe that the cruelty in Gideon's eyes and the twist of his mouth were not real, but an illusory trick of the harsh desert light.

"When did you join the Irgun, Gideon? Right away?" he asked.

"Me? I didn't say I'd joined them," replied Gideon. "Let's just say we're known to one another." Gideon seemed determined to be cryptic on this point, and Dan did not press the subject. He asked instead how Hanna and Gideon had reached Palestine so quickly. It was all luck, according to Gideon. Luck in having good weather for a week following their escape, luck in stealing two unguarded bicycles, luck in finding a goods train under Jewish guard. From Venice they'd ridden baggage cars down to Naples. They'd found a fishing boat willing to take them from Naples to Palermo, and another all the way from Palermo to Tel Aviv. "As our friends the English would say, it was just a piece of cake," concluded Gideon.

On the right they began passing an endless expanse of barbed wire. On some low buildings signs were posted: "Ablutions Other Ranks;" then "NAAFI."

"What's that all about?" Dan asked.

Gideon spat out the window. "British post," he said happily, as though he had raised a small standard of liberty with his gesture. "The empire upon which the sun never sets, as they say. Know why? Because God would never trust the English in the dark." There were blockhouses on the highest hills, and a segregated area for Jewish terrorists, complete with radios and other civilized amenities, amenities with which the British puzzled the enemies of their imperialism.

From there on, the road wound gradually down through the landscape of an alien planet. The contours were sharp and serrated as stone knives, the colors strident: purple, red, yellow, brown, with great cracks of black shadow. At first glance it appeared too poor even for goat foraging, but there were a few wild dogs, an occasional gazelle, and many slow-moving Egyptian vultures with white-and-black plumage. Down in the wadis the Bedouins grazed their flocks and spread black tents. Here and there villagers scratched a pitiful living from gardens on the slopes. Beyond were the marginal deserts of Sinai, full of waterless gullies and sand, with life only for lizards and vultures. Now and then Gideon would point out a kibbutz in a greener patch of tamarisk, stunted acacia, and wind-rolled Christ thorns.

"What about Promise of the Future? Is that here?" Dan asked.

"Damn right. Wettest place between here and Beersheba."

They followed the desert road, on which spice caravans once had marched. To Dan it seemed a place of mystery, where sandstorms rose unaccountably to engulf travelers finally and forever; where the sky was harder, less gentle than European skies.

"Don't look so discouraged, Dan. You'll get to like it. Hell, it's a challenge to all of us. Anyway, keep your eyes open here for a bit. We had a driver killed along this way." They were

131

winding around hairpin turns through an area of low hills. There were caves by the hundreds, the stone above their entrances blackened by the fires of shepherds. From one of them, a sniper had recently found his mark.

Without incident they arrived on flat high ground. Here were houses of burnt brick and hewn stone with red-tiled roofs, the homes of rich Arabs, according to Gideon. Beyond was the main part of town, a dreary prospect of blue-black stone and mud, all in shadow now. They drove through at a good clip, but even at full speed Dan could see there was no beauty in it. It huddled among the stones like a whipped, flea-ridden dog. Farther up the hill Dan saw a mosque. Somehow immune from the squalor below, its dazzling white minaret still held the sun.

"This isn't a bad town," Gideon said. "We get on. Of course they're backward as hell. Illiterate; no plumbing. If a few rats were smart enough to survive at the kibbutz, they'd be able to run the town council here. Damn Arabs scarcely have enough energy to throw a rock at them now and then. That's why the British like them so much. They make perfect colonials."

As they left town, some small boys playing in a puddle cheered the truck and showered it with mud. Gideon looked furious and gunned the motor, regardless of an old Arab who stood with his back turned in the middle of the road. His head was wrapped in a white scarf bound with goat's hair bands, and he didn't hear them until they were upon him. Gideon slammed his hand on the horn and the old man turned around, eyes wide, cheeks sucked into his mouth. He shouted something and waved a stick. In the nick of time Gideon grabbed the handbrake and slued around the figure, which simultaneously dived for the ditch.

132

Dan clutched his seat to prevent being catapulted through the windscreen. They had missed the old man, but a scavenger dog, lean from back-street living, stood before them transfixed by fear. Dan closed his eyes as the dog went under the wheels. Gideon scarcely slowed down. The dog lay there, a blot of blood and burst intestines, kicking slowly in the road.

Dan felt sick.

"I was just joking with the old fellow," Gideon said. "He's all right. See, he's standing up."

"What about the dog?"

"I don't think he did us any harm." Gideon's face was intent, his whole body attuned to the truck as he listened for the thump or squeak of damage. "No, we're all right."

A vast landscape now unfurled itself and helped to put the horrid incident out of Dan's mind. Gideon called it the Negev Highlands. They were green in spring and very dry in summer, when the riverbeds were full of shaggy sparrowwort and tamarisk. When the pioneers had first arrived, there was nothing but burned grass and a few shrubs. There'd been no road to speak of, just scorpions and vipers and Bedouins with their curved blades. Water had come in by mule back. Now they had a well and an electric pump.

"What's all that?" Dan asked.

"Trenches," Gideon told him. "They say the Australians dug them in nineteen eighteen. Look there, down the road. That's Promise of the Future."

It was dusk. Dan squinted ahead but saw only the empty road and the low hills. It was all strange and bare, and quiet as the hush of the seventh day of creation. "There. Over there," Gideon insisted. Then Dan saw a few palms and whitewashed buildings, like so many sugar cubes laid out in a defensive quadrangle. The whole scene was as flat and lacking in perspective as a painted cardboard set.

Dan felt stripped and plundered. How could anyone take roots in this desolate soil?

"But it's ours. That's what matters," Gideon reassured him. They drove on through a fence of barbed wire. A figure in shorts saluted, and Gideon parked before a large building. Gideon turned the ignition key with evident reluctance, and the motor died. Dan eased open the door and stepped very deliberately to the running board and then to the ground. A quick pulse throbbed in his temple. For better or worse, he was home.

"We're here, Sholem," he whispered. "Really here."

Dan had little time to reflect. Someone came running through the shadows. He had a glimpse of long tanned legs, square thin shoulders, and tangled hair. He recognized her in two heartbeats. The first one rose and faltered, and at the second he thought his heart would burst.

"Hanna!"

They gazed at each other with sparkling eyes for a moment, neither smiling but both seeming about to smile. Then, in the way she did everything, by surprise and with thoroughness, she kissed him joyfully on both cheeks in the ancient greeting. "There," she said. "There."

Dan was filled with stupefied delight.

Hanna laughed as he stood speechless before her. "I can hardly believe it's you," he stammered.

"Neither can I. I'm like some old woman: cry when she's happy, cry when she's sad." She wiped her eyes with the back of her hand. "Are you all right, Dan? You look pale."

"I'm the thick-skinned sort," he replied. "The blood doesn't show through. You look fine, Hanna."

Her brown legs were crisscrossed with scars of thistles and thorns. Her body was tanned to a Gypsy shade.

134

"A pretty boy, isn't she?" remarked Gideon, who never liked to be overlooked.

For a moment more they ignored him.

"Sholem's dead," Dan said.

Hanna's head moved quickly in affirmative nods. She knew. "Poor Sholem. If he could only have come this far."

"We all knew he was sick," Gideon said. "Death came as a judgment of mercy. You both know he wouldn't have fitted in here. There's no room for saints, not at the moment."

"Without him, none of us would be here now," Dan said. Between the land of the living and the land of the dead there was only one bridge, and that bridge was love. He did not intend to let that link with Sholem decay.

They started walking toward a long low row of buildings.

"Did you enjoy Gideon's driving?" Hanna asked.

"I shut my eyes and expected to open them on Judgment," Dan replied.

Gideon gave a whinny of pleased laughter and punched Dan affectionately on the shoulder. "Come on. Let's show old buddy boy his room," he said.

As they walked along, Hanna pointed out date palms, and olive and pomegranate trees. Down by the water there was some bamboo. Did he want to examine the bamboo? Or maybe the biblical ruins? Or the Bedouin tents? She was ready to show him everything at once. That night she would start him on his first lesson in Hebrew.

They arrived finally at a small room. One of many, it was little more than a cell containing a table and two cots. He would share it with Gideon. "There's electricity," Hanna assured him. "Only you have to use one thing at a time or you'll blow out a fuse."

Dan looked around him. At least it was clean. Dull, but clean.

135

"Learn to smile, Dan. Do try." She ran a finger across his eyebrows. Her eyes shone very close to his own. "There's a family feeling here. You'll share it soon. Home isn't just a building. It's something between people, something emotional."

Then, her old quicksilver self, she brought him a towel, shoes, and work clothes. The shorts and the cotton shirt he could turn in at the laundry once a week for a fresh set. Dinner was over, so she made him a sandwich.

"Is everything all right?" she asked apologetically.

"Fine, wonderful," he said. "It's just that, well . . . you come so far and count on a place so much and when you finally get there all you feel is tired."

"I know," she said. "Sleep well, Dan." She turned and walked quickly away. Dan never moved. Any doubts he might harbor were overcome by the fullness of his heart. He felt himself glowing with the aura of a new self-possession. No more wandering, no more plotting. He was home at last.

Out under the palm trees, Gideon washed his truck by moonlight. Then he wiped off the two guns he kept inside with an oily rag. Dan was asleep when he finally came to bed.

The following night was the Sabbath eve party for which everyone prepared with hot showers (as long as the water lasted), a change of clothes (if there were enough to go around), and a trimming of dirt-caked fingernails. With the darkness they gathered in the communal dining room. If a kibbutz was a living entity, the dining room was its throbbing heart. Here the feast days were noted if not solemnly honored. Only the old ate kosher, and they were few. Here plans were made and committees formed: kitchen committees, purchasing committees, education committees. Politics

136

were discussed without passion in this room. The conquest of the desert sapped the energies of would-be politicians.

Hanna was describing this to Dan as she pulled him along. She looked scrubbed and clean all through. Dan would happily have skipped the whole affair. "You have to meet your new family," she insisted, "and there'll be white tableclothes and candles."

"I'm tired, and I'm shy." He hated to disappoint her, though. She looked so excited.

The people he met there, a hundred or more with names he quickly forgot, represented no community of age. They ranged from the very young to the very old, but all were tough and determined, used to working hard in the unyielding desert. They wore their best Sabbath clothes, not new or fancy, to be sure, but clean working garments that usually fit. Later in the evening they broke into groups according to age. The older members shared a nostalgia for pioneering days when they were the first and alone, and the future was unmapped. The young regarded themselves as soldiers ready to die to preserve what their elders had built. There were a few new arrivals like Dan who looked and listened, outsiders still. Then there were those who would always be outsiders, for their ears were tuned now and forever to the sibilant hiss of the gas showers of Europe.

From the kitchen with its reluctant kerosene stoves the food came first in a trickle, then in a flood. Coarse and unattractively healthy, it appealed to hygiene, not gastronomy. There were mounds of hard-boiled eggs and fresh onions. There were bowls of *tahina*, a thin sesame-seed spread. On this occasion, there was also mutton.

Though Dan was entirely satisfied, Hanna sounded mildly apologetic. "Everything is improving so fast, Dan. One day we'll have silver candlesticks in here, and chandeliers."

137

"Chandeliers?" scoffed Gideon. "They wouldn't even clear the table tops if you hung them in this room."

"Just you wait, Gideon. This will be a proper ballroom. We'll raise the ceiling. And the chandeliers will be made of crystal."

Since this was the Sabbath eve, dinner did not end the day, but ushered in songs and psalm reading, storytelling and music. A spontaneous joy seemed to fill the room, igniting now and then into explosions of convivial laughter.

Dan was uncomfortable with his knife and fork removed. He didn't know what to do with his hands. At measured intervals a sentinel passed outside the window. There were several patrolling that night. Except for the good cheer, how different was it really from the camps he had known before? Dan's mood grew darker still as the music struck up: an accordion and a shepherd with his pipe. His father should have been there with his piano. Would there come a day when there would be a piano and the sentinels would go off duty forever? It seemed about as likely as the dining room's being fitted out with chandeliers.

Then the dancing started. First were a pair of traveling Druzes who had stopped at the kibbutz because they felt more at home here than with the Arabs. They wore silvery silk shirts and rainbow skullcaps, and performed, hands on shoulders and knives between their teeth, to loud applause. When they finished, the accordion player struck up a polka. As the first couples appeared on the cleared floor, Hanna sat quietly listening. She looked alert and happy, with her head cocked to one side like a puppy hearing new sounds. When Gideon asked her to dance, laughter played in her eyes.

Dan had never danced. The mere thought of it terrified him. But as he watched her dance lightly and discreetly, with

138

a deep glow on her cheeks, he wished he had asked her first; wished, and knew he would never dare. Seeing Gideon perform with a light step, springing expertly on the balls of his feet, Dan was all the more certain he would never ask her. They danced well together, Gideon and Hanna. They must have practiced a great deal over the last weeks. For the first time it occurred rather unpleasantly to Dan that Gideon was, after all, a handsome fellow. He had filled out a good deal in Palestine. His hair was black and curly, and his tanned skin so clear any girl would envy it. Part of his charm was his ready and unpuzzled smile which flashed most often in Hanna's direction.

Such were Dan's inner grumblings that he hardly noticed Hanna's approach until she took him by the hands.

"Now we'll dance," she told him.

"I can't dance. I never have."

"None of that here, Dan. If you can't dance, it's time to learn."

"Honestly, I've never done it in my life."

"Come on, try!"

"I'll step all over you."

"I'm not made of china. Hold out your arms."

"Like this?"

"Higher. Don't stiffen up."

They moved lamely about with the others, Dan's face intent and concentrated. "Are you wearing lipstick?" he asked her, striving for casual conversation.

"No. But I wish I owned some," she replied.

He did step on her sandaled toes, not once, but many times. She didn't seem to care, but Dan was miserable. When he began to limp with his left foot, which had not fully recovered, Gideon took over. Dan heard their laughter as they disappeared into the crowd. He saw them once again, their gay faces swaying to and fro with the music.

They did not return when the polka ended. They did not seem to have lined up for the hora. The circle was made up of many men and a few women, holding each other by the shoulders and beginning to sway right and left, their mouths emitting tuneless groans. Gradually the pace quickened, like a steam engine getting under way. There were shouts and chants and applause from the nondancers who sat on barrels and boxes. Everyone had an arm across his neighbor's shoulders. Those who didn't dance shouted and stamped.

Dan hated this maniacal dance, but he was trapped where he sat. The performers stepped high with energy and precision, landing heavily but gracefully on their feet. They swung and they yelled. There was a raucous thunder in the room as the ring of dancers moved and changed direction. The floor shook and the tin plates rattled.

Perhaps he was too fond of the piano, but to Dan this wasn't music; it was an assault on peace and quiet. When the dance came suddenly to a halt, he felt dazed, as if a chasm of silence yawned at his feet.

He looked for Hanna and Gideon and did not see them. To be alone in a crowd, particularly a happy, prancing one, was misery. When the hora began again, Dan worked his way to the door, feeling like an outcast from life's feast.

Once outside, he moved quietly through the shadows, though it was unlikely anyone was there to observe his departure. Then he stopped short when he heard a voice.

"Look at the moon. Will you just look at that moon!"

Dan looked at the moon as though bidden. It was a great yellow desert version of a moon.

Another voice answered, "I'd rather look at you." A match

was struck. "There. The first to see your face." The match was hurled away and extinguished, another struck. "The second to see your eyes." This one was flung to the ground. "And the last one for your mouth." It, too, was blown out.

Gideon and Hanna.

Dan could tell it was not the first time they had kissed.

The music from the dining hall masked his retreat. As he sat on his bed, Dan could still hear it. He beat his feet in time for a moment, sang some gibberish, *"Jabajaba jaba jaba,"* to the distant music. Then with a groan he fell backward, to lie with his shirt open and his arms under his head. For a long time he stared at the ceiling, feeling very much alone in the world. Then he got into bed for fear Gideon would return and catch him awake. His foot still ached and his legs twitched now and then as the muscles smoothed out. When Gideon finally did come, he closed his eyes and contrived to breathe slowly and deeply.

"You asleep?" Gideon asked.

Dan did not answer, and Gideon did not press him. He undressed slowly, chuckling occasionally to himself, and climbed into bed without once having turned on the light.

From outside drifted the voices of sentinels greeting one another. "My beloved is mine, and I am his; he feedeth among the lilies," one sang.

Dan buried his head under the pillow. Finally, in muffled silence, he slept, but his sleep was dream-ridden. He seemed to see Hanna dancing superbly, wildly, with a tall and powerful partner. Then her skirt caught fire. Her partner began laughing and would not let her stop and the two of them became a single torch. With this vision still before him, Dan sat up drenched in sweat. Outside the silence was complete.

CHAPTER 7

AFTER ONE MORE DAY OF RECUPERATION, DAN WAS READY FOR work. He rose in the bronze light of the desert dawn feeling fit. He flexed his muscles, feeling, as he hadn't for a long time, an intensely male pleasure in his own strength. Then he dressed, and ate cheese, eggplant, and tea with the others amid a clattering of pots and tin plates.

He had often dreamed of working in the kibbutz, and now it was about to become a reality. Usually he had pictured himself farming, turning over the warm red earth with the point of his hoe, uncovering now and then bits of brick and pottery and bone from ancient times. He liked the idea of farming, of being part of the earth to which all life returns; but he knew nothing practical about it, nor had he made his preferences known to the kibbutz labor committee. For that matter, he was unaware of such a committee's existence, but it had not been idle. Among the several notices on the dining hall's large public bulletin board, Dan saw his name at the top of a labor pool list. A line was through it. Looking further, he found himself again, assigned to a brickmaking team. As though to exhort the reluctant, a notation below the assigned names outlined the importance of brickmaking, and indicated that the bricks would be used for the construction

142

of a library and a storehouse. These buildings would complete the solid perimeter of the kibbutz, forging the final link in an almost impregnable fortress.

Bricks! Never in his wildest imaginings had he postulated such employment. He knew too little about it to resist the assignment, and even though he resented its summary nature, he did not know to whom he might register a complaint. So, with the small penciled map of Promise of the Future in mind, he crossed the compound to that spot which corresponded to the red check mark and the legend, "Bricks."

Moses Barsky was in charge. A gruff, middle-aged man with a bushy moustache and an agile walk he was a respected pioneer at Promise of the Future. With a perfunctory grunt of recognition, he handed out picks, shovels, and wooden molds. "Here, you. Take this." Dan was presented with a shovel.

A muddy brew was being mixed by a pair of Russians, who spoke no more Hebrew than Dan himself. Barsky explained to him in Yiddish how to shovel it into the forms, let it dry for a time, and then turn the bricks out on a plank to cure. Barsky told him that a good brickmaker could produce eight hundred bricks before dusk with time to spare. So Dan set to work with a will. His shovel rose and fell. He grunted as it fixed itself in the mud. All about him in the dancing morning air the new peasantry of Palestine were working. Most of them were young and strong, and they labored in the rhythm of those who build a future. Many sang. Their voices, though untrained and without a common language, blended pleasantly.

Never had Dan toiled like this. Soon every muscle of his body whimpered. The sun burned him. His nose filled with dust. By the time he sat down to his sandwich lunch, he had formed no more than two hundred bricks.

143

He must have looked discouraged, for Barsky sat down beside him.

"You think this is hard work?"

"Yes."

"Well, you're right, boy, but it can be harder. Do you mind me telling how it was?" Without waiting for Dan to say anything, he began his narration, slipping into a tonal groove which countless recitations had worn in his memory. "We were twelve in all. Ten men and two women. Six men to plow and two to watch, one accountant and one man in reserve. Plus two housekeepers. That was in 1924. We came from comfortable homes in Warsaw and had soft hands for a hard job." They had sought the Negev fringe, stopping only when they came to the village on the hillside, Tel Jabir, where Arabs lived like passive lizards among the rocks. Here they received shelter for the first year. They took meals in a communal shed, and slept there, too, while they cleared their dusty land. They named the few durams, purchased by the Jewish National Fund from an absentee Persian landlord, Promise of the Future. The Arabs called them Children of Death for their folly, and they were very nearly right. Malaria took one man and one woman. The Bedouins dismembered another, but the Jews fought back savagely. Barsky himself boasted a broken nose and a line of scar across his upper lip and lower jaw where he'd been raked by a Bedouin blade. In the second year they had lived on their own land, though their first rickety cabins had blown away, and they had no crops to speak of until the third year. Then a few of the men were joined by their wives. A few sabras came, for whom life in the north of Palestine was no challenge. Somehow they had clung to the land and improved it, despite the wilderness of savage nature and more savage men. They had dug wells,

144

planted palms, and turned it into something that was worth leaving to their children. Now their roots were deep and secure. If they called on the rabbi for weddings and funerals, they relied on their own hands to push their community into the future.

"Those were the old days, and they were hard, before the Hitler people came," Barsky said, obviously contemptuous of those who came through fear rather than idealism. "Things are easier now. They can get a lot worse. I wonder about you young ones. You're all so ready to kill the English and the Arabs, as though fighting were a substitute for an honest day's toil."

"Don't worry," Dan told him. "I'm no fighter."

Barsky seemed glad to hear it. He clapped Dan on the back so that the boy choked on his sandwich. "Can't spend the whole day eating," he said. "Finish up, Baratz, and back to work." As the man went off to exhort the others, Dan watched him glumly. It was true he wasn't a fighter, but he didn't seem to be much of a laborer, either.

Dan ground down the remains of his sandwich without tasting it. In the sand at his feet an ant lion dug out its cone-shaped trap, buried itself at the center, and waited for the first stumbling ant. One arrived in due course, tentatively explored the rim of the depression and might have left had not the ant lion showered it with sand until it finally tumbled down to its captor. A brief scuffle ensued, and both disappeared under the sand. In a moment the ant reappeared, or rather its empty husk, which was flipped free of the trap. The ant lion remained in hiding, awaiting another victim.

Dan started back to brickmaking, only to be intercepted on the way by Hanna. The sun was behind her head, making a halo of light on the fair fringe of her hair.

145

"*Nu?*" she said, meaning, he supposed, how was he coming along?

"Lovely," he told her with a flatness in his tone that belonged to the night of the dance.

"How do you like brickmaking?"

"Gets a bit under the skin, doesn't it?" He examined three or four blisters on his palms. "It's so very biblical. I feel I've really arrived in the land of Goshen. Where have you been, anyway?"

"Out in the desert, nights."

"With Gideon?"

She took no offence. "Actually, no. We've been laying water pipes. It's against the rules of the Mandate, you know, so it's got to be done at night. Wet blankets held around the acetylene torches, and all that." She wrinkled up her nose for a moment. Then she put her hand on his arm and bent her head. "You don't like it here, do you, Dan?"

"I do," he insisted.

"But it's not the way we talked with Sholem? Is it brickmaking? You don't have to make bricks forever."

"Don't worry about it. It's just me. I have to learn, that's all. I'm in lousy shape."

"I guess you are." She seemed annoyed. The muscle in her jaw tightened, and she looked up at him. "If you could change things, Dan, what would you be?"

"A better brickmaker."

"I mean it." He only shrugged, and she said, "If I could be born again, maybe I'd be an Arabian dancer in a house of mirrors."

"Be serious."

"All right, then. Eve. The first escapist."

"Come on, Hanna."

"Then Noah, the second . . . I don't know. I wish you'd laugh at me just for once. I feel it would set something free."

"Oh, I do laugh at you."

"No, never. You're always so intense. You're a bit like Sholem, you know."

"I'll take that as a compliment," he said.

"Perhaps it was meant that way."

"Everyone needs something to believe in."

"Fine. But why sound so hopeless about it?"

"I'm not. I've discovered something to believe in."

"God?"

"No."

"Well, what?" she demanded.

"Broken barriers between people, so they can reach each other."

"Well, practice what you preach, Dan. I'm sorry. You've only been here a few days. I'm too impatient."

Dan picked up a rock and threw it, picked up another.

"Don't," she said. "Sit down." Gently and firmly she laid her hand on his arm. "Don't make fists. Don't. Give me your hands. Open them. I'd tell your fortune if I knew how."

"I could recite a poem, and I do know how," he offered. When she nodded, he did so, looking all the while at the ground.

> "Your face has grown so dear, it seems
> A vision only seen in dreams;
> So seraph-like, so mild and frail,
> And still so pale, so sadly pale . . ."

"Doesn't exactly apply in this place," he said, smiling. Still he went on with it to the end.

"Did you make that up?" she asked when he had finished.

"Yes."

Hanna said in a taunting tone, "For me?"

"Yes." He was beginning to feel uneasy.

"She gave him a stern look, which was negated by a smile.
"You didn't really write it, did you?"

He was in a jam. "No," he said in a small voice.

"Who did, then?"

"I hate to tell you."

"Oh, come on now, Dan, Was it Gideon?"

"Lord, no. It was a German. Heine, or somebody else."

"A German!" she answered. "How lovely. They are so sentimental."

She began to laugh, then both of them laughed together.
To think of a love poem being written by a German!

"I wish I could be angry with you, you poetic peacemonger. But honestly, Dan, you can't live in an ivory tower
these days."

"What if it's bombproof?"

"I'm serious. You'd be better off if you were more like
Gideon."

Dan said, "If you want to know, his attitudes frighten me."

"He's cunning and resourceful. He knows how to get on."

"As long as he has a flag and a spear. Someday he'll find
himself in a dungeon without a key."

Hanna smiled as if she knew something about Gideon that
Dan did not know. "Are you jealous?" she asked.

"No. Why should I be?"

"Because you like me. I'm glad you like me, Dan."

"It's just that Gideon's wild. You know he is."

"You two are my best friends." She seemed to see no contradiction here. True friends were so rare, she said, and she
felt lucky to have two of them. "You will stay friends with
Gideon?"

148

"As long as I only have to smile, you can rely on me. I just don't want to get involved with fearless people."

"Fearless? Gideon? He's always afraid, always. He thrives on it. If he weren't afraid, I don't think he'd know he was alive. Anyway, he's ill."

"Gideon? He's strong as a whip."

"No, I mean ill emotionally. Listen." She spoke in a hushed, rapid tone, darting continual glances in the direction from which the topic of her conversation might appear. "Did you know he joined the partisans as much as anything to get away from his parents? Not only that, but it was his acts of sabotage that led to their being shot. In a way, he killed them. That was four years ago. Since then, he's killed them a thousand times."

"He ought to forget all about that."

"He'll die first. If he didn't take it out on others, he would on himself. Have you ever heard him screaming at night? That's when he comes face to face with it."

"And that's when I'll have to come face to face with those bricks if I don't get back to them."

"Just one more thing, Dan, while we're on the subject of grim realities. In case you don't know, anybody joining a kibbutz is just about automatically in the Haganah, unless they're some kind of cripple. It would look better if you signed up. They'll be after you, anyway."

"Well, let them. I'm in no rush," Dan said. Marching about, taking guns apart in the dark while somebody kept track of the time on a stopwatch had no appeal for him.

"It's not so bad," she assured him. "The marches are fun. More like picnics. Sometimes you search for old pottery and ruins. I often come back with my pack full of old things."

It was the idea, rather than the doing, that offended him. He wasn't sure how to explain his feelings even to Hanna.

149

"Do you realize," he said, "that ever since I got here I've lived inside barbed wire? It's the same old thing."

"No," she said, "it's entirely different. It's to keep them out, not to keep us in. We'll have to make a stand and fight somewhere, sooner or later. You believe in Israel, don't you?"

"I believe in peace. You have no idea how wonderful it is." He looked at her accusingly as though she had spoken lightly of someone he loved.

"Oh, Dan. The British will keep us here in peace, inside this wire, forever. We'll die here of old age, not a bit better off than we were before if it's left to the British. And the Arabs, well, with half a chance they'd exterminate us. So we have to fight them to survive. There's no choice. It's a matter of natural law."

"You scare the daylights out of me, Hanna, when you talk like that." Yet part of him agreed with her. There had been no real freedom, no feeling of belonging for his father or his grandfather. Here at least they stood on their own land. They were limited now by wire, to be sure, but in future years they might not even be limited by the far horizon. The thought made him giddy. It rushed through him like wine, but along with it came fear, Sholem's fear. He felt now for the first time that it was best that Sholem had died where he did, with his dreams intact. Hanna might be right. Perhaps it was time for Moses to step aside, and for Joshua to take over.

During the cold, windy, and often wet days of February, Dan worked hard as a brickmaker. He never rose to the heights pointed out by Barsky. Six hundred bricks a day was the best he ever managed at the price of an aching back and blistered hands.

He made several new friends. Chief among them was a

young, barrel-bodied Russian immigrant named Pavlov. Pavlov had been in the Russian army, and due to some misunderstanding over his name, he had been assigned to training messenger dogs. Later on in the war, when Moscow was threatened, he was ordered to train suicide dogs whose job it was to carry high explosives on their backs. Thus equipped, the animals were taught to hurl themselves under onrushing German tanks. Unfortunately, Pavlov liked dogs better than most human beings, and so he had become a deserter. Now, in his spare time, he was training dogs again for perimeter defense.

Work and training left Dan with little time or energy for social activities. At night, when the kibbutz was relatively secure from British surveillance, he and the other new arrivals were mustered and drilled in the desert.

By this time Dan was usually so tired that he was dreaming on his feet. The stars seemed just beyond his fingertips. It was a good place for hermits to conceive great concepts of the unity and order of the universe, a good place for Sholem.

Dan and his companions had target practice twice weekly, with pistols and rifles flashing and cracking over the sand. Few shots were allowed; they could not afford the risk of detection or the waste of ammunition. Dummy grenades were thrown. Stick fighting was taught as though they expected the English might one day throw Robin Hood and his merry men against them.

Some nights they staggered wearily on cross-country hikes, singing in thin and discordant voices of the wonder of water sprinklers redeeming the land, and the beauty of Judea and Galilee, which Dan had never seen.

Later the elements of training were combined into maneuvers concentrating on Tel Jabir, the Arab town that com-

151

manded the approaches to the kibbutz. In the moonlight it stood out clearly above them on the stony hillside. The boulders and the rooftops gleamed clear and white. It had been there so long that the dwellings seemed a part of the rock they were built upon. The training commander pointed out that it would be useless to waste artillery on such a place, even if they had artillery. It would only fall to surprise and massive assault, so the nights were spent attacking similar slopes of nearby hills. Their performance was in deadly earnest, for their commander was convinced that once the British had pulled out, Arabs and Jews would reach instant accord: that the only solution was a fight to the death.

All of this Dan hated. He had met only one Arab, and he owed the old fisherman a debt of gratitude. So it was to his great relief that the drill sessions ended and his military duties were cut back to a fortnightly turn at guard duty inside the wire.

During this period he saw little of Hanna, and he missed her in spite of himself. Nor did he see much of Gideon, who vanished regularly with his truck. When his roommate was around, he spoke mysteriously of electric mines and bombs hidden in tree trunks. He was quickly adopting a career of assassination, and Dan was happy when he did not have to hear about it.

During Gideon's absences their small room became Dan's own, and he enjoyed it. That was one real problem with the kibbutz; having nothing personal. Perhaps this was a fault in himself which went back to his mother and her preoccupation with things. Dan had nothing. His old clothes had been burned and replaced with impersonal kibbutz clothes. His father's watch had been dear to him, but it had been left behind in Italy. There was only the picture of his parents,

152

frayed and fading. Occasionally he would look at them, trying to know them better, but the effort only confused him. Somehow they looked like strangers. It was during one of these nostalgic sessions, when the empty room hummed with loneliness, that he resolved to write to his grandfather.

The electricity generator had been shut down for the day, so he lit the oil lamp that stood on the table, trimmed the wick to a golden moth of flame, took out pen and ink, and balanced the pad of paper on his knee. For a long time he sat rigidly, the pen pinched hard, unable to get beyond, "Dear Grandfather."

He longed to urge Jacob to join him, and yet he could not do so with a clear conscience. There were many things he could not record for fear of censors, both Jewish and British. There was the build-up of weapons: rifles, Sten guns, homemade mortars; arms at any cost, even though the paint was peeling from the kibbutz and broken windows were fixed with cardboard. Guns, but no synagogue. Not that he or his grandfather were deeply religious, but the core of tradition was lacking. Here Judaism did not mean God, but nationalism, a paradise compulsory. He dared not mention the armadillo of a bus sheathed in hammered boiler plate, nor the shepherd found after two days with his head severed from his body. Some blamed the vagrant Bedouins, who killed with indiscriminate sportsmanship. Others called it a deliberate Arab provocation, and pondered retaliation. Under such threats the kibbutz thrived with a kind of collective and childlike fervor within its barbed-wire shell. Work went on at a fever pitch. Trenches were dug.

At last, with his legs hooked like a schoolboys' around the legs of the wooden chair, Dan began laboriously to write. He wrote of the good things; the victories over nature won by

153

the first pioneers, who overcame malaria and drought and seeded the land. The labors of Hercules could not compare. Now they all ate well, they had two tractors, a flower garden, and an invincible faith in themselves. Even the present threat from the outside world seemed to work to their advantage. Without it they would soon succumb to the climate, and be as charmingly decadent as the Arabs, who had existed there for hundreds of years.

Dan sucked his pen conscientiously each time he lifted it from the paper. He had met one Arab, he wrote: a fisherman. He hoped to meet others. With luck he would be a shepherd by springtime. Things were well with him, with all of them. Probably the age of miracles was over. If it came to war, the sea would not close on Pharoah's army or on the British tanks. Yet the Jews themselves were a miracle. They had outlived the Romans and the Greeks and Hitler, and they would somehow outlive the British Empire.

"Please come," he wrote against his first intentions. "There are many old people here and they are happy. And, Grandfather, we need clocks that show twenty-five hours in every day. Please come and make us clocks. . . ."

He signed his name "with love," and stared at the paper for a long time. A tear fell and formed over a letter and enlarged it as though with a magnifying glass. Then the ink dissolved.

Dan blotted the paper, folded it and sealed it away in an envelope. "Well," he said aloud, "that's done." He was self-conscious, as if someone had been watching.

The lamp was burning smokily. He adjusted it to a pure-white glow, thought better of it, and put it out entirely. Around him the camp was settling down. An owl called out and was answered by its mate. The night was cold. He could

154

hear the guards stomping as he put an extra blanket on his bed in the darkness. For a moment he stood staring into the night with his nose pressed against the screen until the flesh of the tip was molded into tiny squares. The owl called again, and once again was answered. Then he heard the sudden descending beat of its wings and the shrill of its prey. Far off a jackal howled with hunger, but this Dan did not hear. He had closed the window tight and had gone to bed.

CHAPTER 8

THE WEATHER REMAINED SO COLD AND DAMP THAT THE BRICKS were slow to dry. Dan hated the work more than ever. It was said of a good kibbutznik that, through sheer devotion to the group, he would stay with one job for a lifetime, even if it was only opening and closing a tap to irrigate the fields. He would draw comfort from thinking about the water quenching the thirst of the fields, while one hand grew large from turning knobs and the rest of him whithered, body and mind. This was not for Dan. A shepherd had been killed, so he applied for the job. For him, shepherding was an idyllic notion, filled with tales of David, the Songs of Solomon, and the green pastures. For once he had Hanna's cautious encouragement. She was the one person to whom he could talk freely, though his ideas often made her laugh. But even her laughter dispelled the hollowness inside him.

"You won't get out into the hills until spring, you know," she said.

He didn't mind. A shepherd's thoughts always sought higher pastures than the sheep. So he learned about sheep in winter, from a heavy, unshaven old man in a dark kilt which smelled of manure and had long since lost any trace of a clan tartan. "Call me Tam," he said, with just the trace of a burr.

Part Scot, part Jew, he'd been a Tweed bank herder before World War One, a volunteer piper when that war began. He'd piped Lawrence into Damascus when the war was over. Mustered out in Palestine, he'd never quite got around to going home, and had finally settled down on the kibbutz, where he was needed.

"So your name's Daniel, and you want to be a shepherd. Know anything about it, Danny boy?" Tam looked at him shrewdly. "No, I thought not. Well, it's not all pipes and Pans, I'll tell you that for a start."

Dan's actual apprenticeship was under the guidance of another young shepherd named Saul. Saul was a sabra and proud of it. Even in the coldest weather he wore shorts, from which protruded thick woolly legs. He reminded Dan of the pictures of the mindless, apple-munching German youth of the war years. From the start there was an antipathy between them which Dan felt keenly since he was in the subordinate position. Indeed, there was no flute playing for this apprentice shepherd, no cloudy hillsides, no green pastures. Only a 4 A.M. call, rain or shine, with a black wind invariably lashing the palm trees.

The sheep were of the Awassi breed, which meant they were lean, with low-quality wool. To make them worth their keep, they had to be milked. If they were to be milked, they had to be fed. That involved stumbling down a muddy track to the fold, while Saul bounded ahead as if he could see in the dark. Into the long eating troughs Dan tipped buckets of sloppy *kouspa*, the sheep's favorite blend. Then he would open the doors and the flock would hurl itself, bleating, at the food. Once they were all inside the fold, heads down and eating, gates were slid into position and the sheep could not get away. Dan's next task was to seat himself on a tottery stool

157

behind each ewe in turn, grasping grotesquely large udders in both hands. To achieve any results, he was obliged to support the udder on his forearm, which was unpleasant work in the damp season when the sheep had chronic diarrhea. He had to work fast to keep the milk free of contamination. Each morning, with Saul urging him on, he milked about a dozen ewes. Then, thankfully, it was time for breakfast.

The rest of the day was taken up with cleaning the falls, an intricate maze of enclosures through which old Tam marshaled his flock. Pregnant ewes here, rams—"tubs," Tam called them—there, the youngsters in various age groups. Then Dan was set to mixing their food in a great vat. As he stirred the seething mass with a forked stick, he felt like a witch with a bubbling caldron. By the end of the working day he was far dirtier and just as weary as he had ever been after a session of brickmaking.

"You look peaked, Baratz," Saul remarked. "Don't worry. It's a good life, all in all. Here, feel that bicep." Saul drew his fist up to his shoulder.

"Very hard," admitted Dan, more interested in a shower and clean clothes.

"Hard! It's like iron. Feel my calves. Like iron."

"I'll take your word for it."

"Just watch this," said Saul, suddenly standing on his hands. Things fell out of his pockets as he began to walk jerkily. His upside-down eyes bulged like the eyes of an octopus. "You try it."

"I couldn't do it."

"You won't make it with that attitude, Baratz. You'll wash out as a shepherd."

At that moment Dan didn't care. He could even smile back

158

at Saul's contemptuous look, sustained by the thought of a long hot shower and fresh clothes from the laundry.

The evenings were now taken up with Hebrew classes. He had resisted at first, but Hanna had convinced him as usual.

"Really, I think you'd better turn up."

"Is that an order?"

"Not from me, but if you like to put it that way, yes."

"I smell of sheep," he told her. "Nobody'll be able to concentrate."

"How charmingly pastoral," she replied, laughing.

So he went, as much to be with her as for any other reason. Gideon, too, was there at first, smoking and looking off into space. "You don't need to speak Hebrew to kill Arabs or Englishmen," he commented after the second session, and from then on Dan had Hanna to himself. That was enough to keep him coming, and it also emboldened his tongue.

"You're beautiful," he said once, eyes glued to his language notebook.

Hanna's voice was sharp with surprise. "What are you talking about?"

He said it again and stared at her so fixedly that she threw back her head and laughed.

"Do you really think so?" Her glance challenged him to say it again.

"I was only fooling. You're ugly."

"I deserved that," she said good-naturedly. "And I am, really. Now let's get back to work."

Hebrew came naturally to her, but for Dan it was a struggle.

"Isn't Yiddish and Polish and English good enough?" he asked her.

"We won't be hearing English very long around here."

"It's the language of commerce."

"We're farmers."

"Why not learn some Arabic, then?"

"Still looking for one world, Dan?"

"Yes, I guess I am. And one God and one heaven, too."

"All right," she said. "As long as the language they speak there is Hebrew."

Sarah Klein, their Hebrew teacher, was the only surviving female founder of Promise of the Future. She was also the mother of many among the growing kibbutz population, including Saul the shepherd. Once a woman of great beauty, the sun and the desert wind had wrought in her an ageless sandstone elegance. Her relationship to Saul had prejudiced Dan in the beginning, but her endless patience with his first lingual blunderings had quickly won him over. More than anyone else at the kibbutz, she reminded him of Sholem. In her classes she taught not only language, but a gentle acceptance of life, as she and the first pioneers had accepted the desert and the Arabs who lived there. They had soon come to terms with their neighbors. A dispute had occurred in the fields, a Jewish sheep had been stolen, and an Arab had been shot in the arm. A feud might have resulted, but a formal peace ceremony had been arranged. After all, Isaac was brother to Ishmael, and it was from Ishmael that the Arabs traced their descent. At Sarah Klein's insistence, the kibbutz had even set up a special school for Arabs, teaching them sanitation and the use of heavy machinery. The school flourished still, with the result that the Arabs winked at Jewish flocks' pasturing on greener Arab hills. Now this relationship was threatened as never before. There were only a few, like Sarah Klein, who still praised Weizmann and his readiness to

160

cooperate with both the Arabs and the British in adjusting the future of Palestine.

So in those last wintry days Dan learned his first words of Hebrew: the words for "friend" and "peace" and "hope." And so spring arrived, with a bumble bee flying into the classroom, registering its mistake, and quickly flying out again. It was the month of lambing and of pasturing the sheep. "Here is March: an hour of sun, an hour of rain, and an hour of the partridge calling." So went the old Bedouin proverb. Dan made ready to drive his flock toward the hills.

CHAPTER 9

THE WINTER OF RACING WINDS AND RAIN TURNED ON ITS HEELS, giving place to a springtime conceived in Eden. Nature went wild in a brief pageant of scent and color. The sea breeze was clear and cool, swelling the palms like sails, laughing among the flowers where butterflies flickered like petals come to life.

Suddenly and all at once the ewes began to lamb. With the first helpless *mee-ee-eeing* cry of the staggering newborn, Hebrew lessons were forgotten. Dan's time was taken up entirely with the sheep. Tam introduced him to the mysteries of lambing.

"Now the care and nurture of lambies is a fine art," Tam told him. "You see this crooked lambin' stick? Now a wee lambie is fast on his feet, but with this—" and as he spoke, the stick darted out and around Dan's neck. With a sideways twist, it held him fast. "But not too savage, mind. They have wee neck bones, the lambies do." Once caught, there was the lambing bag for transport. "You get him inside, don't you see, and he's as gentle and contented as he'd be inside his mother."

Dan learned to coax a motherless lamb with a bottle of warm milk, and how—after one painful shock—to avoid the charge of a ewe deprived of her young. He watched with awe

162

as Tam cut the skin from a stillborn lamb. The old man sewed the dripping pelt about the body of another ewe's twin lamb and convinced a bereaved mother that her child was reborn. "No ewe can nourish two lambies in this country," Tam explained. "But this way, everyone's happy."

When the "tubs" were fenced and pastured, Dan and Saul, carrying Italian carbines on their shoulders, drove the hungry flock of ewes and lambs out to spring pastures. The lambs could not go far at first, and there was no need in spring, when there was ample pasturage nearby. Dan loved this season and, almost unnoticed, his happiness began to reestablish itself. He caught himself whistling again, and was surprised. His throat ached to shout out loud a cry of deliverance, and when completely alone he gave vent to it, a long call to nothing but the elements.

The pastured sheep had one unpleasant surprise for him. He had always imagined them as a solid creeping carpet of wooly backs, but their inclination was obviously to wander as far as rivers, fences, and food would allow. Often he heard Tam sing the praises of his old dogs in Scotland, the Border collies, who could run a hundred uphill miles a day in pursuit of errant sheep. Here the land was too hot for the little collies; and the only half-trained sheep dog the kibbutz had owned had vanished when the previous shepherd lost his head the season before. Tam had requested dogs in a meeting of the general committee. The Russian, Pavlov, had offered to train them. Dogs had come eventually, but the sort that could only be trained to kill, and for a long time Pavlov refused to have anything to do with them. So, there were no dogs to help with the herding.

Dan began to learn about real walking and running. His life was strenuous, but in those few moments when he rested he took secret pleasure in the muscular awakening of his

163

body. The surprising advent of biceps caused him no little pride, which he was careful not to display in Saul's presence.

Toward the end of April, with the prospect of the summer's drought and leaner pastures, the flock was divided. Saul took the larger half, leaving Dan with "all you can handle." Their parting was almost friendly. "You're not so bad, Baratz. You may make it yet," Saul told him with rare indulgence. He gave Dan a painful smack on the back. "Just look after your sheep first and yourself second, remember. And keep that gun handy."

With this advice he left. For a time both herds grazed near the kibbutz, returning for supplies and protection at night. Otherwise they had no contact.

It was a pleasure to be on his own, with no one to criticize and no one to sneer, though he had gotten used to Saul. The only thing he didn't like was the gun. It seemed an anachronism in all this pastoral blue and gold. Yet a shepherd had died not long ago through carelessness, so he clung to the gun from fear.

The Negev was wide and green in the early days of May, and no one threatened him or his flock. He watched the pageant of birds in migration, a great cloud of storks darkening the sky on their long flight from Africa. Crested larks with their call of *cheever, cheever* darted like arrows into the folds of trees.

Then one day, with the advance of dusty summer and withering vegetation in the Negev, the Bedouins arrived out of the wastes where David had fought Goliath. They were the Solubbi, mixed descendants of Ishmael, of whom it was said in Genesis, "And he will be a wild man, his hand will be against every man, and every man's hand against him." The rest of their bloodline came from Christian Crusaders who had fallen in love with the desert hundreds of years before.

164

Their sheik arrived first, in a flawlessly polished black 1929 Dodge touring car. Fiercely mustachioed bodyguards, their torsos laced with bandoliers and daggers, rode on the running boards. When the sheik emerged, he was enveloped in a white cloak.

Dan watched them from the dense violet shadow of a hillside boulder, clutching his gun in terror. It was said of the Bedouin that he would kneel before a stranger, either on the ground as host with a platter of delicacies, or on his chest, shouting, "In the name of God!" as he cut the stranger's throat. In this case, they ignored Dan or did not see him at all. A single stake was driven into the ground, and as suddenly as they had appeared they departed, the car raising a long plume of dust.

The following day Dan drove his sheep to higher pastures. It was as well that he did, for the Bedouins returned; the Dodge first, then a troop of lean, haughty men on horseback. The rest of the tribe arrived before dusk, less spectacularly but just as mysteriously. The smell of spring flowers gave way to the reek of goats. Dan knew they had come before he saw the flock of black goats with their long drooping ears and backward-curving horns. With the goats came the women and old men. The plain was quickly dotted with black goats' hair tents; "houses of hair," the Bedouin's called them. Women began preparing supper. Dan could hear them as they made fires of pungent camel dung. "Ah-a, ah-a, ah-a . . ." A tuneless, almost toneless chant arose from the desert.

Dan needed the kibbutz. He drove the flock home that night by a roundabout route and felt the shadows pursuing him every step of the way. He lost a sheep in the process, arriving dead tired and thorn-raked, only to be chided by Saul, who had come in hours before. Wasn't he going after the lost sheep? Saul offered to go with him; they'd both take their guns and have it out with those thieving Bedouins. Tam refused to hear of it. This was a friendly tribe, as well mannered and trustworthy as Bedouins could be. They'd pastured their flocks here in early summer since time immemorial. One sheep more or less was a tribute due, in their eyes, and a little goodwill would do no harm in such troubled times.

It was mid-May when the first real heat set in. The Bedouin tribe clung to the Negev fringe, so Dan moved his flock as inconspicuously as possible back into the hills. Sweat streamed from his forehead into his eyes as he climbed. This was really summer, with the grass shriveling and receding toward the hills.

The new pastures brought Dan closer to the Arab town, Tel Jabir. "Don't worry about the Bedouins. The Arabs are the ones who'll shoot you in the back," he'd been warned. Yet the town, like an incomplete crossword puzzle, attracted him. It was evocative and strange; near, yet completely remote; and it seemed full of threat and promise. Small figures moved about in it, as tiny as though seen through the wrong end of an enormous telescope.

At such a safe distance there were only a few things he could learn about the people of Tel Jabir. They loved noise, he discovered; the banging of doors, shouting, encouraging dogs to bark and donkeys to bray, slaughtering loudly, wailing toneless Arab tunes like wind under a door. He learned, too, or rather he had it reaffirmed that among Arabs it was the men who lounged all day and the women who toiled in the fields. He could see their bright head scarves like flowers under the sun. In the dusk, when the women came home to make supper, he heard a mandolin serenade them, scratching its soul out on the evening breeze.

166

One day in early June the sun came out of the desert with its usual savage onrush of light. The air was glassy clear and cloudless. It was a day like any other summer day except that on a hillside opposite there appeared a flock much like his own. It was guarded by a shepherd of about his size, armed like Dan with a rifle. Dan had a strange feeling of seeing himself in a mirror.

He stared at the Arab boy and the Arab stared back. All day they watched one another, a chasm of silence between them.

The following day Dan drove the flock to the kibbutz for supplies. It would be for the last time. Thereafter Tam would come out with the truck until shearing time in late July. This was tigerish summer, when even in the hills the sheep grew lean. He meant to take leave of Hanna and Gideon, but neither of his friends was there, so it was with a particular lonely feeling that he set out again for the hills. The river he had so often crossed by bridge was nothing but a muddy stream. Three Arab girls were wading as he passed. They shrieked and ran, tearing the water apart, when they saw him. As Dan crossed, his flock moved ahead to the flowering hibiscus that grew where the winter bed of the torrent had been.

Now he climbed to higher hills where the smell of sun-weary flowers was in the air, and once again, like a mirror image, he saw the other flock and its shepherd with his gun. Impulsively Dan waved, but he got no sign of recognition. Before going to sleep, he clicked a cartridge into the chamber of his carbine and lay down with his hand on the gun. The action made him self-conscious, as though Saul were there to criticize. When he finally fell asleep, he slept hard, and when he awoke the sun was high. He knew without moving that it would be fiercely hot, so he drove the flock to a small cluster of trees where, by midday, the sheep lay stunned. He didn't have the heart or the energy to force them farther, but sat in the shade himself, watching his Arab counterpart through a haze that made the distance dance and tremble in mirage.

Only a *hirdaun* lizard stirred in the midday blaze. It nodded its head constantly in a way Dan had heard the Arabs hated, for it seemed to them the lizard was mocking prayer. Unseen by the *hirdaun,* a monitor lizard approached, its head held high on a skinny neck. Too late the *hirdaun* turned to flee, and there was a flicker of green lightning on the white-hot stones. The *hirdaun* was caught in powerful jaws and devoured. It was always that way between creatures here. The wasp waited in the dust for the unwary spider. The hawks drifted overhead until a goldfinch broke from the cover of a tree. In this land it was wise to assume that everything bit or stung, and that when a creature looked dead it was only carefully watching.

He watched the Arab shepherd, feeling uncomfortable when he disappeared from sight, knowing that he, too, was watched. At the same time he felt a growing fondness for the other's campfire, and caught himself smiling when at dusk he heard the Arab calling to his sheep. *"Y-o-o-o-a . . . y-o-o-o-a."* Imperceptibly an affinity grew between the two flocks, so that they did not stray far apart in their wanderings—until one day in early July.

The stones of the desert were as hot as loaves of freshly baked bread and the sun seemed an acetylene torch striking down through a blue glaze of sky. The slightest motion brought on a rush of sweat, and Dan had taken refuge with his sheep in a pine grove. The Arab was nowhere in sight, but overhead lazy vultures floated on the rising heat.

168

Perhaps the Arab was in some kind of trouble. How could he be? He probably knew more about sheep and these hills than Dan would ever know. Still, the vultures, flying lower now in tighter circles, looked ominous.

Toward evening a breeze from the sea brought down showers of dust from the pine branches. Dan called his flock and drove them listlessly toward higher ground. Presently they began to trot ahead of him toward a natural stone archway. Try as he might, he could not turn them aside with crook or curse. But the sheep were right. Beyond the stone arch was a green dell where a spring was gushing. The place was in shadow now, and the air was cool enough to make him shiver.

The overall effect was miraculous, worthy of Moses at his best. Dan would have gratefully settled down for the night, but a memory of lowering vultures would not let him rest. Most likely a sheep had died of thirst, but he had not seen the shepherd for a long time. What if he had fallen, or been stung by a viper?

"It's none of my fool business," Dan muttered, and at the same time he found himself turning back. There was no danger that the flock would stray from their water. "Damned fool," he kept saying as he moved along, guided by the vultures. He'd even forgotten his gun. If he went back for it now, darkness would intervene, and so he continued until he saw a gray-white blanket of sheep sheltered under the pines.

The Arab shepherd stood up defensively when he saw Dan approach. The rifle was under his arm. He had a rather delicate face: narrow Asiatic forehead with indrawn temples, large, somber eyes with a trace of brown pigment in the whites, a narrow pink mouth made for flute playing.

For a moment they stared at one another with questioning, slightly hostile, faces. Dan had forgotten the language problem. He spoke first in Yiddish. The Arab's jaw tightened, his dark eyes measuring.

"*Sholom aleichem,*" Dan said, one of his few Hebrew expressions.

"*Salaam aleikum,*" replied the other in Arabic.

Beyond this they did not progress until the Arab spoke in English with waspish authority. "The English call me Saïd," he said. His real name was Achmed. But his father, who admired the British, now also called him Saïd. So it was in a tongue foreign to them both that they became acquainted. Dan told of his discovery and offered to share the spring. Together they drove the thirsty flock uphill, leaving two dead sheep behind for the vultures. By nightfall, their flocks were mingling by the small spring.

"It has been dry for years," the Arab spoke in wonder. "Ever since before the war." He'd run errands for an Australian outfit during the fighting. His father was Muktar of Tel Jabir, an important man, known and respected at the kibbutz. Mustafa Abdel Kader. Dan nodded sagely that he had heard the name, which was a lie.

"You can see I'm not a shepherd by trade," said Saïd. "If I were, I wouldn't have lost those sheep. It's my father's idea. Experience, you know. He's very . . . well . . . Western. In a few years I'll be going to the university in England."

"You speak English well," Dan said. "Did you learn from the Australians?"

"Actually, no. From English archaeologists before the war. I helped them find some caves. I could show them to you. They're very interesting." He seemed ready to start out in the dark. "Would you like to go?"

"Very much, yes," Dan told him. "Tomorrow."

At dawn they built a barrier of brambles across the en-

170

trance to the spring and set out over an upland of thistles and scattered stones. Shortly they came upon a graveyard full of turban stones, like granite people trying to struggle free from the ground. It was an old and long-abandoned Turkish cemetery, Saïd explained. If it weren't so isolated, its stones would have been dragged away for building materials long ago.

Dan thought of the graveyard at the kibbutz. The earliest occupants were a mother dead in childbirth, a man who had succumbed to malaria, and Moshe Czerniakow, who had lost faith in Promise of the Future and taken his own life with a shotgun. Dan's predecessor was the most recent addition. One day it, too, might be abandoned and trampled over by strangers on their way to somewhere else.

That "somewhere else," Saïd's cave, was farther than Dan had reckoned. His throat was full of dust and his face became burned by the sun. He began to lag, but Saïd urged him on. "Come along, Dan. Come along. Just a bit farther." And Dan went so as not to be bested by an Arab. Also, there was something about Saïd's enthusiasm that was hard to resist.

The last stretch was up a flat strip, which Saïd referred to as a Roman road. It led past the crumbling ruins of a Crusader fort which had later become a Saracen castle, and then down into a cave. Here Saïd displayed the cave's treasures with an air of proprietorship. With the aid of pocket matches, Dan could see some wall paintings done in the Egyptian manner, a few great jarlike containers, and some bones and bits of pottery.

"Some say Joshua, your Joshua, was buried here," Saïd said. "I thought you'd like that," he added in response to Dan's smile. "Others say it's the place where the kings that fell at Armageddon were brought; not dead, really, but

171

asleep until they hear the last trumpet calling them to fight again."

From that time onward they kept their flocks together. On the hottest days one would watch while the other slept, or lay back under a tree in a heat-drugged stupor. Sometimes, with a confidence the land and the times did not warrant, they both slept, coming alive with the ending of the day, when the great rocks began thrusting their shade toward the desert. The sun hung for a moment on the horizon, its glow enlarging and losing power as the sky changed from glaze to pale blue with patches of pure gold and streaks of emerald. Then the hills turned from dirty gray to rusty red, and a few fireflies began to glow.

"I never knew the sun could set in so many ways until I came here. Red, green, pink, gray . . . amazing, isn't it?" said Dan. Saïd only shrugged, for he had never known anything else. Then he would perch on a rock, black against the green crystal of the sunset sky, and play his pipe under the first twinkling light of Venus.

This was sheepherding as Dan had imagined it, and he would applaud loudly. "I wish I could do that," he said.

Saïd offered to teach him, adding, "When one is warm to me, I am warm to him in return."

At first they had clung to their guns, but their growing mutual confidence made the weapons a small indecency between them. Dan finally left his rolled in his blanket, and Saïd said of his, "No one would dare to shoot this thing." It was an old banded flintlock made many years before for some desert warrior. The muzzle was so big a champagne cork could have been rammed into it.

They talked freely about everything but politics; there, an odd politeness kept them apart. Saïd said only that his father

172

was a progressive thinker, and that his mother had once been cured of a desperate illness by a Jewish doctor. To match this, Dan mentioned his Arab fisherman. That was sufficient between friends, but when Tam brought supplies, the Arab boy stayed out of sight.

Their favorite topic was Petra, blood-red Petra, ancient wilderness city of Nabataeans. Saïd had been there, and he called it, in the Arab way, Khaznet Firaun. Dan had only heard his father talk about it, as he had talked dreamily in those far-off days of Timbuktu and the Vale of Kashmir. Petra, distant, unattainable, filling men with wanderlust, was only a hundred miles away. Only a week's journey on camel-back.

"Let's go," Dan said. "Soon."

"In the spring."

"Good. When it's still cool."

"When the Arabs are churning, as they say," Saïd replied, for when the Arabs were churning milk in the good spring days, they were more apt to invite a stranger in to share.

"What shall I tell them at the kibbutz?" Dan asked.

"Say you're going south. That's all the Bedouins say. We can walk to Beersheba and go to the Bedouin market. We'll rent camels there."

"Camels can go five days without water in summer," Dan offered. That was all he knew about camels.

"Longer than that in springtime. We'll plug our noses like the Bedouins because of the smell of the city." Like maestros, they would tap the camels with little sticks until the last houses fell away and there was nothing ahead but the unending desert. Then with their cloaks streaming from their shoulders, they would sing a Hijeini, a camel riding song.

"Do you know one?" Dan asked.

173

"Actually, not yet. I'll learn one, just to be ready."

"We'll need to take plenty of food."

"No, we won't. We'll be the guests of the Bedouins."

"They may cut our throats."

"The Ikhwan always attack at dawn."

"Will we fight," asked Dan, "or run?"

"Neither," Saïd told him. "It will only be old Sheik Suleiman and his twenty-nine wives, each one a better cook than the other. They'll feed us thick black coffee and fresh-killed sheep on rice until we're ready to burst. Then they'll apologize profusely for the poorness of the meal. Do you like sheeps' eyeballs?"

"I'd be sick."

"No, you wouldn't. You'd be polite and swallow it down like a pill. They'd slice you from ear to ear if you didn't."

"I'd be sick later, then," said Dan.

"So would I. Maybe they won't give us sheep at all, but grilled lizard or hedgehog."

"Let's take plenty of food," Dan insisted.

From the desert they would cross the Jordan River and strike out into that largely unmapped wilderness where the basic element was heat shimmering over bare rocks. The mountains were hewn as if by some mad axman. They were an ideal place to perish for uncomplicated reasons: thirst, hunger, heat, and cold. The only paths would be goat tracks strewn with granite boulders. They would move at night under the moon, and the dim blue light would cast warped and eerie shadows across the ravines. According to Saïd, they would be looking for the double granite hump of Jebel-i-Ded, from where they would see another, higher peak, Jebel Haroun.

"You'd call it the Mount of Aaron," he said. It was the gateway to Petra.

174

"Will there be wild animals?"

"Most of them are gone now," Saïd replied. "I didn't see anything there but a few jackals. But the Bedouins are wild enough. Nothing like the friendly ones in this area. They smuggle opium, and they'll kill a stranger for his pocket watch."

"I haven't one," Dan confessed.

"Neither have I. My father has a gold one, but you wouldn't catch him within fifty miles of Petra."

The last mile would take them through a narrow gorge cut in the stone where even at noon the sun was scarcely visible. They would ride single file while the camels' hooves hammered and echoed on the stone. Then, when it was least expected, it would appear in the widening gorge: Petra, city of the desert pirates. Hewn from the rocky cliffs, pillars and obelisks, altars and secret chambers were carved like a giant's cameo. They would arrive at sunset, when all was blood-red.

"Blood-red!" Saïd insisted. "You won't believe it. And it's half as old as time."

"We'll do it," Dan said, unhesitating. He would act out his father's dream.

"Yes, we'll do it," echoed Saïd. Then he added a phrase that kept it a dream and not quite a plan. "If all goes well . . ."

Dan returned to the kibbutz in late July for the shearing. He had looked forward to talking with Hanna, but she was interested in nothing but politics. There was much talk of an English withdrawal from Palestine, and a plan to supply Jerusalem by truck if war came. Gideon was feverishly happy. Dan felt sure he had wormed his way into the Irgun at last, though he didn't say so and Dan did not ask. In the end, Dan sought refuge with his sheep and Tam, who lived outside of politics.

"You've done a good job, Danny. Wool's first class for a summer like this one. Yes, it is. And not a lambie lost." This was high praise from the Scot. It was even more savory as an indirect condemnation of Saul, who had lost three lambs and a ewe.

Some kibbutzes had power-driven clippers, but Tam didn't like them. "One slip," he said, "and you've lost half a pound of mutton before you can find the bloody switch to turn it off." He used instead razor-sharp A-shaped shears, turning the sheep first on one side and then on the other. Thirty good cuts and a sheep stood there naked, shorn of a four-pound fleece.

The shearing took three days. When they were done, Dan's hands were soft and pliant from the lanolin in the new wool. Hanna held his hand to her cheek. "Just like a newborn baby's," she said.

"Give them a few more months of sun and dust," Dan said. He was setting out with the flock in the morning.

"I don't like you out there alone. Not anymore."

"You don't know what it's really like," he said.

"Neither do you," was her reply.

Dan was not afraid of solitude, but he looked forward to seeing Saïd again. It would be a relief to get away from the somber talk of the kibbutz. Even the sheep, shed of their heavy coats, seemed frisky and glad to return to their pastures. In the days of late summer the sun had lost its edge and the cool evenings came earlier. Dust rose behind the moving flock as high as the treetops, for not until September would there be heavy dew to blanket the ground.

The watered dell no longer provided the forage, but for Dan and Saïd it was a safe rendezvous at night. They never talked politics, only history and sheep and a future full of

176

discovery. Dan's only contact with the kibbutz was Tam and his truck. The old Scot did nothing to break the spell except once when he said, "These are strange times, lad. Keep your eyes open. I'm not of a mind to be breaking in another new shepherd."

In mid-October Dan returned for the sheep dipping, a long-threatened ordeal which would rid the flock of parasites. A dry day was needed for the job. If it rained, the chemicals would not soak in. In hot sun, the sheep would roll in the dirt, picking up more parasites. If there was a chill wind, the sheep might take sick. October was by all odds the best month.

Tam stood at the far end of the dipping trough. He pulled out an ancient gunmetal watch from his pocket, consulted it, and raised his hand. "All right, Saul. Let 'em come."

Dan was stationed at the falls between high wooden dikes. It was his task to urge the sheep onward as they came up a ramp onto a diving board to plunge into the dipping trough. The first sheep, a determined old ewe who had been through this many times before, arrived like a charging bull, her head lowered. Dan grabbed her around the neck and was almost dragged into the trough himself. Two more ewes followed in quick succession, and then a small flock. Was Saul determined to have him trampled to death? In no time, Dan was working ankle-deep in mud and excrement, for the terror-stricken sheep lost control of their bowels long before he could wrestle them into the vat. In time, even revulsion passed. Foul from head to foot, he stood ready to wrestle a charging water buffalo if need be. The sheep were coming now thick and fast, bleating with terror, and they backed him up against the dike and pushed one another up the ramp and into the dip so expertly he wondered if all his struggling had

177

been necessary. Perhaps he had only been meant to keep count.

By midafternoon the last sheep was dipped. Saul enjoyed several of his own labored jokes. Bruised and groggy, Dan laughed along with him. What a sight he must be. Green and almost iridescent with slime, he was an apparition to frighten little children. On his way to the showers, he affected the groping stride of Frankenstein's monster.

"You're all right, Baratz," Saul told him as they shared a lump of soap. "I may get to like you yet."

That night was the Sukkoth feast. There was little religious ritual in the kibbutz, but the dining hall was decorated with flowers and fruit. "Isn't it beautiful? Soon we'll have those chandeliers. We really will," Hanna insisted. And it did seem warm and beautiful until a first course of thick brown lentil soup arrived. Then Dan had to excuse himself from the dining hall.

The days of sheepherding were numbered. Saïd had left their favorite watering spot when Dan returned, and they did not meet until November, when the weather had changed. The wind was punishing and cloud laden. There was a chill in the air.

"Palestine is to be partitioned. Did you know that? What will happen to us, I wonder?" said Saïd, breaking their old taboo.

"I don't know," Dan replied. "Some people"—he was unable to say "Arabs"—"shot at one of our trucks on the Haifa road." Of course Gideon had gotten away and made a big thing of displaying the bullet holes in the hood. Pilfering had taken place in the kibbutz fields, and, despite the protests of Sarah Klein, the language classes as well as the school for neighboring Arabs had been closed down.

So it was in a somber mood that Dan and Saïd sat and

178

talked on their reunion. They pretended at first that everything was as it had been, but whatever they said sounded false.

"I was going to invite you home to meet my family," Saïd began.

"I know," Dan answered. He'd had the same idea, wanting Hanna to share in their Petra plans. Now she seemed just as war-minded as Gideon. The two were always together, and Dan rarely had a chance to speak to either of them alone. In a few days, when the flock was enclosed for the winter, he, too, would be shouldering a gun. It was only because of the kibbutz's strategic and almost indefensible position that he and the others had not been called into Palmach. But Promise of the Future needed a garrison to keep any hope of a future alive.

"Soon, probably tomorrow, the rains will come. Then the grazing season will be over."

"It's not going to rain," Dan said. "The sky's still fairly clear. We'll be together a few more days."

But Saïd shared the intelligence of all wild things when it came to weather. "I can smell the sulfur in the air," he said. And that night there was distant thunder, so that Dan, reminded of other thunder, was afraid.

Morning dawned still and clear. Dan woke up, listening. It was so still. The desert and the hills seemed to have suspended their breath.

"There's a storm on the way," Saïd told him. "We'd better move the flocks." For confirmation he pointed to a small black cloud that rose like a hand over the desert. Faintly rolled the first thunder, a distant hint of the forthcoming orchestration. Jews and Arabs and Englishmen, all the animals of the hills and desert, heard at that moment the first drum taps of the oncoming storm.

179

It took Dan and Saïd some time to separate the two flocks, which had grown used to mingling, and the sky was dark and threatening over the plain when they drove down toward it. There were no more shadows, for everything was in shadow. The first clear shafts of rain were joining the sky and hilltops.

"To the ford?" Dan yelled through the rising gale.

"No time," Saïd called back. "The bridge!"

The bridge was much farther, but Saïd had been right about the storm and Dan did not question him now. At least the wind was behind them, and the sheep hurried along, bleating excitedly. Dan felt the first gusty shower on his back. The rain was quickly absorbed into the dusty earth. Puddles formed, and then rivulets. The ridges in the hillsides filled quickly and spilled into the dry riverbeds.

Across the river, Dan could see Arab women running from the fields. Children were running with them in shrill and cheerful panic. He caught the mood, performing great bounding leaps.

"Hurry, you idiot!" Saïd urged him. He was not amused, and even Dan's gaiety was soon quelled as the rain thickened. Its roaring crescendo was so uniformly dense that it amounted to a profound silence, blotting out all ordinary sound.

Dan's first view of the river came as a shock. The green whiteness of a lightning flash revealed what appeared to be a motionless surface of rusty steel. Then he saw the banks beginning to crumble, and deep down below the seeming placidity he heard a subterranean rumble, deeper than the rain itself. Around the bridge the newborn river worked with savage power, digging at the supports. Before his eyes the bank was being devoured. Bushes fell and vanished, whole trees rolled by. Dan thought he saw a struggling sheep.

Too late to heed Saïd's warning, Dan's sheep were already on the bridge. Dan looked back once and then plunged after his flock. The whole structure was whispering and the slender pilings were beginning to vibrate. Through sheets of rain he saw Saïd's flock following, perhaps in panic, perhaps because of his example. Saïd was midway, struggling to carry his gun as well as a reluctant lamb, when the bridge went down. An entire tree must have struck it full force, for it seemed suddenly to explode. Saïd and several of his sheep disappeared.

Dan ran frantically along the bank. He caught sight of Saïd, then lost him, saw him again, and began to shout. "Saïd! Saïd! This way!" His words were lost in the wind. The river moved faster than he could run. His friend was helpless in a yellow turmoil of mud and shrubs and sheep. Cutting across a hairpin bend, Dan caught up again and thrust out a long stick which Saïd flailed for and missed. At the next bend they made contact. Dan was dragged along the bank and only saved by the roots of a tree. Hard and tough, the roots held, and Saïd, clinging to the end of the stick, swung in a pendulum arc toward the shore. Dan hauled him out, and they both lay panting on the bank, washed by the rain, which seemed no longer to fall in separate drops.

"The sheep!" Saïd exclaimed.

Dan had forgotten all about them.

"Saïd, are you all in one piece?" That was what was important, not the sheep.

Saïd did not seem to hear him. "I've got to find them," he said, and started back along the bank like a sleepwalker. Dan followed. Lightning ignited the swollen river and the huddling sheep, then quickly blew them out again. While it still rained, they made no effort to separate the flocks.

Saïd stood staring into the rushing haze of rain. Finally he

181

said, as though just returning to his senses, "You know something? You saved my life."

"I owed one to a fisherman," Dan replied. "Do you think many sheep were lost?"

"Three or four, I guess. And my father's gun. I'll get hell for that. It happened so fast, it seems like a dream now. I never had a chance to be afraid."

Dan had lost no sheep, and had even found his gun in the mud.

"I might be dead now," Saïd said. "Just imagine—dead." It was an idea too large to comprehend.

"May you never die until I shoot you," said Dan. "And that's the wish of a sincere friend. You know that."

"I'll live forever, then," Saïd replied. "I owe you my life. I'm sure my father would want . . ." He was stumbling for words. "Listen, you must come to my house, soon. My father would want it. You will?"

Dan promised.

By now the storm had passed, and great blades of light were cutting the clouds into ribbons. The flocks were easily separated and driven off in opposite directions. Dan ran laughing, heading his sheep homeward. When he passed some village Arabs, busy reinforcing the roadway that paralleled the river, he waved exuberantly. They waved back, all sharers in nature's cataclysm. Dan was wet and spattered with mud, but he was happy, full to the brim with the brotherhood of man.

CHAPTER 10

IN THE EARLY MONTHS OF 1948, THE WEATHER AND THE NEWS
were bad. Dan patrolled the sheep pens at Promise of the
Future eight hours a day. He was never really off duty. Most
fortified kibbutzim had been safe thus far, but they were
taking no chances. According to the radio, that old crackpot
soldier of fortune, Fawzi al Kaukji, had led an Arab army of
liberation into northern Palestine. After blunting his nose on
a kibbutz or two, he'd turned to looting the easier homes of
local Arabs. It wasn't the sort of war they'd fought in Warsaw; Dan was sure of that.

An uneasy peace prevailed between Promise of the Future
and her neighbors in Tel Jabir, thanks to sober meetings
between the kibbutz council and the Arab elders. They even
cooperated in rebuilding the washed-out bridge. Dan volunteered to work there, as did Saïd, for it was the only chance
they had to see one another. Even Gideon toiled indifferently
for a day, and on their way back to the kibbutz Dan told him
about Saïd and their summer friendship.

Gideon listened with apparent interest. Then, smiling as
at a child who lived in a world of make-believe, he said,
"You're funny. Do you know that?"

"You've told me before I'm pretty comical."

183

"Funny in the head, I mean. Not that I'm accusing you of being an Arab lover, or anything like that." Dan would not have denied it, but Gideon left with this shot, taking his ugly thoughts with him.

Dan expected more understanding from Hanna. He wanted to tell her about Petra, and about the tombs he had seen, and that he hoped to have dinner soon in an Arab home. Perhaps he chose the wrong moment. She seemed pre-occupied and nervous, her strong freckled hands in motion, her fingers creasing the cloth on the dining-hall table.

"I'd like to tell you something," he began.

"Well, what is it, Dan?" she said as though she had a train to catch.

"I can't tell you so quickly. Please sit down, Hanna. Relax —the way you were always telling me to do."

"What is it you want to tell me?" He was fascinated by the perpetual activity of her hands.

"Take a couple of deep breaths. Then I'll tell you."

She listened quietly until he spoke of visiting Saïd's home. Then she jumped to her feet.

"Do you want to commit suicide?"

"Saïd's a good friend," he protested.

"It isn't sensible to make such friends."

"What is this leaden rule? Fear thy neighbor as thyself?"

She walked quickly to the window and back. "You irritate me, Dan. I'm sorry, but you do."

"You want us to be enemies with them?"

"We're something they've got to get used to."

Arguing with her, he decided, was like arguing with a tree. Most of the time she did not even bother to deny what he said. She simply listened patiently and then talked again in that cool, even tone, as if he had never spoken.

"I want you to stay friends with Gideon," she said. "He needs to be trusted, by you in particular. You're his oldest friend." God help him, thought Dan, if I'm his oldest friend.

"If he thinks you've lost faith in him, he may do something reckless."

"Reckless?" Dan almost laughed. You didn't even have to scratch Gideon's veneer to find the warpaint underneath.

"What do you expect after what he's been through?"

He'd been through no worse than the rest of them, and yet there was a passion in Gideon for the dangerous which amounted to a flirtation with death. He drove his truck everywhere with complete abandon, and there were few roads which were not mined. Thus far the Arabs had completely failed to grasp the instantaneous action of electricity. Since they believed a charge crawled snakewise from fuse to point of detonation, explosions regularly took place well before the arrival of moving targets. But even Arab stubbornness would eventually yield to practical adaptation, and then the roads would be deadly.

"One day he's going to get himself killed. That's the way he wants it," Dan said. "But not you, too. I don't like you going out on that truck to lay water pipes."

"Don't be silly, Dan. Someone has to do it."

"But not you."

"We're armed. We're all right." She seemed to appreciate his concern. Her voice had dropped as low as a boy's, and he had a sudden image of her playing boy's games as a child.

"And we have the armored bus now."

"For laying pipes?"

"Well, no. Not exactly."

"I suppose I shouldn't interfere.

"Then don't."

"You're the stiff-necked one," he told her, using the Hebrew phrase with horrendous pronunciation. At this she laughed so gaily that Dan had to laugh, too.

"You've grown a new laugh. An honest, hearty one," she said. "Confess that you're happier, Dan. You look happier."

"I might be, if you'd tell me where you're going in that armored bus."

"That's a military secret."

"Hanna."

Her eyes shone with mischievous delight. Putting her lips to his ear, she whispered a hint. "Do you know what standard the Romans raised over the temple of Jerusalem when they sacked it?"

"Jerusalem!"

"It was the image of a pig."

"You can't go to Jerusalem, Hanna. Nobody's getting through."

"I didn't say we were going there." Then, giving up the game, she said, "When I'm nervous, I talk too much. Do you mind, Dan?"

He might have said that she was all that mattered to him, all he had except for his grandfather, who had not answered his letter. He might have said that he loved her, but the words stuck in his mouth. All he could manage was, "Mind? I haven't any mind. I'm the kibbutz idiot."

"Then stop frowning. It makes you look grouchy and old."

"I feel old."

They were walking now side by side toward the barren fields as if by mutual impulse.

"I have a peculiar idea about age," she said. "Everyone has

186

an age they're made for, that they really are all their lives. Take Sholem. He was always old, about seventy. And Gideon's about eighteen and always will be. 'In his hour,' as the Arabs say."

"What about me?" Dan asked.

"Oh, thirty-five or forty. An older man. That's why I like you."

"And you?"

"I can't say about me. It's hard to tell about oneself."

For a while they walked silently.

"Should we talk?" Dan asked.

"If you want to."

"You'd rather I didn't," he said.

"Sometimes being together is nicer than talking together."

She walked moodily by his side. He took her hand and they crossed the soft, lumpy fields as laboriously as insects.

"Is your hand always so warm, Dan?"

"I suppose."

"It'll be spring soon. You can smell the earth already. It's ugly here, Dan, but I love this place. I'll never leave it." She was gazing at something in the distant blue haze.

"I love it, too," he said. They stood for a time looking into the distance. "Hanna, I love you." It seemed at first that she had not heard him, and he felt relieved. Then she dropped her eyes and squeezed his hand. "Dan," she said, and nothing more.

Committed, he looked at her boldly, and when she would not look back at him, he traced the line of her eyebrow with his finger, rubbing it softly against the grain.

"Do you never blink? Do you never shut your eyes?" she asked.

"Yes, at night, when I'm able to sleep."

A spot of red had appeared in both her cheeks and she bit her lips with apparent vexation.

"I'm sorry," he said. "I know you're Gideon's girl."

"I'm not," she protested. "I'm no one's girl. I belong to myself. Oh, Dan, I don't know what to say. I'm fonder of you than anyone. You may not believe that, but it's true. Don't be jealous of Gideon."

"It's healthy to be a little jealous. It means I love you." Dan was doggedly determined not to retreat.

But the conversation had no chance to develop further. Gideon had seen them and came cutting across the field. He carried a long crosscut saw on his shoulder. It made a musical sound as he approached.

"Well, it's Dan and our friend Eve. Have you run out of apples today?" Gideon put his hands on Hanna's waist and walked his fingers around it.

"Don't, Gideon. That tickles."

"Are you going to Jerusalem?" asked Dan.

"That's supposed to be a secret. Our little Hanna is quite a verbal athlete." To take the sting out of his comment, Gideon made a joke or two at Dan's expense, but for once Dan interrupted him.

"When are you going?" he asked.

"I'm not," Gideon replied.

"Tomorrow night," said Hanna.

"To Jerusalem?"

"Yes."

There was no talking her out of it. She was a strong and determined person, and she had volunteered with a dozen others. Dan cast about for arguments, but none of them proved strong enough. Jerusalem, the most hallowed city, was surrounded by Arabs. She was starving. Promise of the Fu-

188

ture lay near the Jerusalem road, and the kibbutz had an armored truck capable of transporting food and arms and hope through the blockade. Hanna was battle-tested while others were not, and that was that.

The following evening was typical of the indecisive weather between seasons. Clouds opened and closed, laden with explosive shafts of gold and silver. Those who were going stood about the bus in a variety of costumes: sheepskin jackets, capes, peaked hoods; everything from the nondescript to the exotic.

Gideon was standing close to Hanna. When Dan approached, they looked up. Gideon sighed deeply, so that Dan felt he was violating the sanctity of a tryst.

Passengers were already boarding, all of them with guns. Gideon was telling Hanna to shoot on sight, to keep low and shoot low. Everything was happening too fast. They were speaking in telegrams to express volumes.

"It can't have come to this," Dan pleaded.

"Listen to who's talking. He wants to know everything and knows nothing," Gideon said. "He never listens to the radio."

The passengers were lining up.

Gideon gave Hanna a kiss, and she twisted her head away with a little gasp.

Finally she kissed Dan, lingering a moment, her forehead against his as he stood there forlornly; and seeing the dismay in his face, she said, "Don't gloom. I'll be fine."

"Come back, Hanna."

"Of course, silly. And don't worry. Just stay away from Arabs."

"Away you go," Gideon exhorted.

"Long live our friend the machine gun. Long live our

189

friend the revolver," the passengers chanted. They were all young and wild; if not a menace to others, certainly a danger to themselves, thought Dan. As the bus ground its gears and gathered momentum, he waited in the hope that he would have a last glimpse of Hanna. He was not disappointed. She leaned far out, waved and blew a kiss, all gaiety, as though she were a child going on a holiday. Then the bus swung through the barbed-wire gates and rapidly diminished as it set out toward the Jaffa road, that rocky entrenched road where Arabs waited. Finally only a blue pall hung in the air where it had passed. The crowd began breaking up. A few sang the Hatikvah, "The Hope," as they trudged in to supper. Dan and Gideon sat together; Dan gloomy, Gideon in high spirits.

There was speculation about the bus, its mission, and how it would fare. When someone said, "I have a feeling they'll never . . ." Dan froze. It was what he had thought but could never voice. Gideon shut the speaker up, adding to Dan with unusual and humane intuition, "Don't worry. People always have premonitions, but I know a few things."

What Gideon knew, he wouldn't enlarge upon, as though it were a military secret he couldn't give away. He said only, "Hanna can take care of herself. She can kill if she has to."

"But she shouldn't have to."

"Listen, I've never told you how she shot a German. There were a bunch of them stationed on a hillside as lookouts. We had to take care of the place and she was, well, a decoy. They thought she was their friend, just a neighborhood farm girl. She was teaching one of them how to ski when we blew the place up. She had a pistol, and when she pulled it out, he must have had the surprise of his life. Can you imagine him trying to get away? He fell down with his skis in the air, and just lay there. They were friends, but survivors tell tales. She had no choice. He closed his eyes and covered his face with his mittens. Then she shot him. If you can do that, you can take care of yourself."

Nevertheless, Dan worried about Hanna as he paced the sheep pens that night, a cocked carbine under his arm. He worried as he worked with a shovel near the bridge the following day. Saïd was working there, too, and during a respite he brought an invitation from his father. They wished to honor Dan at dinner the following night. In such times, was it possible? Unhesitatingly, Dan said that it was. It seemed the one sane thing he could do in a world that was going mad.

They met toward dusk on the road that led to Tel Jabir. Small irregular fields were marked off by heaps of stones. When they entered the town, purple shadows already masked the meanness of the streets where the elders slumped, supported by the walls of their dwellings, and stick-thin children played at being beggars, frightening each other with toy guns. Dan saw no hint of violence. They looked too drained of human sap to promote it.

Talk preceded and followed Dan and Saïd. The moment of their passage was hushed, as though a stone had fallen into a pool full of croaking frogs. But they were stared at, in a particularly Arab fashion, as though the watching eyes saw through them to something infinite.

A larger bulk loomed abruptly amid the hovels. "A church?" Dan asked in surprise.

"It was," replied Saïd. "It's our Madafa now, a town guesthouse."

High above them gleamed the mosque. It was still etched in sunlight, vertical and emphatic.

191

In the center of town the street opened up around a well, black, mossy, and cool. In the market square boys floated balls of paper in stagnant tanks. An ancient beggar whose cataracts looked like clots of mucus put out a dry hand as they passed. Impulsively Dan pressed a coin into it, and the beggar seized his hand and raised it to his lips. Dan was flabbergasted, and he felt like giving the old creature everything he had.

Above the square the houses were larger and withdrawn behind dense gardens. The house of Kader was the very last before the road wound away into the empty hills. It was surrounded by a wall and a gate, a garden full of olives, and a grove of fig trees. From the gate only a single dome was visible, rising out of the trees like the tomb of a Mamluk. A strange silence hung about it. The murmur of the town and the shrill cries of the children broke against its walls and were dissipated like ripples on a seashore. In the garden were white metal chairs, somewhat rusted, and an awning that was bleached and tattered. The shutters of the house itself were closed.

Saïd did not enter, but solemnly knocked. "My father will come," he said.

The man who opened the door wore a striped silk *kibr* and a sleeveless *aba*. A jeweled dagger was thrust into his belly-band. He looked to Dan like the personification of a Bedouin sheik brought to anchor amidst Western enlightenment. In every way Mustafa Abdel Kader was a surprise. He looked more Egyptian than Arab. His jet-black hair and beautifully sculpted eyes were like the illustrations Dan had seen from the burial chambers of the Pharaohs. He had high cheekbones, full lips, and the expression of a man who is waiting to listen and to laugh. In fact, the only thing purely Arab about

192

him was his greeting: a bow and a dropping of the hand, then a touching of the heart for affection and the head for the appreciation of wisdom. He took Dan's hands and clasped them.

"Welcome the blessed hour. A welcome to you," he said in English, leading Dan into a sitting room filled with peacock-blue armchairs and tasseled lamps. There was even an upright piano with gilt claws for feet. On little brass trays were heaps of crystallized fruit and Turkish delight. Strong mint tea awaited them on a low brass table.

Mustafa Abdel Kader was a charming host, not only because he was a good Moslem who believed that when a guest enters a home God comes with him, but because he obviously liked to entertain. "Life must have moisture to survive," he said, pressing a cup of black tea upon Dan. Then he passed the sweets. When all were served, he began to talk. His mind was a rich vessel filled with many treasures.

He spoke of his family with pride, of their heritage of revered and prosperous ancestors, all desert men. He discussed his five sons, all stalwart, but a mixture of joy and sorrow to him. The first two had rebelled against his Western ways and had ridden off into the desert, never to return. The third, after a European education, had settled in Saudi Arabia, where he would be an important man in oil one day. Another, a year older than Saïd, even now was attending school in England, where Saïd would be going next year. "You may wonder why I set my sons to sheepherding," he said. Then he explained that nearness to nature and the humble ways of the ancients were good for any man. "With Saïd, all that will come to an end. Poor sheep. On the day my last son puts aside his crook, there will be a feast that men will remember."

193

The Muktar spoke also of his wife, who was nowhere in evidence. Dan presumed she was dead, a feeling that was strengthened when the Muktar told him that she had come to him through murder. "In the old days, when a member of one family group killed a member of another, either a feud resulted or reparations were made. A life for a life." One way to repay was for a woman of the offending clan to marry into the victim's family until she gave it a child. Such had been the fate of Saïd's mother, except that his father had become attached to his bride. They had had ten children, two of whom had died at birth before the Jewish doctor had arrived in town. Eight lives for one; good odds, it would seem. There must be three daughters unworthy of mention, Dan thought. "You see it never pays to murder a Kader." At this witticism the Muktar managed a mild smile. The Prophet never laughed, but the Muktar seemed to draw delight from Dan's amusement. "Allah, you laugh," he said.

He could joke lightly about his family, but he had pride in his heritage and the family connections with the Beni Sakhr tribe, the "Sons of the Rock" upon whom the enemy always foundered. He knew the Englishman Glubb Pasha well, and his father had rallied the green banners east of El Kerak. By way of substantiation he produced an enormous pistol. It was almost as large as a small musket, and its sight protruded like a wart. He pulled the hammer back, a small cobra head of steel, and let it fall.

"I have no love for these things," he said. "Has Saïd shown you the orchard?" In that he took particular pride. The orchard and his wife's cooking made life worthwhile. Consulting a fat pocket watch, he clapped his hands.

Almost immediately a small plump woman appeared. From above her veil flashed enormous hungry eyes set in kohled darkness. She moved with the rolling gait of a Japanese wrestler. Magically, food appeared: steaming hot loaves of round bread and a great platter of rice with what looked like an entire lamb ensconced upon it. As quickly as she had appeared, the woman vanished, with the finality of a cuckoo returning to its clock.

"Brave men and good food don't last long," the Muktar proclaimed. "Eat while it's hot. My wife is a fine cook, have no fear of that."

"Was that your wife?" Dan asked.

"You didn't know?"

"Why doesn't she eat with us?" Dan asked.

"She prefers it that way," the Muktar explained. "She comes from a traditional family. I can't cure her." With his right hand he carefully detached the morsels nearest the lamb's backbone, choice pieces for the honored guest. Dan was not allowed to refuse, and he ate until his eyes were swimming. Even then his host seemed disappointed. Dan had just launched upon the tragic tale of a puppy he had once known that had literally died of a burst belly when there came an intrusion.

Saïd's mother ushered in a stranger, a thin nervous man in Arab costume, evidently someone from the village who held the Muktar in high esteem. He called him "Bey." His message apparently was an unhappy one, for the Muktar wagged his head gravely and sounded apologetic. Dan could not understand the Arabic, but he saw the serious look in Saïd's silent almond eyes.

When the messenger withdrew, the Muktar explained to Dan that a man had been killed.

"The old beggarman. You remember him," Saïd said.

In the village he'd been something of a saint, and now he lay dead in the market. He'd been run over.

"By a bus?" Dan exclaimed in horror.

"No, by a small truck from the kibbutz. You know—the blue one."

Dan knew.

There was no way of guessing whether or not the deed was deliberate. An accident, probably, but the truck had roared on without stopping. Accident or not, there were hotheads in town who would accept the incident as murder. There was no telling what would happen.

From this news the evening never recovered. Not that the Muktar didn't try. He described the old days of the *ghazzu,* the game of raiding which the Bedouins played among themselves. When they had tried it on the Jews, the Jews had struck back. He made the fight an epic thing, and Dan sat precariously on the edge of his chair.

"Tel Jabir was nothing but fire and smoke, and the dead lay knee deep in the market square."

Saïd played the part of spoiler. "I thought you told me only one man was killed here."

"What's that you say?"

"Some shepherd who just happened to be passing through. A poor man who had nothing to do with politics."

"Come now, my son."

But Saïd continued. "You told me when the fighting was over, both sides claimed him as their own."

"You know very well your own grandfather was severely wounded in the battle."

"I thought a spark from his old flintlock rifle set his beard on fire."

"And he was severely wounded as a result," his father insisted. Dan realized this was all a game they had played before, but now the Muktar became serious. His fine eyes searched Dan's face. "You see, it's not very easy to make sense out of history. You're old enough, I think, to distinguish the

196

good from the bad. I want to put what for you will be the other side of the case. May I do that? After all, we Arabs have lived here a long time."

He admired the Jews, he went on to say, and they had developed the finest form of Western socialism. However, this was not a warrant to occupy land which didn't belong to them. He had seen the Jews perform miracles in agriculture and medicine. Arabs and Jews could well pull together in this land. "We Arabs have more in kinship with the Jews than we have with the black slaves of North Africa or the tattooed Tuareg, and yet we are brothers in Islam with them and enemies to the Jews. Why? Because the Jews are a closed society. You understand, my friend, I don't mean you personally. You take more than you give, and hang on to what you take like a bulldog. You'll not share your God as Allah has been offered to the world. Now, if one listens to the United Nations, over half of Palestine, the better half, is in your hands."

Though the Muktar yearned for peace and understanding, there were already zealots on either side banging their heads together. Now an Arab was dead. He had been old and useless, perhaps, but a life. Though he did not approve of the ancient ways, a life was owed. Would the Jews be as reasonable as the tribes of old had been? Would they give a wife to the Arabs?

"I conjure you by Allah to ask them that! But I should apologize for my vehemence to a guest. We have our hotheads here as well."

Dan had never embroiled himself in political arguments, and he now felt unable to hold up his end in such a discussion. "I suppose I should be going home," he said uncomfortably from the midst of a long silence.

"Saïd will go with you," the Muktar replied. "An Arab

197

host is responsible for his guest as long as his salt is in that guest's stomach. Longer, much longer, in your case. We owe you a life already."

All three of them stepped outside. The sky was clear and star-studded.

"Did you know that in Islam every man has his own star? It appears when he is born and goes out when he dies." The Muktar pointed to a pair of bright stars. "You two. They're far too bright for me. Stars pale, you know, as one gets old. Mine must be quite dim tonight." It seemed to Dan that his host's personality had changed. His was the sort of charm one expects in the old or very ill, the charm of the defeated and the lost.

The Muktar remained at the front gate. "Praise God for your safety," he said in parting.

The boys walked in silence through the town, which was very quiet. The few faces they saw were expressionless, and Dan felt more than ever the stranger, the intruding Jew, the Western man.

At the first field, Saïd stopped.

"I'm sorry about what happened tonight," he said.

"I'm sorrier than you are. Will you be taking the flock out this spring?"

"Soon," Saïd replied.

"Good. Then we'll see each other."

"Go with God."

The road from Tel Jabir to the kibbutz was dark and silent. There were dovecotes near the fringe of town. He thought he heard the birds stirring until the sound grew into a low wail of lamentation. Perhaps they were mourning the old man. Dan seemed to feel Arab eyes upon him, not full of

198

hate, but as though the sight of him were painful. Would they demand a life, then? Perhaps his, if he was not careful. Since Cain, there had been injustice, robbing, killing. There would be an endless sequence of revenge until people were able to sit down without rancor to build the future by forgetting the past. That had been Sholem's dream. It seemed forever destined to be no more than a dream.

Dan hurried along the road, a solitary traveler. Bats stitched through the darkness. He was passing the bridge when he first heard it, an odd sound that filled the air as though the earth itself had suddenly developed a pulse. As he walked on, the air was filled with the muffled shocks and lingering vibrations of a drum from a darker, more spacious world than his. The Bedouins were back. He crept up close enough to see their sheltered camp. There were the black tents and the camels snorting and gnarring. Music and the odor of human beings wafted across the night toward him, rich with the memories of country fairs he had visited with his parents as a child.

They had returned early this year. He wondered why. There were more vehicles this time, a veritable fleet of "armored cars," which was the local way of describing an old Chevrolet truck body enclosed in overlapping scales of flattened petrol tins.

Fires burned among the black tents, and Dan caught the copper glow of the big camel drum. There were other musicians lost in shadow, for he heard the spank and gulp of a finger drum and the lament of a one-stringed fiddle, the chords running along the string like little footsteps. Guttural, visceral voices raised an atonal chorus. It had an odd dream-like slowness, as if it originated in the cosmos and had to cross space and time to reach him. Dan knew the song from Saïd

—it told of ten camel riders galloping together, though the words were quite beyond him. Then an old man entered the circle of firelight. He stamped and clapped until he was joined by a girl. She began to dance, rolling her head wildly. Another song began, the voices hoarse and masculine. "Our enemy came to the country, We drove him back from Bab al Wadi, O Tellal, son of the sherifs." Finally the songs faded as the dancing quickened, raising clouds of dust that turned the fireglow from yellow to somber red. The sheik stepped into the dancing circle and gave his jeweled sword to the girl, who slashed the air, a disk of flaming silver.

Dan watched from his hillock, hypnotized, as an old camel was trotted into the firelight. He could hear its bubbling snorts as it knelt peacefully by the fire, its forelegs folded under it like a cat. Then, as he watched, the horde of dancing men attacked it with axes. The camel made no sound, but stared hard at the stars while a leg was lopped off. Dan's stomach sickened at the sight, but he could not pull himself away. The beast made no effort to avoid the blows, uttered no cry. The axes bit into him as though his body were made of balsa. Whole members were hacked off as indifferently as fruit might be struck from a tree. Women and children scampered off with the pieces to the various spits and boiling pots around the camp.

Dan had seen enough. Were it not for the unworldly quality of what he had witnessed, he would have been sick. He could now believe all he had ever heard of the Bedouins. It was a not uncommon sight to see one of them staring moodily into the desert. Though he could ill afford it, he would suddenly ignite a priceless box of matches. From this his soul would catch fire, and he would race his camel up and down the sand waving his scimitar. When whole tribes fell into such a mood, it meant holy war and a knife across the throat.

200

A dog began to bark. It seemed very close. Dan ran, cautiously at first, but with the sound of horses' hooves and louder barking, he fled in panic. Once he fell on some loose gravel, scrambled up and ran again beneath the mad desert moon of April. A shuddering throaty laugh out of blackness, a hyena, perhaps, or his own imagination, kept him plunging blindly for the protective wire of the kibbutz.

A great eagle owl out for a kill swooped low overhead with its boo-hooing cry. Dan could hear its hissing breath, the sound of a sword cutting through air. He dodged to the left, tripped over a bush, and flung himself headlong into the barbed wire, which gashed him across legs, arms, and throat.

"God . . . oh, God." He hung there a moment, and the hooves that he heard pounding were only the beating of his heart. Painfully he detached himself from the barbs. Far off rose the forlorn bark of a dog complaining of hunger and loneliness. There was no sign of a sentry, so Dan dragged himself silently under the wire. It was late. The brittle stars of early spring flowed down in a slow cascade over the western horizon.

He took two stealthy steps into Promise of the Future, and then a hasty one back as he was confronted by a roar of murderous hatred and the report of cracking leather.

"Damn you! Damn you, dog!" came a shout from the dark, and then, "Who is it? Speak up, or he'll tear out your throat."

Dan identified himself as a lean shape leaped forward, snapping sideways in midflight as the leash caught him. A great snowman figure stumbled behind the police dog.

It was the Russian, Pavlov, padded like a deep-sea diver, out training a guard dog.

"It's a miserable job for a man and no life at all for a decent dog," he said.

"I imagine not," Dan agreed.

"You see, there's no mustering out for a dog soldier. You can't break him of killing. You can only shoot him. God knows the way we corrupt our poor dumb beasts to serve our beastly ends."

Once more Dan could only agree. He was too tired and shaky for philosophy, so he took his leave of Pavlov and his still grumbling charge and made straight for the compound across the plowed fields.

CHAPTER 11

On the surface it was just another springtime, with sheep demanding green pastures. Dan would have preferred to handle them alone, but he was ordered to take an armed companion.

The companion was Gideon, who was no use as a shepherd. His only training had been to kill Germans, and he idled about with his gun, sighting at imaginary targets. War for him was a matter of days, and he for one would welcome it. How else could a man be truly tested? He could hardly wait to impress the chaos of his soul on everything around him. All he needed was a target, any target; but Dan was the best he had for the moment, a purely verbal one.

"Hey, did Hanna give you that?" he asked.

"Sorry?"

"That bite on your neck. Looks like her work." He gave a great snort of laughter and banged his knee until dust flew out of the folds of his trousers.

"Actually, some barbed wire," Dan explained, reddening.

"I knew it wasn't shaving," Gideon replied. "Good old Hanna. I wouldn't put it past her."

She was out for the third time on the Jerusalem road. With each convoy the trip became more deadly, even though they traveled at night and, as often as possible, near British military trucking. Many such convoys were attacked. One had been annihilated in a seven-hour fight, with Gadna boys of sixteen manning the guns at the last.

Dan worried whenever he thought of Hanna out there, and that was most of the time.

"She's tough as nails," Gideon reassured him. "Too tough for me."

"What do you mean by that?" Dan wanted to know. "I thought she was . . . well . . . special with you."

"I don't know. I like a girl who's feminine and voluptuous. You know, one that walks like a girl, not like a boy athlete. Hanna's a good pal, but that's about all. Anyway, she prefers the shy, retiring type like you."

"Go on." Dan was pleased, but he didn't want to show it.

"Oh, she likes you all right. You ought to hear old Hanna on the subject of you."

"Criticizing. I can just hear her."

"Sure, but would she bother if she didn't care?" said Gideon. "Look, he's beginning to blush. I can see it. You're blushing, Dan. You're sweet on her yourself."

"Sure, I'm fond of her. We get on."

"Is that all?"

"I love her," Dan said defiantly. "Is that what you want me to say?"

Perhaps Gideon had not expected this. In any case, Dan thought he read in his friend first surprise, and then a decision to lie. "You should see the one I've got in Haifa," he said, rolling his eyes for emphasis. "Nice. You know, you ought to come with me one time, when I get going again."

The truck was no longer Gideon's to drive. He had always

been suspect in the eyes of the kibbutz council as one who was too eager to take up arms and hunt his neighbors. The death of the Arab beggar in Tel Jabir had been the last straw. Though a state of war existed between the ill-trained and motley armies of the Arabs and the vastly outnumbered but savagely determined Jews, a veneer of civilization still existed between Promise of the Future and the Arabs on the hill. Every day a truckload of Jewish and Arab notables drove from one place to the other, appealing to both sides to remain calm. Dan had seen both Sarah Klein and the Muktar among them. Old and better times would come again, he assured Gideon.

"You'd be just the one to believe that," Gideon said scornfully. War was afoot and hungry. No truck full of hand-waving seniles was going to lull it back to sleep. He mentioned old secrets casually, as though they had outlived their importance. He admitted his membership in the Irgun, which Dan had long suspected. He told about the arms he had smuggled through, covered with onions in the back of his truck: stolen English Webleys, German Schmeissers, Czech rifles, and Italian pistols. For the first time, he spoke of Chavera as an old friend. Yes, he was Irgun, and proud of it. He would have been in the thick of the fighting long ago were he not more useful as a liaison with certain sympathizers at Promise of the Future. Even so, he'd been in a scrap or two. He described English soldiers wounded by time bombs as though they were before Dan's eyes. "His insides strewn all over the place; all over. And him calling for morphia."

"I don't want to hear that," Dan told him. "If you have to talk, talk about something pleasant."

"Well, let's compose a war song. We need one," Gideon said.

"A war song? What for?"

205

"Call it an anthem, then."

"Why not? The 'Horst Wessel Lied' was a catchy tune."

"You're funny—you are."

"I'm serious. People are always stealing war songs from the Germans."

"You'll have a surprise one of these days. We're going to surprise the whole world." Gideon hinted dimly at things that were about to take place at Acre prison and an Arab town called Deir Yassin. "Chavera mentioned your name to me. He wondered if you would reconsider making grenades."

The question was a simple one, but Dan was not sure of the right answer. "I can't," he said finally.

"Look at yourself," taunted Gideon. "Look at Israel's hope. You have no courage, isn't that it?"

"Not the sort that longs for a rifle."

Gideon extended his hand, aiming it at Dan's face like a pistol. "You can be damned sure when the English are out of here, matters will be a hell of a lot worse."

"We've been getting on with our Arabs," Dan insisted. "Even after what you did with that truck."

"Damned old fool just stood there in the road. He's probably better off."

"You really hate all Arabs, don't you, Gideon?"

Gideon hesitated and thought a moment. "As a matter of fact, I do. The only way I can describe it is this. Somewhere inside my head there's a cluster of little cells. I can't control them, but whenever an Arab comes within earshot those little cells begin to vibrate. They beat up and down and ruin my digestion. That's just the way it is." He gave Dan a brotherly punch. "You can talk, but wait until an Arab shoves a gun in your face."

206

"I'll wait."

"You'll stand there asking yourself moral questions. But will he?"

"I don't know," Dan said.

"You can be damn well sure he won't." Gideon stepped forward until his sunburned nose was thrust almost into Dan's face. "We'll have our war, and it will be with that town up there unless the Irgun chases them out first. There's no choice. We've got to fight. Some of us will have to die."

"And if we don't fight?"

"It'll be like Poland. They'll slaughter us, and their women will come along with baskets to pick up souvenirs." Gideon felt the whole future of Israel depended on the war. The protagonists were well matched, like two insects prepared by nature for a struggle, with weapons and weaknesses that corresponded. They had simply evolved unknowingly to the point were war was natural, inevitable; the survival of the fittest.

Dan was no match for Gideon in argument. He listened, but he was impervious to the other's conviction. Gideon listened to no one, or at most only to what complemented his own beliefs. Dan had a soft, rather hesitant manner of speech, which Hanna called mumbling; Gideon talked as though he were addressing a large and hostile audience through a megaphone. Dan felt as if he had been bludgeoned. He bowed his head because he could think of nothing more to say.

"Glad to see you agree with me," Gideon concluded. "Oh, by the way, there's an insect on your shirt. I'd kill it if I were you."

"What for?"

"Don't take chances; it may be poisonous."

Dan flicked it away. It was only a tiny bug.

207

When the grazing season had begun, Dan hoped he would meet Saïd, but Gideon's presence and the fact that they returned each night to the protection of the kibbutz made it unlikely. So the trip to Petra passed by default. Occasionally Dan had glimpses of the Bedouins; some on horseback, others in cars going off on mysterious errands.

That night Dan patrolled the barbed wire. He had fired the gun once—they were short of ammunition—and had missed a man-sized sack of straw. That had been in broad daylight, and since then he had not fired. He managed to maintain a façade of slow dignity, though it hardly matched his nervous heart. No moon shone down. No night bird called. He peered off into a landscape without form or shadow. Behind him rose the stark silhouette of the kibbutz water tank. A guard was stationed there. The stilted tank and the wire enclosing them all was like the old days. They were prisoners in an Arab world, and yet the Arabs, too, were prisoners. So was everyone within an endless series of Chinese puzzle boxes, smaller and smaller, until at last was reached the confining flesh of the body.

Suddenly his thoughts were erased. There was a shadow where no shadow should be, and it was moving. Falling to the ground, he aimed the gun as he had learned in maneuvers. He called to the stranger to identify himself in a rapid succession of languages. For such an emergency, he had even learned Arabic.

The shadow answered in English. "Dan, is that you?"

It was Saïd.

"Saïd!" Dan exclaimed. "I nearly killed you. Be quiet. There's a guard on that water tank."

"Don't worry," Saïd said in a whisper, as if danger just now had entered the scene.

"What are you doing here?"

"I've come to warn you not to send out that truck again. There's a plot to destroy it."

"Because of what's going on?"

"Yes. And because of the old man."

"Surely your father can stop it."

Even at the kibbutz, the Muktar was respected and trusted as *Sahib,* good friend. He had long been thought to control Tel Jabir.

"Not anymore." Saïd's face was lowered, seeming to brood on the ground at his feet. "My father will stay to do what he can. Many who can afford it have driven off to Trans-Jordan until the trouble is over. Others have taken their place in the councils. Have you heard of the Arab Brotherhood?"

Dan nodded.

"They're wild men, out of the desert and the slums of Cairo. They talk in imitation of the Prophet. Do you know what I mean? 'O Arabs, sons of Ibrahim, chosen of the Prophet and noblest of warriors, give heed to the instructions of your friends. We sit in the high places, and neither are we idle.' They keep threatening another Ezzion."

The Ezzion were four kibbutzim guarding Jerusalem from the south, a fortress more than a community. Ezzion had been overrun by Arabs, and the defenders slaughtered.

"They speak of you here as another Ezzion. I haven't heard their plans, but it could be anytime."

"And you're warning us," Dan said. "You could be shot for that." Of course, it was only what the kibbutz had been preparing for all along. Touched by his friend's devotion, Dan wanted to give something in return. Judging by what Gideon had said, the Irgun, together with a younger and more militant group from Promise of the Future, were planning an attack on Tel Jabir. "I'm sure the council is against it," said Dan. "They may not even know what's intended. I don't know how, or when it will happen, Saïd. I wish I could tell you more, but I'm not really in Gideon's confidence. He'd kill me for saying this much."

Dan could not see Saïd's face in the dark and could not guess how he was reacting. Probably nothing he had said had come as a surprise.

Uneasily, he spoke again. "I wish you could persuade your family to leave Tel Jabir."

"We have relatives in Trans-Jordan," Saïd answered. "But can you imagine my father deserting his people? He'd never go."

"Then take care."

"Don't worry about us. If need be, we have a place to hide. You remember the caves."

"Of course. The tombs. I'd forgotten them."

"Whatever happens," Saïd said, "we two will never fight."

"Never," Dan echoed.

They stretched their hands to each other through the wire. Their cold fingers locked hard.

"Give my best to your father and mother," Dan said. "You're lucky to have them."

"Next year, Petra," Saïd replied. "Or the year after that. You are my friend, and I shall never change even if you do."

"Go with God."

"Allah be with you." Then, as if anxious to provide a phrase which would bridge the unhappy gap, the Arab added, "All will be well one day."

Saïd withdrew into shadow and Dan continued his patrol, each left with a secret he did not know how to use. It wasn't long before Dan heard footsteps. They were quite unguarded, first dull on the hard soil, then ringing clearly on the new roadway. They came from the kibbutz compound. He was not particularly alarmed until he heard shouting. "Hear the radio! Hear it!" It was Gideon, calling him away from a duty Gideon had always held sacred. As he jogged along beside his friend, thankfulness that Gideon and Saïd had not encountered one another blotted all else from Dan's mind.

The dining hall was packed and hushed. The radio, tuned as always to *Kol Israel,* was going full blast. It was the fifth day of the month of Iyar in the year 5708, the fourteenth day of May, 1948, and the radio, though static crackled between the words, was proclaiming the free state of Israel in Palestine. The voice over the radio was like a great bell that was struck and ringing in all their heads and hearts.

The decisive weeks in the history of the Jewish nation had arrived. They could hardly hold themselves in check, standing while the rabbi prayed for a peace that was already lost. There was a point from which there was no turning back. That point was past. The rabbi knew it, and fell silent. Then the place went mad, with everyone hopping about like dried peas in a pan. "Praise Him with the blast of the horn, praise Him with the harp and lyre. Praise Him with the timbrel and the dance . . ."

The rejoicing was infectious. All that was lacking was Hanna, whom Dan had expected back before this. Without her he could not throw himself into the celebration wholeheartedly. Also, he was troubled by the warning he had received.

He had decided to return to his post, where he could peer into the night for the masked lights of an armored bus making for home, when something happened that changed the situation abruptly. The power failed. The radio went silent and the room was black except for candlelight. Surprised silence and amusement at first; they had overtaxed the generator. The generator! Sabotage! Chairs were knocked over in a rush for weapons and for the door.

In the darkness, panic spread as though all five Arab armies were converging on Promise of the Future. Only the day before, the Ezzion block had finally fallen, and now it was their turn, a modern Masada, to stand or fall.

Dark corners were searched and posts were double-checked. The truck was sent out with its lights on to give the effect of reinforcements arriving at the settlement. It rumbled back and forth with lots of laughter and song. More than once Dan took it for the bus returning. There was nothing wrong with the generator, only a fuse blown out. With this replaced, the celebrations continued with diminished zest. Though the alarm had been a false one, they were aware that this evening bore a price which had not yet been paid. The radio made that clear enough, with reports of Arab armies penetrating all the frontiers of Palestine.

Off duty, Dan joined the throng around the radio. It was well toward morning. Reports kept coming in through heavy static. Each report was discussed so vehemently that the announcement a bus had been ambushed and its occupants annihilated at the top of Scorpion Pass went almost unnoticed.

"Did you hear that?" someone cried out.

Dan stood transfixed, cold as marble. He was barely able to hear through the static and a hollow roaring inside his head.

"From here? Did someone say our bus?"

The static was terrific. Only the closest listeners could decipher the reports, and so they were coming to Dan secondhand. A bus had been destroyed. An Arab legion had the

212

identity cards of Jews of many nationalities. All presumed dead . . . their armored bus . . . Hanna . . .

Something had gone wrong with Dan's knees. If he did not leave, he would have to hold on to something, and he did not want to stay with these people. Gideon, who had been watching him silently, followed and helped him when he could not manage the knob.

"Gideon, has she a chance?"

"She's better dead than alive in Arab hands."

A fate worse than death? To Dan there was no such thing.

He could not cry. His senses were numb, as though awaiting some event yet to come.

Dan sat on the edge of his cot. Everything was still and quiet here, but behind his eyes ran pictures evoked by the flat words the radio had spoken. He saw it all so clearly that he felt he must have been there himself: the road narrowing to an overgrown track, the bus moving tortuously beside gray outcroppings of rock, lurching in the ruts, and then ahead a great rocky ridge, and beneath it a dry riverbed. Nightfall was coming. He could see eyes peering out through slits in the plating, watching for familiar landmarks, and then, over the growling din of the bus, the rattle of machine guns. The careening bus, the bursting tires, the motor in flames . . . he saw it all, and yet somehow he could not see Hanna anywhere.

The minutes dropped away as the scene replayed in his mind again and again. He was immobilized by the weight of the tragedy, which had not yet fully expanded into his understanding. Outside, dawn was breaking, and normal life went on unheeding. The guard was changing. He could hear voices, even laughter. Dan turned to the wall and struck his fist against it.

As though the blow were a summons, Gideon appeared in the doorway. He looked at the floor politely, waiting for Dan to notice him. Receiving no recognition, he cleared his throat.

"I wish I didn't have to bother you, Dan."

"Then don't."

Gideon's eyes glittered, but for once his voice was low. "Dan, the Arabs have begun shelling Jerusalem." Dan looked away, but Gideon went on talking, his face still as stone. He talked about Hanna, who for him had already become a symbol. She had held out until the last for Israel. He distorted hard facts with sentiment. "Dan, she isn't really dead. She's stationed beneath the seat of glory."

"Don't give me that garbage."

"Well, we can't let her down now. There's work to do."

"What's the use? You just keep spending love and energy and getting nothing back. You never get paid back."

"That's right; because we're paid in advance."

"Like hell. With what?"

"Being born; life. Listen, Dan." He looked at Dan with the calculating assessment of a machine. "There's only one reason we're here at all. Because we Jews have become fighters at last." He took his penknife out of his pocket and dug the point of it again and again into the door frame until he had gouged out the name "Hanna." "We're going to get ours back. We're going to attack that town up there tonight. Not a massacre, just a lesson. This Arab business can't drag on and on. There's got to be a final solution. Clearing out that place is a good start. You don't like that, do you? Well, what if I say revenge is good for the soul? Out of revenge grows forgiveness. We'll be doing God's work."

God's work. Surely God had abandoned this desert land

214

centuries ago, along with the insects, the birds, and the beasts that struggled here for survival. That part of himself that remained loyal to Sholem hated these ideas, and yet the more he hated them, the more undeniably rose the desire to kill.

His long silence was an admission to them both.

"Well, Dan?"

"I'm with you. Whatever you say."

"I was sure you would be." Gideon's voice hissed between his teeth. "You won't regret it. Chavera's coming out with the others." Dan could see again the wind-gnawed face with the bleak cold eyes. "I know you don't like him. I didn't either, at first. I'm not fond of fanatics, but his dedication is marvelous. And don't forget, you'll be doing this for Hanna."

He held out a gun to Dan. "Take it in your hands," he said. "It's cool and heavy. It's wonderful how they make these things to fit your shoulder."

Dan loaded the magazine, then clicked out the bullets onto the bed, where they lay with a brassy gleam. He seemed to hear Sholem pleading inside him. "Shut up," he said. "Shut up."

"What's that?" Gideon was looking at him.

There was one virtue in war. It offered simple answers. Now that hatred had flowered in him, he had to turn it loose on someone. Methodically he reloaded the gun.

CHAPTER 12

THE FIGHTERS ARRIVED FROM THE COAST WHEN THE AFTER-
noon sky was beginning to redden. Chavera led them. Dan
recognized him from a distance; a head taller than the
others, his leathery chin ginger with bristles. Beside him was
the thick-set woman whom Dan had once mistaken for a man.
The others called her Sheherazade, but they did so without
smirking. They were a motley crew, young and old, male and
female. Most of them wore the brown stocking caps made
popular by the Haganah, but all were members of the Irgun;
fierce-eyed, pledged to the death. A group of volunteers from
the kibbutz joined them, untried young men who knew they
were ignorant of war and hoped they were brave. Several of
these instant warriors cleaned and oiled their clean and oily
rifles as Chavera spoke to them all.

At first he sounded like an old coach trying to bridge the
gap between himself and a green football team. "We're all
one family," he said. "There are no generals and no privates
here, only brothers and sisters of Israel, the land of our
fathers." He stood very tall and straight, his eyes slitted from
staring into sharp light or down rifle barrels. The great muscles of his body were tense with pride. It was very obvious
who was the commander. "We will beat them, not only to-

216

night but in the final victory. Many of us may die, but we shall march through horror to triumph. We shall fight in the knowledge that it is more dangerous to lose than to win. Let me tell you of a Jewish garrison where all but four died, and of those four, only one stayed at his post." Here he brought down his fist. His eyes were terrifying. "Each one of us will be the one who stays. We will create synonyms for the word "Israel," and they will be pride, and courage!"

After this rhetorical peak, a hot geyser of chauvinism presumably bubbled in every breast. Chavera descended to practical matters, the logistics and objectives of this night's affair. There was to be little shooting, he said. What they wanted was a strategic location, not dead Arabs. They would attack with noise and fire, and the Arabs would flee in their nightshirts. It was all very simple and painless as he described it.

Until this moment, Dan had not been aware how much depended on him. With his topographical knowledge of the area, he was to serve as pathfinder. The purple twilight hour was turning black and ominous when he was handed a synchronized watch and told what was expected of him. Weapons were being handed out to the others, as well as knapsacks packed with rations for a day: rolls, salt, onions. Some received homemade hand grenades and firecrackers with which to frighten the Arabs into flight. Ammunition was too scarce to waste.

They finally set out under a white, withered moon that gave little light. Dan walked beside Chavera, acutely aware of the man's physical presence. His head and shoulders swayed from side to side like a bear in a ring. He was silent, as though stalking game in a jungle. Gideon was there, too. In the moonlight, his face had the complacent sheen of a waxworks figure. Dan didn't like it. The urge to kill had many

217

masks, and the calm, smiling one was the worst. Occasionally Gideon's mouth opened and closed in ugly trembling yawns.

"It's breathless tonight," he said in a whisper.

"What is?"

"The air. It's so close. No wind."

Dan hadn't noticed. He only knew that his grief and fury had passed into dullness mixed with hunger and fatigue. Though it seemed callous to sleep while a loved one lay unburied, he longed for a bowl of soup and a quiet spot to curl up and sleep for centuries.

The attacking force was divided into two groups: one above, the other below the village. Dan was with the group above. The line was sparsely manned, but spirit filled in the gaps. There was a persistent rumor that an Arab tank was due. Its demolition, should it arrive before 2 A.M., would signal the attack. For a long time they waited. Now and then Chavera would put his ear to the ground. Their trap was set, but nothing moved into it. Stars went about their business drifting west.

They waited.

They waited.

Then Chavera jumped up. "It's coming!" he said. The word swept down the line. After a few moments, Dan could hear it. This was the way their bus must have sounded to Arab soldiers waiting in just this way. It was not a tank. The Arabs called anything a tank. It was another homemade armored car. Slowly it passed down the hill, running in neutral, its passengers undoubtedly breathing a sigh of relief that they were almost home. With Tel Jabir in full view, they ran right into the trap: two drums of petrol wired together so that a passing vehicle would pull them to its sides.

Dan dropped to the ground at the first roar of tracer bul-

218

lets. Then a probing blade of flame leaped up from the road. It reached in through the truck's window and pulled out a shuddering scream. The truck swerved crazily and men jumped out. They did not jump in any orderly way. It was as though a great spring had been released. They hurtled out in bizarre attitudes, waving their legs and arms like clowns, spinning in the air and then falling onto the road in new postures more fantastic than before. The machine gun never paused in its work. In the center of the road antic figures leaped and danced. Dan could hear their panting shouts. Through a gap in the low trees he saw a man hurling himself along, a figure of stark loneliness, all feathered out in fire. Then he fell, rolling along the ground as the flames devoured him. Now the truck itself exploded with a dull pulsating roar. In the white heat of its explosion, a solitary human figure glowed white-hot, disintegrating.

Stillness for a moment. Only the lapping of the flames. Then Dan heard what he thought were the firecrackers going off nearer the town so that the superstitious Arabs would flee into the dark they feared. Tracers spat into a field behind him where sheep had been grazing. There was bleating panic, a pounding of hooves, and an Arab curse. The Arabs readjusted their sights and stopped slaughtering sheep. The tracers found their way among the rocks where the Jews were hiding with a staccato patter that forecast death.

So the Arabs had been expecting them. Chavera's band, however, was not about to pull back. Dan held his fire while a machine gun hammered behind his ear. He could feel the hot breath from its muzzle. The shocking noise made his eyes blink and his teeth rattle.

For a few moments both lines held. The darkness was filled with bright stabbings. *"Allah akbar!"* came shouts from the hill, and the Jews answered, *"Ag'u-el-Yahud!"* "The Jew has come!" Dan wondered why the Arabs didn't break and run as they were supposed to. Was it because he had told Saïd of a possible attack? Because of his warning, were people dying? The stalemate was broken when Chavera unveiled a new weapon, the "little David," a homemade mortar that threw a tumbling hammerlike projectile full of dynamite. The explosion of the first shell was devastating. It stunned even the Jews, who had expected it. The Arabs broke when their first men went down, horribly wounded.

After that, it was a rout. Sheherazade led the Jews into town, her Irgun comrades close behind her, confident as wolves. The soldiers from the kibbutz came last, with a cowering walk that exposed them for the novices they were. It was as though they were acting out alertness, imagining what it must be like to be in danger with very little real comprehension of what they were doing.

And so they descended upon Tel Jabir.

Dan went reluctantly. Beside him, Gideon moved with a tread as light as his voice. "Faster, Dan. Come on. How does it feel to be in the lion's den?" Dan made no answer, but his legs hurried him along in spite of himself until he was in the fight again and obliged to take pride in that variety of fear that passed for courage.

What followed was a slaughter. The Arabs ran this way and that. Some fought, some fell down and prayed, others fled screaming, back and forth. Monstrous pictures etched themselves into Dan's brain. He had seen people die before, but never this way. It had always been a slow fading out of life, an escape from pain and hopelessness; not this terrible dismemberment. Here they screamed and wriggled and burst open, their blood crimson in the crimson flames. The woman they called Sheherazade was down on her hands and knees.

220

She turned to him a mouth that was now a jagged hole, and the sound that came toward him with a tongueless mixture of pain and astonishment might have come from the mouth of a run-over dog.

Presently it was finished. Far off, a rifle cracked twice into the subsiding night; probably one of the girls, a little late but demonstrating her warlike intentions. Peacefully the village burned, as much of it as was combustible, and the red ashes swept up toward the stars.

Dan dragged from the flames what he thought was an unconscious child, but it was only a large doll. Beads of wax had formed on its cracked forehead like drops of sweat. Dan threw it back into the fire. The dead and wounded could not be so simply evaded. They were everywhere. The injured that could be moved were taken to the broken-down church. The dead were heaped in the square, entangled with each other like maggots; men, women, children, every age it seemed, except the age of loveliness. Rather than transport them farther for mass burial, someone suggested throwing them down the deep well. Dan watched in horror. The rights of Jewry seemed utterly irrelevant to these gaping mouths and stiffening limbs. For one life, a dozen had been taken; now a hundred in return. Dan clenched his jaws to stop their shivering. The horror was deeper than tears. It was a revelation. He wanted to call out loud to whatever gods there were, powerful listening gods who would hear and understand and explain how this cycle of revenge could be brought to a close.

Dan could do nothing for the dead, so he went to the church to see what he might do for the living. The small building was full of wounded. Some lay quietly, but others screamed, an echoing litany of pain and dying. He had no medical skill, but he could bring them water. Some whose heads he held to the cup drank thirstily. Others were beyond anything but surgery, and there were no surgeons. When they died, a handkerchief was placed over their faces.

Sheherazade was there and Chavera was beside her, kneeling down with her head in his lap. He stroked her hair and whispered softly to her, "Be peaceful, my girl. Be peaceful now." She could not answer, but she held his hand. Dan approached with water, but the man nodded him away. She had closed her eyes. "Sleep, old friend. I'm here with you." The woman who had seemed so indestructible was dead. There was no handkerchief for her ruined face. Chavera picked her up and carried her outside. Dan did not watch him, for the strange leathery man was crying silently. Tears poured from both eyes, the bad as well as the good.

Out in the square he raised the body in his arms. "See what they have done!" he shouted. All told, ten Jews had been wounded. Three of them were dead. The Arab casualties were beyond count. The only solace Dan could draw from this was the report that the Muktar and his family were not among them.

It was a complete victory. The grimy conquerors sat about, weary, yet grinning with a radiance lit from within. Some raised their rifles in salute to one another. "Victory! After two thousand years, victory!" A few were too tired and shocked to care. More than one cried, none more unrestrainedly than Saul, the shepherd. These were the boys from the kibbutz who had lost their youth this night. Except for Gideon, they had been strangers to killing. He was of the sort whose mind and body worked at its highest pitch under the stimulus of danger. Now his face, seldom gentle or composed, seemed about to explode with the sheer ecstasy of fulfillment the night had brought.

"Wait until the Arab radio gets hold of this," he said to Dan. "There'll be a stampede right out of Palestine."

"There wasn't to be any fight at all," Dan said.

"Damned fools weren't supposed to fight back."

"Joy in his eyes, blood on his hands," Dan said.

Gideon had evidently not heard him. "Will they be stampeded!" he said again. "It'll be lovely."

Dan placed his hands on Gideon's shoulders. They were blood-smeared from the work he had been doing in the church. Slowly he drew them down over Gideon's shirt front.

"There, that's better," he said. "Now you really look like a butcher."

Desperate days were to follow. An Egyptian mechanized army rolled out of Sinai and attacked Yad Mordekhai. When Dan pressed his ear to the ground, he heard the rumble of artillery. The people of Promise of the Future were under arms for an attack, both behind their own barbed wire and within the rubble and rocks of Tel Jabir.

Many Arabs had stayed in the town. Some were wounded, some apathetic and fearful. Others remained simply because their lord, the Muktar, had not fled. He was in the hills somewhere nearby, though only a few, including Dan, knew where. If the Irgun had known, the Muktar would be a dead man, but the Irgun had vanished, leaving the Arab town and its disposition to Promise of the Future. A skeleton guard was posted. Dan was among those patrolling the upper road. Though an uneasy cease-fire had been declared all over Palestine, even he could not believe it would last, with so many wounds still open and bleeding.

All day, vultures hung overhead in sweeping gyrations,

223

looking for their due. The sweet smell of corruption had lured them from afar, but they found nothing beyond a few carcasses of the sheep which the Arabs had mistaken for Jewish attackers. The village well had been covered over, and the Arab dead who had escaped the Irgun's hasty disposal were buried in decent graves. The town looked relatively tidy from a distance. Only the charring here and there was an indication of what had happened; only that and the smell, inaccessible and untraceable, a smell Dan knew would never wash out of his clothing, perhaps not even out of his skin.

Promise of the Future did what it could. Sarah Klein had organized volunteers who came with disinfectants, bandages, and food. They set up a dispensary and treated the wounded around the clock. Saul was there and old Tam, not through idealism, Dan supposed, but because it was their habit to be on the side of the weak and helpless.

Dan, too, helped with the wounded when he was not on duty. He longed to visit the Muktar and Saïd, to tell them that their home was still standing. He was posted nearby and would keep an eye on it. But permission was necessary to go off post, and Dan was afraid of drawing unfriendly attention to the caves.

The cease-fire was obviously failing. It was only a breathing space for stockpiling food and arms and for digging out bombproof shelters for the children. Any day the fighting would break out again.

One moonlit night in mid-June, toward the end of this shaky peace, Dan stood guard near the upper road. If an attack came, it would come from there. If a sniper crept down from the hills looking for a target, he would look there first, so Dan avoided the open moonlight. He hunched against the wall beside the little shrine of the village holy man. Across

224

the gray strip of road was the Muktar's orchard. Behind that, the dome of his house showed ghostly in the moonlight.

It was the luminous sort of night when dwellers in caves would be stirring in their high places among the rocks. Dan kept warning himself not to relax, to stay on guard. Maybe he'd listened too much to Gideon, who kept reminding him this was no game of cowboys and Indians. "None of that stick-up-your-hands stuff," Gideon had said. "Shoot him in the back if you get the chance, and shoot to kill. A wounded man can get you with a pistol or even a knife. Don't take chances." But Dan wasn't about to shoot anyone in the back. He had not killed yet, and he hoped he would never have to. He dreaded the moment of choosing: your life or mine.

The night wind blew through the leafed darkness of summer with a sad murmurous sound, and in his imagination silent shadow shapes crept and darted, always nearer.

Was that the snapping of a branch underfoot? He laid his hand against the damp barrel of his gun, then wiped the cool moisture across his face. He did not like the moon that night. It was too bright. Nor did he like the wind that carried sounds upon which his anxiety fed.

Staring toward the deserted orchard, he thought he saw a sudden small movement in the still night air. The saliva in his mouth was thick and glutinous, but he dared not spit or make a sound. The shape he saw moving beneath the trees was not shadow but substance, and he heard a very audible click like a hammer being drawn back.

"What is it you want?" he called from the deep shadows.

The figure crouched for a moment, then moved quickly in a stooping posture. He saw the flash of a gun barrel under the moon. At that moment all the sweat that had accumulated in his brows splashed down into his eyes, covering them with a

225

stinging blinding film. Every nerve in his body was quivering. His grip tightened on the gun until the trigger fell away.

The whipcrack report was followed by a piercing cry. It sounded like a woman, but pain takes the sex out of a voice and Dan could not tell.

Without a thought for Gideon's warning, he ran to his victim. A man lay on his side, knees pulled up tight. He uttered inarticulate sounds that turned into words. "Allah, help me." He rocked to and fro. "Allah, be merciful. My stomach."

Dan knelt down beside him. It was the Muktar. He had been looking for things buried in the orchard. His gun was nothing but a small shovel.

"God forgive me!" Dan tried to see how badly the man was hurt, but he continued to hug his knees. "I'll get help," Dan pleaded. "I'll get a doctor."

"Don't leave me. Don't . . ." The voice was frail and crinkling as tissue paper. The blood from his wound rose, forming dark bubbles in his mouth, flecks of tar in the moonlight. Dan held his head. Though he was losing more and more blood, the Muktar was becoming steadily heavier.

"Here," he gasped. "Give this to Saïd. You're his friend. Don't let the Jews get it." He spoke as though Dan were an Arab, not the Jew who had murdered him.

The Muktar's gold pocket watch was pressed into Dan's hand.

"I'll see Saïd gets it," he promised. "Now, please, let me find you a doctor."

But the Muktar held his hand as though it were a life preserver. He was babbling, sometimes in Arabic, sometimes in English. "Why? Why?" were the last words Dan understood.

226

For some time he held the wounded man in his arms. They were both silent, motionless. Then Dan spoke again. "I'll get a doctor," he said dully. "Can't you hear me? I'll get a doctor for you." But he couldn't talk a man back to life. The last sustaining pillar from the Arab community of Tel Jabir was dead. In death he resembled a wise old child, staring secretly and significantly from under half-closed lids upon the revealed secrets of the universe.

Dan had killed mindlessly, without even the intent of killing. He felt he had become less than a Nazi, for even the Nazis had some satanic purpose in their slaughtering. His gun lay on the ground beside him but he ran from it down the hillside, falling and picking himself up again, his fists clenched. When he came to a low stone wall overlooking the plain, he leaned against it, gasping for breath. He had run away, but there was no getting away from himself. He had become as vile as his life's enemies. In this paroxysm of self-hatred a sound came from him that was not a word. It was more like the sound of vomiting when there is nothing to emit but emptiness. This was followed by a high and interminable moan, which Dan himself could not hear. Then he crumpled down, burying his face in his hands. He began to pray, a prayer so dismal that it became a blasphemy.

CHAPTER 13

At Promise of the Future the funeral services were over. Three had been buried: the Irgun leader called Sheherazade and two young fighters from the kibbutz. The flowers were still fresh and colorful. A price had been paid, but a small one, for victory. The dead would not be forgotten, but the communal hall was already bursting with happy people. The great door had been removed from its hinges to allow the passage of a piano which had been salvaged from the Muktar's abandoned home. Its elaborate decorations looked incongruous in the otherwise utilitarian room.

Dan moved amid the excitement, but it could not draw or touch him. He did not smell the flowers, only the blood upon his hands which he could never entirely wash away. Desire for all things seemed dead in him. He had scarcely slept, had not eaten for days; yet he sat down at the long table and his stomach made a liar out of him. He ate, but he could not sing.

When someone began to play the piano, he got up without excusing himself and went outside into the furnace of the Negev summer. Sunlight splintered down in fiery flakes. The air was nearly too hot to breathe. Singing had begun inside and it pursued him into the glare. He crossed the road, passing the new tractor. The driver sat on his iron seat, proud of the machine he did not own, prouder still of the power he controlled; power enough to flatten walls of stone. The tractor chugged up the road toward the hills. It left a smoky blue ribbon of exhaust quivering in the air behind it.

Dan walked diagonally across the fields and slipped under the wire near the guard tower. The guards, Pavlov among them, knew him and waved listlessly. Heat shuddered across the desert. Dan headed toward the low hill from which he had once watched the long-vanished Bedouin camp. Little lizards sunning themselves on the stones ran into their holes as he blundered past. He paid little attention to where he was going. Up there somewhere, he knew, was a tree with shade. If a sniper took a shot at him, it woud be welcome. He would not raise his own gun, though he had it with him. One was suspect these days if one did not carry a gun. He pictured himself falling down, happy in the nullity of being dead; but as he well knew, the Bedouins had withdrawn into their sandy sanctuaries long ago, and there were no more Arabs. They were dead or gone.

It was difficult for Dan to grasp why so many had fled the land. Certainly in the beginning the Jews had not wanted a panic, but the Arab radio had called on its friends in Palestine to clear the roads for its conquering armies. Some rich Arabs had left to avoid stray bullets. Their people, docile, ignorant, dependent on the judgment of their superiors, had followed. That was before the tide had turned for Israel. According to Gideon, it was the initial phase in clearing out what he called "greater Israel." The second phase began with the Irgun's unprovoked annihilation of the Arab population of Deir Yassin.

Gideon tried hard to rationalize this action for Dan. "I

don't want you to get the wrong idea. We weren't motivated by cruelty. It was just a lesson; a cheap one in the long run."

Whatever the reason, panic had spread all over Arab Palestine. Their radio screamed atrocity to inflame their warlike resolve, but the result was only greater panic. It was deliberately augmented by the Jews, who sent loudspeaker trucks with records of bombs and explosions to boom over the countryside. At towns such as Lydda they announced, "The Jericho road is still open. Fly before you are all killed!" And the Arabs, men, women, and children, all blind with fear, obediently scuttled down the dusty roads and into the wilderness.

Dan had seen them in flight, black dots moving always toward the east. About them swirled the dusty *hamsin*, the desert wind that killed birds in flight. Some would die in the wilderness. Most would struggle on to Ramallah or Jericho, bearing the cross of their despair, a despair he knew would harden in time into a determination to return no matter how. But now they were only children chased by the night and the little black Piper Cubs, the so-called "primus" planes of the Israeli. The planes renewed their panic, kept them going, and then swept home, dropping bottled messages of hope upon the isolated kibbutzim. Dan had found one such message. "Victory," it read. "Victory for Israel."

Dan reached the tree at the top of the hill and collapsed in its shade. His gun lay across his knees. A small bird had also sought refuge in the shade. It looked at him curiously, flicked its tail, opened its beak and whistled two or three mocking notes. To the east was the desert, a griddle at last beginning to cool. To the west was more desert, still aglow with sun, and the hills, black but fringed with light, beyond which lay the green sea and Europe. Toward the kibbutz a truck was moving; Gideon's old truck. If only it had blown a tire at high

230

speed months ago, how different things might be. Yet it had survived Gideon's maniacal driving as well as Arab revenge. Now dust like red-hot ash rose behind it. The truck itself seemed on fire in the sun's last ferocious rays, and the passengers in the back glowed like so many torches; the devil and his disciples motoring in their own country, thought Dan bitterly.

He took out the Muktar's gold watch, which he kept constantly with him. The hands of the watch said five in the afternoon. He might tap the crystal on a stone, collect the glass fragments and put them into a hole. He might twist off the hands, but the ticking would go on behind the blank little dial. He might grind the works beneath his heel, but until it was delivered to its proper owner that ticking would go on for him as surely as the beating of his own heart.

Thoughtfully, he reversed the gun and looked into the black depth of its loaded barrel. How could he hold it? The muzzle against an eye, perhaps, so that the bullet would crash with greatest ease through the watery cells, carrying white lightning into his brain. He tried to reach the trigger with his finger, and couldn't. Then he remembered some pictures he had once seen of Japanese soldiers who, monkeylike, had used their big toes to help themselves die. He began to loosen his right shoe. The ultimate desertion—I from myself. As a child, death had not been for him a bearded man with a scythe, but a young man dressed in red. He held long iron pincers, the sort dog catchers would use on rabid animals. Saïd had once told him that death was a desert caravan laden with incense and myrrh. One simply mounted a jet-black camel and rode off into the desert. That was a good way to think of it; that, or oblivion. A few seconds, and I'll not be. He would shed life like an ill-fitting garment. But even with

231

his shoe half off, Dan knew he was only playing a game.

He was simply not ready to die. There was an insect he had heard of that lived only ten minutes. Youth, adulthood, senility, all in that fraction of time. Maybe a simple organism could exhaust all its possible experiences, but he was a man. He had scarcely begun to live.

Suddenly, because he had tempted death, he feared it, whether in the form of an Arab's bullet or a viper's sting. There was beauty in the world that he had glimpsed as a child, a beauty that could run through life like a thread of light. He wanted to see it and touch it and taste it again before he died. Would it be possible for him to find it here, or in Poland with his grandfather? The thought of that long road in reverse was a crushing defeat. If he left the kibbutz, it would be with far less than he had brought with him.

It was at this point, toward dusk, that he saw a slight figure coming down the road with the sun behind her. He saw the long shadow of her body as she turned from the road and started toward the hill. He saw her as he would see a ghost or a vision from a dream. As he stood up, she began to run, her pretty legs flickering in the light. He could hear her feet slip on the shale as she hurried up the slope. It was Hanna, far from dead and glowing with health.

"Dan! Dan, are you here?"

He must have been almost invisible in the shade of the tree. As he moved into the light, he reached out his arms toward an embodiment that seemed not quite real. Very close to him now, Hanna stopped with a queer dignity. As he touched her, a soft sound, half amazement, half laughter, came from her throat. Then Hanna threw her arms about him and burst into tears. Dan knew that his own face was wet, and he buried it for a moment in her hair. Then, with an abruptness

232

that was awkward, he kissed her full on the mouth, on the cheeks, on the eyes, and then on the mouth again. Her eyes opened wide and he saw the black pupils so closely that she appeared to have only one eye, dark and startled. Then she gave a laugh of sheer joy, and kissed him back. Dan felt as though somewhere a window had been flung open and fresh air allowed to pour into a long-sealed room. They stood embracing with more repose than passion, like an old married couple who had found one another again in dangerous times.

Hanna's story was not a long one. The bus had been attacked by the Moslem Brotherhood, all right; attacked and surrounded. It would have burned with the Jews inside it had not a detachment of the Arab Legion arrived on camelback with their saddlebags all red and black and white. They'd wanted the bus whole, not in ashes, so they offered mercy to its defenders. The Jews had surrendered, those few that were still alive. The Arab Legion had treated them amazingly well, particularly with the members of the Moslem Brotherhood shaking their rifles and screaming for "Isaac's blood." They had remained prisoners until three days ago, when they had been turned over in a local exchange.

"And now we have won," she said. "The land is all ours."

Dan's sense of guilt had been lost in her nearness, but now it clawed at him again.

"You didn't see those poor damned Arabs at Tel Jabir," he said. "I see them whenever I close my eyes."

"I know."

"They were terrified of me, that's the thing. They looked at me and saw death grinning at them."

Grave and unabashed, her gray eyes were very close to his own. "I know all about it," she said. "They told me every-

233

thing when I asked about you at the guard tower. We just got back, you know."

"I saw the truck. I never thought it was you."

"I heard about the Muktar and how you've been acting. Dan, I killed a German soldier." Dan nodded. Gideon had boasted of it more than once. She had known him for some weeks, seen pictures of his family. They had laughed together over his clumsiness on skis, and when the others had blown up his post with his comrades inside, she had aimed a pistol between his unbelieving and pleading eyes and shot him down.

"Gideon would say it had to be. We couldn't have witnesses. I don't know anymore. We might have faded away into the forest. Nobody made us do the things we did. I remember how he wouldn't die right away and how I sat in the snow holding his hand until he did. That was six years ago, but it's as vivid as yesterday. I suppose it always will be." The Muktar's death would be the same to Dan. There was no denying that, but it was done, past. The land was won, and they would learn to live with their memories.

Dan felt her confidence sinking into him like the reassuring warmth of a fire in winter. Hand in hand, they walked through the sunlight of early evening down toward the dusk which had already fallen into the shadows cast by the hills. Mid-heaven still blazed with light. On the brink of darkness they hesitated a moment, motionless in the vast emptiness.

"It's all ours," she said.

Then they stepped down into the shadow. It was a delicious element to walk through, a twilight designed for wooing, consenting.

"Look, Dan. Isn't it beautiful?" Hanna said, pointing to where the moon rested like a great white egg upon the hills.

234

"You're a moon gazer," he said cryptically, remembering another time. That, too, was past.

"I wish I were a bird," he went on. "One without any feet, so that it could never land. So light, the wind would always carry it. I wish I were a bird like that."

"It's good enough for me just to walk here, without wire fences or guns, in our own land." Hanna's voice was full of quiet satisfaction.

Surely it's still Arab land, Dan thought, but he didn't say so. He spoke instead of Sholem. He wanted Hanna to know what his friend's last words had been. He had talked of a land of milk and honey, where men were shepherds in grass knee-deep. A land where all creatures were friendly. "Just over there, Dan. Look. It's just over there." "You'll make it, Sholem," Dan had told him, but Sholem had replied, "I can see it now. How beautiful it is. You'll go there for me."

He had gone in search of that dreamland, but he had not found it. "And I don't know where it will end," Dan concluded.

"In the grave," Hanna told him. "Where it doesn't matter whether you're an Arab or a Jew." Life was a strange gift. Perhaps she had not learned how to use it well, but there was no other. As far as Hanna was concerned, nothing was important except the happiness you got out of life. "There aren't any paradises, Dan. There's only the present. That's what's important. Every day, in a way, is a miracle. Waking up in the morning. Eating breakfast. Going to work. There's no use feeling guilty about things that are done and can't be undone. Everybody goes through pain and suffering. You just have to try to make up for it with kindness and love. That's the only thing I'm sure of."

Probably she was right, and yet Dan could not entirely dismiss Sholem as a mad dreamer. He had kept Dan moving

235

toward Palestine with his golden dream when nothing else could have persuaded him. If tomorrow the sun failed to light the earth, surely some madman's dream woud give the world its sunshine.

Far off in the hills an explosion shook the ground without affecting the calm of the sky. Dan was startled, then remembered they were using tractors to level the Arab town, dragging the outskirts with chains in case of mines. By now it was no longer a town, only a cemetery.

No doubt the land would be better used than it had ever been before. New immigrants were coming by the thousands from Cyprus, where they had practiced warfare with wooden arms and stones the size of hand grenades. Anguished and cynical, made cunning by their double imprisonment, they were coming to this narrow strip of soil on the Mediterranean. Redeemed from the gas showers of Germany and Poland, and the Asian cesspools of humanity, many were crippled in mind and body. But they had kept their souls intact, and they brought with them hope, anger, and determination expressed in a babble of voices; all of it compounding into the roar of a newborn Jewish state.

"It's a miracle," Dan agreed. "But isn't it a large enough one to include a few poor Arabs?"

"It wouldn't work," said Hanna, always a realist. "The Arabs would never be willing to share."

"We could try."

"It's our homeland now."

"It's always been the Arab's home."

"And always our spiritual home. Since David and Goliath."

It was hard to think of the ragged Arab refugees as Goliaths.

236

"Not by right."

"I think so," she insisted. "The end sometimes justifies the means, Dan, whether you like it or not."

"I'm not sure what the ends are."

"Then call it a natural necessity. Call it fate, or natural law."

"You mean Germany put us here."

"If you like," she said.

"*Lebensraum,* is that it?" he said. "Just because the Germans have taught us about immorality, that's no reason for us to inflict the lesson upon the Arabs."

"I'm not saying it's right. It's a question of the greater wrong. Or, if you don't like that, the greater strength."

"And what if the Arabs become stronger?" he asked.

"They mustn't."

"If we drive the Arabs to despair, won't that make them strong? I've been asked to make grenades again. I don't want to." Her clear gray eyes were studying his face. He would never be able to lie to her. "I've thought of going away, Hanna. Would you come with me?"

"To paradise island? There's no such place, Dan. And you're the kind we need here. Not the Gideons, who are hardened beyond curing. I'm arguing with you, but I want to believe a lot of the things you say."

"Do you believe this war was the last?"

"Yes," she said. "The next is still ahead of us. But we'll fight it like the last and win. And we'll win another after that, until they learn we're here to stay."

"I'm not fighting any more wars," he said. "I have a weakness. I keep recognizing myself in my enemies. It's a real infirmity." His voice had grown soft and husky. All the tiredness in him seemed to rise into his throat. What did wars accomplish, anyway? Only death and new hatreds. Victory was an illusion of generals and fools. He was wearied by all the wounds that had not yet been opened. Peace was to him the most beautiful word in the language.

"One day it will come. It doesn't seem so far when you look ahead."

"The trouble is, I keep looking back."

"Then you'll see the moon over your shoulder," said Hanna, who had talked all she cared to of war and peace. "Just look at the sky and the night coming on. How lovely it is."

They stood for a time gazing at the horizon. Its bright colors seemed reluctant to die.

"The fact is," Hanna whispered, "I'm fonder of you than anyone on earth."

Dan felt exultant and deeply moved. Above all, he felt happy. Looking into her shadowed face, he saw his own happiness reflected, a happiness that was all embracing; it erased everything else.

"I love you so much," he said.

"Say that again, Dan."

"As often as you like."

"Love . . . I think that's the most beautiful word."

Their arms were around each other.

"I always thought you were sweet on Gideon," he said.

"Not really. Sometimes, now, I think I hate him. I hate what he's become."

"But you loved Sholem."

"Yes, the way you love a holy man."

Dan held her face between his hands. He saw the bright evening star reflected in her eyes, and the night clouds. As though she saw the same thing, Hanna looked up and asked,

238

"Where did all the stars come from tonight?" She was young, full of summer and happiness, and she was right. The sky seemed to have grown a brand-new set of galaxies. "Falling stars! Everywhere! Make a wish, Dan."

The earth circling on its tour of the heavens had encountered the Perseids, a silver rain upon which lovers everywhere made their wishes. A lifetime ago he had watched the same display with his family in Warsaw. The memory came to him warm and comforting. Perhaps he lived in a ghetto still, but at this moment it seemed a very large one.

"They say it's dangerous to remain standing in starlight," Hanna said. "What time is it, Dan?"

"I don't know."

"I hear you ticking."

It was the Muktar's watch. "I can't see in the dark. It isn't even my watch. It's something I've got to return."

It occurred to Dan that now there was time for clocks in Palestine. He must get used to calling it Israel, now. He would write to his grandfather, from whom he had never heard. He would urge him to come. He would tell him the fighting was over. He would tell him that whatever else happened, Dan himself was staying. This land was his home. His roots had taken hold, whatever the future might bring. Like the prickly desert cactus, he would hang on as long as Hanna was with him.

They walked back through the starry night. Sounds crept up to them from the kibbutz; the clank of pots and pans, laughter and song, all the sounds of life.

They had passed through the wire and reached the brighter lights of the compound when Gideon ran up. His eyes were wildly staring and he stood in an odd crouching way that reminded Dan of a panther he had once seen in the

Warsaw zoo. When Gideon spoke, it was through clenched teeth.

"They got him," he said. "Nothing's left but a little jam with hair on it."

"Gideon! What are you talking about?"

He was talking about the tractor driver, a fellow named Cohn. He had been ambushed up near Tel Jabir. Now it was rumored that the Moslem Brotherhood was stealing down toward the kibbutz like a pack of wolves. He urged them to the trenches.

"I just can't believe it," said Dan "I want to check inside."

"We'll see about that." Gideon's declaration was a threat, not a promise. Still, he did not wait for them, but rushed off into the dark with his gun.

A great lugubrious groan sounded in the air.

"What's that?" Dan exclaimed.

"The ram's horn trumpet," replied Hanna.

"What for?"

"War. What else are trumpets for?"

"It sounds very sad."

"Youthful," Hanna insisted.

"It sounds pathetic, like a ship lost in the fog."

From somewhere far off came the crackle of gunfire. There was no mistake about it. Then crouching figures poured from the buildings and plunged into the dark.

Hanna, and then Dan, turned back toward the barbed wire. Both were armed. They began walking steadily, side by side.

Overhead, the sky was serene. The night seemed to smile, a silver rain of meteors showered down on Jews and Arabs alike.

EPILOGUE

IN JERICHO, HEAT SHIMMERED LIKE WATER OVER THE DARK-green oasis of banana plantations and orange groves, over palms and cypresses. Where the camp clustered, the wilderness was dusty brown. From a distance Saïd could scarcely see the homes there, all of them mud-baked, with small dark window holes. There were many of them, far too many.

Saïd was returning as a soldier that summer of 1955. His careful walk went with his new boots and the hallowed kaffiyeh headdress, held by its loops of goats-hair rope. He had only a twenty-four hour pass and bore his rifle with him due to the state of emergency.

Entering the camp, he passed a nurse in white who was dispensing cod-liver oil from a watering can into the back-tilted mouths of naked children. They looked like a flock of plucked birds. He walked between the rows of squalid huts. Men leaned against them, too listless for games or conversation. Two old women sang softly, like shells murmuring on a windy beach.

"*Al Jeish al Arabi!*" shouted a younger man. "The Arab Legion is here." Either he had not lost faith, or he had a sense of humor. Saïd turned toward the voice and recognized an old friend from the flight into the wilderness.

241

"They gave you fine boots," said his friend. "Tell me, Saïd, will there be war again? Will we go home?"

"If Allah wills, and the King thinks the time is ripe."

The young man nodded his head in agreement. Saïd felt a rush of pleasure at being a soldier and having an old playmate assume a posture of respect and deference.

He felt close to this boy, for they had been together on that dreadful day in forty-eight when the Jewish armored cars had come to town, shouting at the Arabs over loudspeakers to "Leave your homes or the fate of Deir Yassin will be yours. The road to Jericho is still open. Fly before you are killed." The Muktar was dead by then. Saïd had found him in the garden, shot down by the Irgun, he supposed. Without his father's voice to steady them, the remaining villagers had fled into the heat of the goat-tracked wilderness. It was 120 degrees in the shade. Many of the old and the very young did not make it. His widowed mother, desiring death, had to be dragged along. After passing through the lines of the Second Regiment of the Arab Legion, they had found a muddy cistern where hundreds of refugees dunked strips of clothing to suck them for moisture. In a valley farther on, a crazed mob had struggled around the trunks of carob trees to obtain the huge datelike seed pods.

All the while his mother was screaming and babbling in the dialect of her desert childhood. But he would not let her die.

Finally they had come to the miracle of Jericho. They were not the first, and the people already there defended their property against their suffering cousins as they might have against an invading army.

More and more refugees poured in. The well-to-do shielded themselves from the sun with parasols. Many wore

242

European suits, kicking sand from patent-leather shoes. There were muktars and sheiks and the multitudes of patient poor. Mothers laid out blankets on the sand, offering cucumbers to children too tired and confused to eat.

Tents dotted the Jericho plain, and local food supplies quickly ran out as the refugee camps grew. They drank from the fountain where Elisha had drunk. Some found caves in the hillsides, others were sheltered in mosques, or in shacks of flattened petrol cans. There was nothing permanent. After all, they would soon be going home in the wake of the victorious Arab armies.

Such hope died slowly. When the temporary shelters took on the permanence of towns, the refugees kept to themselves at first, like hunted animals safe for a time in a hollow tree from which they peered suspiciously. Their somber eyes smoldered with hostility and distrust. After a while, the women began boasting about the fine houses with plumbing they had been forced to abandon. They described gardens and olive plantations where singing birds and the music of running streams made happiness flourish. They spoke of estates that might never again be theirs, and kept their eyes fixed on the west as if they could still see this luxury and magnificence. It was not merely boasting for effect. It was the torment of homesickness.

Only Saïd's mother never talked of those days. She scarcely talked at all, and seldom ate. For a time he fed her by hand, and yet she wasted visibly. They were all suffering from malnutrition, especially before the United Nations sent help. Flies crawled on their scalps, eczema covered their bodies. They sat apathetically, their shoulders sagging, spidery legs drawn up into bundles of acute angles. When Saïd looked at them, he felt afraid. These were his people, and they were

243

slowly dying. They were not warriors or criminals. They were nothing now but pale shadows of disease and starvation and disillusionment propped up in the sun.

Saïd had expected much at first; food and jobs and medical care from Jordan and the other Arab lands. But Jordan was rich only in pride, and the oil-wealthy Arab countries turned their backs. Israel promised help, but gave only a token. The United Nations did what it could, which amounted to keeping those with the will to live alive.

Saïd and his mother had no relatives in Jordan. Some of the young men were returning to Jewish-held territory as bandits, or to liberate what was rightfully theirs, but his mother kept him from this with her tears. He was just as glad. No sheep ever saved its neck by bleeding, as the saying went, and there were other ways. They had a few things of value saved: his mother's jewels, some household utensils. These he had taken one by one to the Bedouin sheik who camped nearby.

"I am here and must eat," Saïd had said to the man.

The sheik nodded understandingly. "What would you fancy? Fresh lamb? Dried greens? Dates? Olives? I have them all."

"Whatever you will give."

"And what will you give?" The old sheik smiled.

Saïd had shown him a copper dish from Damascus and his father's narghile.

The Bedouin sighed, and directed a lazy arm to such objects piled high. Other refugees had been doing business. "Too much already," he said.

"I have a small prayer rug, made in Persia long ago," Saïd offered.

"Hashish? We might do business with some hashish," the sheik suggested.

244

In the end it was his mother's jewelry that went, piece by piece. It was a dowry that had been accumulated in the family for generations; gold for bags of barley and the haunch of a goat. Still, they survived until the dole was increased. It was the general practice to bury dead refugees under the dirt floor of the tents and keep the ration book as though they were still alive. Saïd obtained an extra book for a gold locket.

As time went by, the camp, which had been conceived in emergency and thought of as a transient affair, took on a kind of weary permanence. Tents gave way to mud-brick huts. Government schools of a sort were instituted. A warehouse for clothes appeared, and a clinic. Yet no one gardened, no one strove for beauty. To do so would be an admission that this was home, that they could expect no better, that they no longer hoped to return.

A resistance movement was discussed. The Egyptian fedayeen raiding Israel from Gaza were much admired. These were the commandos, the forlorn hope, the "self-sac-rificers" who terrorized the Jewish Negev. The Jews called them cutthroats. They were that, too, for they killed the lonely shepherd and the girl harvesting oranges. For every death they caused, the Jews retaliated, not with one death, but with several.

To Saïd this seemed a useless game that would never bring the refugees home again. War was a better way, a young man's way, and he was hot with the desire for vengeance. They all were. To sit on the border behind white markers and watch Jews harvesting their olives and their oranges, to lie there at night hearing the putt-putting of their own water pumps irrigating Israeli crops—this was maddening. They would fight again. Time and time again they would return. In the end they would win, for the Jews were a nail driven

245

into their hand. The Arab nations were the separate fingers of that hand, finally brought together by pain into a clenched fist.

Believing this, Saïd had joined the Arab Legion. The appearance of his new uniform in camp created admiration in the young, who ran behind him, and respect in the old, who stepped aside. Among contemporaries, it seemed to enhance his wisdom and judgment. "How much did such a fine gun cost?" one wanted to know. Not wanting to seem ignorant, Saïd replied, "As much as three camels." He showed off the bullets. Each one was worth six hen's eggs, he told them. And there were bombs carried by airplanes that were worth more than a house, more than a tractor. But most of them asked him about war. When would it come? In spring, when the days were balmy and the fields full of promise? When there were plenty of strong young men full of dreams? Would it prowl out of the deserts of Sinai like a lion? They spoke of Nasser; an Egyptian, it was true, and despised a bit for this, yet a leader. Nasser would surely bring them victory, the young men agreed. When Saïd confirmed all this, they saluted in the old way, unsmiling.

"Es salaat wes salaam," they said. "Peace be with you and the glory."

At the end of an avenue of mud houses Saïd saw his mother's dwelling, pillbox-shaped like the others. He had to stoop low to enter. First he straightened his necktie and pulled down the front of his battleblouse. His mother was there as usual, sitting quietly in the twilight. She gave a little cry on seeing him.

"Mother," he said. "You look well."

In fact, she looked tubercular, shrunken into bony ridges and networks of veins.

246

Solemnly she poured him a glass of cold water and stood while he drank it.

"Do they feed you well?" she asked him.

"Most days we have meat."

Her eyes opened wide. "Surely you exaggerate."

"Truly," he insisted. "You should see the camp. Trucks, and bulldozers. More than a dozen for the war effort."

"Then there will be war?" she asked him.

Saïd shrugged. He could not say. There were those who blamed the defeat in forty-eight upon defective weapons and the corruption of King Farouk. Now there was Nasser. Some believed he was the Mahdi who would save them from the Jews and from Western imperialism. Hatred blared from every radio and screamed from every headline. Miracles would occur if the enemy could only be rooted out of the land of Canaan. He could not lie to his mother about all this. He never had. Sometimes he even thought the holy war was a madman's vision, pouring out the national income for guns and aircraft when people were starving and dying of a dozen curable diseases. And yet there was Israel with her Messerschmitts and her American tanks maneuvering in the desert. If one could believe the radio, Israel intended one day to expand to the Nile and the Jordan; perhaps even to the Euphrates.

Saïd feared war not so much for his own sake as for his mother's. She would not live through another war. But it seemed impossible to avoid. Negotiations had been tried. From the Jewish point of view, it was a simple affair. The Arabs had been beaten. Those were the facts, and the Arabs ought to follow the rules like a game of chess. But not knowing when they were beaten, not understanding the rules of Western games was an Arab fault. Perhaps worse was the Jewish one: not knowing when they were victorious.

247

The Jews spoke efficiently, penetratingly. The Arabs politely twiddled their pens and offered a rebuttal that was full of hyperbole, hypnotizing themselves with their own words. Saïd's father had once remarked that his countrymen were like the characters in *The Mikado,* who persuaded themselves that an execution was an accomplished fact simply because the emperor had ordered it and his word was law. With such logic the Arabs could never lose a war.

The Jews always had good European arguments. They would point out that many Arabs had stayed in Israel and had prospered. They ate better and lived longer than before. Yet it was hard to be ruled by newcomers in what had been one's home. After all, the Arabs, too, were the "seeds of Abraham." Saïd believed they could never survive as second-class Europeans.

His thoughts went back to the time when his best friend had been a Jew. If it were up to Dan and himself, they could still work things out. He smiled when he thought of the Petra talk. He'd been there since. At least Petra was one thing the Arabs had held. No Jew could go there now and hope to return. Strange, the deadly arbitrariness of frontiers; strange, when he thought of Dan. Then it seemed that hate was little more than unachieved love. At any rate, it was too much to think about when one was home on leave for only twenty-four hours.

Saïd's glass was empty and his mother refilled it slowly so as not to waste a drop.

"I will take the pitcher to the well," he said, "before I leave."

"To fight the Jews?" she persisted.

"As I said, a soldier does what he's told."

"I wish you had found a job. Surely there would be something in Amman."

248

They had been over this before, too many times. Perhaps the return was a forlorn hope and his mother was the realist, not he. Perhaps they should resign themselves to a future in Jordan. Then he saw his father, murdered and robbed by the Irgun, and he knew he would return. For his father's watch, if nothing else, he would return even if it meant his own death. So he could not talk to his mother of a future in Jordan. He could only display the rations he had brought for supper. "The army feeds us well. Look, Mother, what I've brought."

He would have prepared them himself, but that was women's work, his mother insisted, and she drove him out into the world of men.

Saïd hunkered down outside the hut. It was cooler now with evening coming. Here the old people sat quietly dreaming, listening to sad music he could not hear. They seemed to have already died, and in dying, to have lost all fear in the knowledge that man can die only once. "Patience demolishes mountains," the old saying went, and there were those who said time was on the side of the Arabs, as it had been during the Crusades. Perhaps. But it did not seem to Saïd to be on the side of the old, for whom time was short, or the young, who were impatient.

With a flicker of its wings, a sparrow alighted beside a puddle in the rutted road. It drank a bit of evening sky and cocked its head at Saïd. Its eyes were bright and round. It watched the young soldier, first with one eye, then, flick, with the other.

Evening was coming fast now. The sky was a tranquil glory, the opening of a golden fan. For some it was time for supper and sleep and dreams. For the impatient ones, it was time to crawl across no-man's-land to steal an orange from a Jewish grove, or to plant a mine where buses passed. Saïd looked at the silent figures hunched against the walls of their huts, and knew they would never leave the camp. To do so would be to admit defeat. They would be patient. They would wait in the dust as the years rolled by, content in the belief that Allah disposes.

Another sparrow flew down to the puddle in the dusty road. His throat pumped faster than a pulse. He pecked first at the water and then at the other bird's bill. They began fighting in the dust, not playing, but picking and rolling, while the first red star appeared in the east. It hung over the desert like a drop of blood. The mountains of Moab turned rusty red in the last glory of evening, and behind them Petra glowed like fire.

Saïd was dazzled by the sun's final fading. For a moment he was in the hills again with his sheep. Then he was back, aware of the feuding birds and a ragged urchin, one of the wild boys who stayed alive by luck. The boy had a stone and aimed it at the fighters. Saïd could not stop him. God knows, the boy might not eat otherwise. The stone flew and splashed in the puddle, shattering the sunset. The birds took flight. Undaunted, the child went on his way. He would try again.

It was dark before Saïd heard his mother's call. The stars were very bright, and so low, it seemed he could reach up and pluck one down. As he watched a star fell, a thief star, the Arabs called it, trailing glory across the sky.

The young soldier watched its fall and made a wish. Then he went inside for supper, for his leave was short and running out, and there was talk of war.